Darling, impossible!

Eva Novy

Darling, impossible!

Eva Novy

[Lacuna]
2014

Published in 2014 by Lacuna
  http://www.lacunapublishing.com

  Lacuna is an imprint of Golden Orb Creative
  PO Box 185, Westgate NSW 2048, Australia
  http://www.goldenorbcreative.com

Cover artwork from an original photograph by Linda Kythe Nix.
Cover design by Golden Orb Creative.
Author photograph (back cover) by David Gross, used with permission.
Text design and typesetting by Golden Orb Creative.
Typeset in 11.5/13.8 pt Adobe Garamond Pro (text) and 36 pt Halo Handletter (titles).

National Library of Australia Cataloguing-in-Publication entry:

  Novy, Eva, author.

  Darling, impossible! / Eva Novy.

  ISBN 9781922198167 (paperback)
  ISBN 9781922198174 (ebook)

  Family secrets--Fiction.
  Families--Fiction.
  Hungarians--Australia--Fiction.

  A823.4

For Robert Treborlang.

Chapter One

"Imagine." This should be the first word anybody learns when they learn Hungarian. "Imagine" as in "Imagine, he wasn't his real father" or "Imagine, they haven't spoken to each other in fifteen years".

"Imagine," my grandmother whispers, clutching onto my arm with sharp, red fingernails. "Imagine, he was only eighty-*sree*." After fifty-two years in Australia her accent is still so thick it's hard to tell if she's speaking English or Hungarian. "Imagine, Lily," she continues, "he was a real bastard, that one."

We are hovering around an expectant grave with a pack of elderly Hungarians waiting for the funeral to start. She is unsteady in faded crocodile heels on the moist grass, grasping me so tightly it hurts.

"A bastard with a tiny shlong! Imagine!" Still whispering, careful not to be heard by the others, she is feigning extreme laryngitis so she doesn't have to explain to her friends why her twenty-two-year-old unmarried granddaughter just quit medical school.

"I hate funerals," she hisses.

I smile and squeeze her hand. Funerals are one of the few social events she goes to anymore. There is a group of them, eighty-something-year-old Hungarian women who brave the long drive from the breezy bayside Eastern Suburbs through a good hour of sweaty traffic on Parramatta Road to the cemetery on the other side of Sydney. Though all are here to contemplate the life and death of the Bastard with the Tiny Shlong, I imagine the real question on everyone's mind is: who's next? We don't talk about this, my grandmother and I, but the atmosphere is always heavy with inference. One day soon there will be only one of us standing here.

I sneeze. The air is thick with the smells of wet earth, body odour and hair spray. A fat gardener with ear plugs and builder's crack is trimming the grave with a deafening whipper snipper only five plots away from us, totally oblivious to the fairly large crowd now gathered around the young rabbi.

"Friends," the rabbi yells. "Come, friends. Closer. Don't be shy! I have competition here." He stares intently at the gardener, but doesn't get the eye contact he is after. "Let's gather to talk about our beloved … uh …" – he glances down at his notes – "Frankie Symonds." He throws the gardener an irritated look and then turns back to the crowd with a toothy smile. "Let's remember Frankie Symonds."

The crowd shuffles in. Sighing. Sweating.

"Frankie was a good man. A kind man. A generous soul …"

Three people check their phones. Two others, their watches. I brace myself for the coming drivel. I know the drill: only heroes and women of valour ever pass away, never the selfish, the miserable, the bitter, or the mediocre.

It's going to be a long morning.

The young Australian rabbi with a cultivated Yiddish accent continues from General Eastern European Old Man Sermon Number 3. "… an inspiration to his friends, a rock to his family. We remember the tragic circumstances of his early life in war-torn Budapest and his heroic survival of the death camps. We remember the terrifying years of post-war Communism, the panic of revolution, the uncertainty of escape and immigration. We remember how he managed to turn the life of a poor refugee into the life of a successful member of the community. We remember the way Frankie managed to turn fear into faith, hatred into love, desperation into success."

But I don't remember this.

I remember Frankie the Ordinary. I remember Frankie the tired, old landlord who used to waddle into our kitchen uninvited through the back door and drum his fat fingers on the window sill. I remember how one of his eyes didn't open all the way, how he'd timidly cast unreciprocated glances in my grandmother's direction, how he'd hesitate when telling my mother our cheque had bounced. Again. I remember how he managed to turn a perfectly peaceful Sunday breakfast into a never-ending morning of trite anecdotes and phony civility. That's what I remember.

I look at my grandmother's face. She remembers Frankie the Bastard.

The rabbi continues from his notes. "Frankie Symonds was born in Budapest in 1926. The son of a businessman and a homemaker, Frankie grew up …"

But I know the story. It's our story too. My grandmother, my father's mother, came here in the fifties with her family as a refugee from behind the Iron Curtain. My mother, born here to immigrant parents also from Budapest, still carries scars of persecution and survival and they define every part of her being. I was born and bred in Sydney, but my hair is a little too curly and my skin a little too dark to escape the question: where are you *really* from? My grandmother likes to tease me that there may be some Gypsy blood somewhere in the mix (on the other side, of course), but really it's Hungarian Jews all the way back.

I stare at the faces around me, a sea of oversized sunglasses in an assortment of kitsch. I can imagine what lies behind those gaudy imitation Chanels and diamante-studded goggles: sweaty, over plucked eyebrows and mediocre facelifts. Behind those, there are memories of similar lists of dates and countries, wars and revolutions, immigration and reinvention. It's their story, too.

But I know it's not the only one.

So I wait for the eulogy to end, for the crowd to meander lazily into the hall a few metres away for much-needed drinks and not-so-needed nosh because I know that's where the other stories are told. The *real* stories come out little by little after the second scotch, between spoonfuls of chocolate torte and mouthfuls of air kisses.

They are what I'm here for.

The ones about how he regularly visited a certain infamous Surry Hills brothel and how he once charged his own brother interest for a gambling loan. I'm here to listen to the way they talk about his dreadful singing voice and how they call him "simple", always after carefully looking left and right, and always in a whisper. The *real* Frankie Symonds stories.

"I went to school with his second wife, you know. What a disaster!"

We don't join in because of my grandmother's sudden bout of selective mutism, and we waddle around arm in arm listening in to the various adjuncts to the rabbi's eulogy. Occasionally a friendly hand squeezes hers or an understanding smile salutes us with a knowing tilt of the head. She responds silently, stoically, as sympathetically as she can muster, and we move on to the next group.

"Well, you know he came to the café several times a week. I tell you, never a tip! Imagine, not a penny! And you want to know why?" – followed by something in Hungarian.

My grandmother punctuates every overheard comment with a disapproving *humph* but never explains what is said.

"That must be her granddaughter, Lily … so skinny and still not married. Imagine!"

I cringe.

"Frankie never liked him, you know, he told me *mindig csak az adóján*."

"Well, she just went and quit her studies. Just like that. What a story!" And then something else in Hungarian.

Humph.

But I don't speak Hungarian.

When I was ten years old, I asked my grandmother to teach me Hungarian.

"Don't be an idiot," she replied, irritated.

I went to my mother.

"Teach me Hungarian," I said, full of the naïveté that I was told is reserved only for children and peasants.

Mama didn't even look up from her novel.

"Don't be an idiot, Lily," she replied, irritated.

It's the only time I remember my grandmother and Mama agreeing on anything.

"You know Hungarian is impossible to learn."

I had heard it all before: Hungarian is impossible to learn, and Hungarians themselves are impossible to talk to. Hungarians, Mama would explain, are the worst. For Mama, Hungarian is the language of idiots and bigots, all of whom hate the Jews more than anyone else. It is the language of obsessions, complexes, and ridiculous Old World superstitions that had made her feel afraid and guilty and ashamed in the New World, and the language of smelly homemade lunch boxes that had made her Australian classmates not want to sit next to her in the playground. For me, Hungarian is the language of family secrets. It is the language of surprise visits and anticipated presents, the language of family controversy and conspiracy theories. Hungarian holds the reason Mama and my grandmother hate each other and the endings of the sentences I can never understand.

"Let's go," I whisper to my grandmother as she shamelessly stuffs an assortment of cookies into her handbag. "I have to get to the gallery." Since I quit my promising career as a medical student a month ago, I've been working part-time at an art gallery on Danks Street, hoping to earn a few dollars as I embark on the not so promising career of a painter.

Humph.

I try to drag her away from the buffet table. Not far to go to the door: three more rumours and two more humiliations and we are there.

And that's when I hear it. It's loud and rough and throaty. I turn to see an elderly woman consoling Frankie's son.

"Don't be an idiot, daahrlink," she tells him.

About the same vintage as my grandmother, she looks outrageous squeezed into an elegant designer suit several sizes too small, a dead animal draped over her shoulders and a mass of teased hair. I recognise her face, but I'm not sure from where. She could be a relative. Maybe a distant relative. Definitely another Hungarian. I watch her pour two whiskies and sit down.

"*Vot* a bloody mess!" she booms.

It's the voice. I know that voice. It carries me straight back to the rummy table from my childhood home in Reina Street. It's then I realise I once loved her. Her tone of voice takes me to a safe place, the smell of stale smoke on the green felt table cloth, the long, red fingernails with manicured half-moons clutching a glass of medicine, the coolness of beads on my back as I watch the game from her lap.

I motion to my grandmother. "Look," I tell her. "She's here."

My grandmother growls and tenses and vigorously pulls me towards the door.

I suddenly know where it was I last saw her: in an old family photo album. She had been an integral part of our story, like Mama and Papa and my grandmother and then all of a sudden, about halfway through that light blue album, she disappeared from the pages and from my memory. I haven't seen her since. I haven't heard about her since, at least not in English, anyway.

I can still hear her from the doorway.

"Was that her Lily I saw with her? I didn't think she'd be so skinny, but I always knew ..." and then something in Hungarian.

Humph. "Idiot," my grandmother says. She is supposed to be mute today, but she just can't help herself. I look around to see if anyone has noticed, but it doesn't matter anymore. We are almost at the car.

My grandmother is visibly agitated but insists on driving me to work. As we step into her beat-up '82 Datsun, I wonder whether this is the time the car finally breaks down for good. All the way to the gallery, my grandmother swears even more than usual at the broken air-conditioning and the anti-Semitic traffic lights. I hear murmurings of "what a bloody nerve" and something else in Hungarian. "I'm awfully mad," she keeps saying, over and over again. That's my grandmother: she is never just regularly mad. It always has to be awful too.

I have a busy few hours at work, followed by an appointment with Dr Horvath. I am starting to feel panicky, and I don't have the strength to interrogate her. My grandmother doesn't like too many questions.

If only I knew why this mysterious woman made her so much angrier than the others. If only I knew what she had said about me. If only I could speak Hungarian.

Chapter Two

The week before an opening is always mayhem. I wander in through the huge glass doors to find Camilla, the gallery manager, tip-toeing atop a three-metre ladder in high-heel boots and a mini-skirt. She is adjusting ceiling lights as she directs half a dozen sweaty, half-naked delivery men carrying in the enormous canvases from the storeroom next door.

She doesn't skip a beat.

"Lily, dear, the new invitations are ready to go out today, before three this time please! And pop over next door to photocopy the price list, you know, the *other* one, and finish the email lists." She turns to chide the young man who is supposed to be holding the ladder. "Concentrate," she snaps in that school-teacher tone of hers. "Trust me, you do *not* want me to fall. And Lily, call the caterers and tell them not the salmon croquettes this time. They were disgusting. Choose something else. I trust you, and darling, please don't wear that shirt again. Honestly, it's positively hideous! Tell them, I don't know, tell them spring rolls are fine."

I reach to turn on the computer, but she is motioning to me from the other side of the room as she glides down the ladder. "And I forgot to tell you," she continues, "the Internet is down again. Call the computer guy, would you, and tell him I've had it this time!"

I sit on the cold, chrome stool and try to gather my thoughts. I still have to pick up the artist's bios from the printers, check off the RSVPs from yesterday, and arrange a time for the dry-cleaners to drop off the curtains.

Meanwhile, Camilla ruffles her carefully coiffed golden mane and pouts towards the mirror behind the front desk. "That horrible woman from PR is coming in a minute, deary me." Her flawless, porcelain skin is taut with Botoxed perfection. "Honey, how do I look?"

She looks immaculate, as usual, like everything I've always wanted to be.

"You look tired," I lie, but she's already gone.

I pick up the phone, but I am only half-heartedly going through the motions. My mind is elsewhere. In about three hours, my best friend Sam will be here to take me to my doctor's appointment. I can't stop thinking about what the doctor might say.

I have become somewhat of a regular at Dr Horvath's office. He's a good doctor, tall with kind eyes and soft hands. It's Dr George Horvath on the prescription pad, but to me he's simply Georgie. He always greets me like family because he came here from Hungary on the same boat as my father and featured prominently in Papa's recoveries and relapses. I suspect that's why he feels obligated to sugar-coat his prognoses for me the same way Mama would crush aspirin into a spoonful of honey to hide the bitterness. It never works, and it destroys the taste of honey forever.

My father died when I was five years old. Mama protected me from the funeral, and neither she nor my grandmother spoke much about him again. I've seen many (though always the same) pictures and heard numerous (though always the same) stories, but I don't remember much about him at all. I have been told we have the same eyes and the same slim build. I know that he, too, used to sneeze ten times in a row after a big meal and that he, too, loved to draw. But I don't know how he held his head when he walked. I don't know how he smelled in the mornings. I don't know the sound of his laugh. I know there are stories, whispers behind closed doors, and strings of Hungarian gibberish as I leave the room. In a funny way, being at Dr Horvath's surgery makes me feel close to my father. There's a lot I don't know about Papa, but I do know what it's like sitting in that waiting room.

I finally put down the phone and look at my watch. Ten minutes to go. A group of three middle-aged women hover around the entrance, trying to sneak a look through the glass doors. I know the type: bored, WASP-y housewives with an afternoon to kill.

"Get rid of them, Lily," Camilla orders. "I don't have time for this."

I block the door. They take one look at my shirt and try to push past me.

"Can I help you?" I ask.

"Not sure," says the fat one, deciding that a smile is probably just too much trouble.

I try to field their questions with as much patience as I can muster. No, we are not open. Yes, we are preparing for a new exhibition. No, they cannot have a sneak peek. Yes, it's an Aboriginal artist from Arnhem Land. No, he's not a poor, primitive thing, but a successful, internationally-renowned painter whose works will sell for the price of a small townhouse. Yes, they can take a brochure. No, they can't speak to the manager. I watch them walk away in a huff, back to their immaculate BMWs, off to pick up their private-school kids, on their way home to tell their husbands about the interesting, cultured afternoon they'd spent at an art gallery.

Sam is waiting for me on the curb. Two freshly lit cigarettes in his hands, one for him and one for me, he is impersonating the women I've just encountered in that unashamedly camp style of his.

"Oh darling, this is simply unacceptable. Who do you think you are?" He brushes his soft, blond hair from his eyes and takes a long, exaggerated drag of his cigarette, channelling his inner drama queen.

I'm nervous, but I manage a smile. His irreverent theatrics always calm me down.

"Hurry up, I don't want to be late," I tell him, knowing all the same that we will probably spend forty-five minutes in a colourless waiting room.

"What the fuck are you wearing?" he says as we climb into his Jeep convertible.

"Tell me what you really think!"

I know I can count on Sam.

On the way to the surgery, I tell him about my morning at the funeral, about the unfinished sentences and my unexpected encounter with the mysterious old Hungarian woman who made my grandmother awfully mad again.

"Why do you care who she is?" he asks, as we turn off towards Bondi Beach. "Do you have to know *everything?*"

Sam doesn't understand. It's not his fault. He doesn't know anyone older than his parents, whom he has seen a handful of times since he left home at sixteen, and never wonders what the people in the next car are talking about and whether or not it's about him. For Sam, history consists of Marilyn Monroe outfits and the list of websites he has visited that day. Sometimes I'm jealous of his clarity and his naturally blond hair, his superhero-like sense of what's hot and what's not, and how he gets to make things up as he goes along. But not today.

Today I just want to know.

We park illegally outside Dr Horvath's office building. The waiting room is packed. In one corner, an old man is coughing and spluttering. His wife is sitting beside him screaming into the phone in Russian, cleaning his collar with a McDonald's serviette and spit. In another, a young mother decked out in diamonds and Gucci is pacing up and down with a wailing baby. Another five mother-and-child combinations take up all the available plastic seats in between.

"Lily, I'm so sorry," says Mary, the receptionist, an old acquaintance of my mother's from high school. She isn't exactly a friend (Mama maintains Mary's still jealous over a boyfriend scuffle from when they were fifteen years old) but she has always been nice to me. Today, however, she has disappointing news. "He is completely run off his feet. An early flu outbreak, it seems. Would you believe it?" She stops to look Sam up and down. Her grimace doesn't hide a thing: who the hell is this handsome yet obviously non-Jewish boy nobody's told me anything about? "Tell me," she continues. "Can it wait till tomorrow? Is it urgent?"

Only a matter of life or death.

"It can wait," I say, arranging something for the following day.

Sam is relieved. He doesn't want to stay and catch something dull from the middle class.

I turn to leave, but am distracted by a guttural bark from the doctor's now open doorway.

It's her.

I freeze.

Not for fifteen or so years and then twice in one day!

I panic.

Should I say hello? Could I say hello?

Dr Horvath ambles out into the waiting room with her at his side. She has an unlit cigarette in one hand, a paper in the other.

Can I pretend not to have seen her? Will she notice me? I'm scared. I'm curious. I'm delighted. I'm frozen.

Sam nudges me. "Come on, Lily, let's go. You'll be back tomorrow."

"It's her," I mouth. Why am I so nervous?

"What are you doing?" Now he is irritated. "Her who?"

"Her," I whisper. The taboo. The unmentionable. Suddenly her name comes to me.

"It's Eva," I say.

He's not interested but I can't move.

Why does Eva get to see the doctor today and not me?

Dr Horvath smiles hello in my direction and lightly touches Eva's shoulder. "See you next week," he says. He says *ve-ee-ek* like it has three syllables.

Before I have a chance to think, she turns to me. She looks right at me. "*Jaj*, Lily daahrlink, *ugy nézel ki mint as apád a te korodba*. Imagine!"

Sam screws up his face. Wogs have always embarrassed him.

I stare at her with a blank look.

"You don't think?" she continues.

"Lily doesn't speak Hungarian," the doctor explains, almost apologetically. "Isn't that right, Lily?"

I nod sheepishly. I feel like a child.

"Never mind." Eva bends to rearrange the hem of her skirt. "Ne-v-er mi-nd," she sings. Through gritted teeth, Sam mumbles something about having to leave.

"Good!" announces Eva. "Give me a lift to the pla-za will you, daahrlink? Come on, kids," she continues, jabbing Sam lightly in the ribs, "let's go." It's like she has been expecting us, like this is all so natural, as if we have done this a hundred times before.

I have no time to think. No time to plan. What will my grandmother say? It's not my fault.

She winks at Sam as he helps her into the front seat of his Jeep. "Where are we going? Safari?" She laughs, followed by a coughing fit. "I was at the hospital the day you were born, you know," she tells me. "We were all very tense and excited, especially your grandmother who is a nervous wreck at the best of times, imagine! And then your Papa came out all sweaty and fidgety. He didn't have the stomach for this sort of thing, poor kid, but your mother. *Jaj!* Like an ox! 'It's a girl! It's a girl! It's a girl' he kept saying over and over. Imagine, we were all very relieved, you know."

I catch Sam's expression in the rear view mirror. I know that look, the what-the-fuck-is-going-on look, the this-is-too-weird-for-me look. We stop at the traffic lights on the corner of Bondi Road. Two more blocks and we'll be at the Junction. It's almost over, but I don't want the trip to end. I want to hear more.

Sam reaches over to light Eva's cigarette, the same unlit cigarette she's been waving around since she came out of the surgery.

"Don't be ridiculous, daahrlink. What are you trying to do, kill me?"

I light myself a cigarette, take a deep drag, then speak.

"When was the last time you saw me, Eva? You know, the *last* time?"

"You were still very little, daahrlink."

"How old?"

"How old? I don't know, maybe four or five, I imagine, *little*." She shrugs.

So Papa was still alive.

"What was I doing?"

"I remember it well. I was sitting at the Cosmopolitan and you ran across the road and jumped into my lap. I remember."

"What did I say?"

"Your mother was very angry, daahrlink. You know how she gets. You asked me for some ice-cream. You loved it when I bought you ice-cream. Pink ice-cream, you asked for, always the same."

Sam turns back towards me, confused, narrowly missing the mirror of a parked car.

"Ice-cream?" he asks.

I wave him away and continue my interrogation.

"Did you buy it for me? Did Mama let you?" Eva's right, I do know how Mama gets.

"Your mother said something about being in a rush and you went away."

"And that was the last time?"

"And that was the last time."

Sam is right to be confused. The story can't be true. I've never liked ice-cream.

I try to imagine what her story means, and whether it has anything to do with me. They say that you should never let the truth get in the way of a good story, but this one isn't even good. Was our last meeting too meaningless to remember or was it too painful to recall?

Sam pulls up to the curb. I have to think fast. In a few seconds, Eva will be out of the car, out of my life again.

In my family, stories about Eva, like those about my father, always end badly, and never in English. They end in a language familiar yet completely incomprehensible.

Suddenly, I know what I have to do.

"Teach me Hungarian, Eva," I say.

Chapter Three

It's the following evening and I'm on my way to my grandmother's house for dinner. I didn't turn up to my appointment at Dr Horvath's surgery this afternoon. After the excitement of yesterday, I wasn't in the mood for news.

The smell hits me head-on as I enter her apartment building through the side door. Margo, her downstairs neighbour, must be cooking lamb again. I know what that means for my grandmother: another bad mood. Hungarians hate lamb.

It's hot and dusty in the concrete stairwell. This two-storey red-brick eyesore from the fifties was built to make the winters colder and the summers hotter. Par for the course in this neighbourhood of run-down apartment buildings, old weatherboard semi-detached cottages and peeling pastel store fronts only three blocks from a beautiful sprawling ocean beach with powder-like white sand and blue-green surf. Side by side, the ugly, the uninteresting and the magnificent have made this place their home over the last hundred years. Impressive thirty-metre-high cliff faces define a coastline coated in graffiti and chewing gum. Bushy and vibrant banksias, bottlebrush trees and jacarandas overlook vast concrete schoolyards with wirenet fencing and rotten football poles. Newly renovated homes of glass and chrome sit above cracked footpaths with the fluorescent painted markings of half-finished utility work. This is North Bondi. This is home. I know my grandmother and I fit comfortably somewhere in the middle of this ragtag community, somewhere in there with the stoners and the supermodels, the Orthodox Jews in black coats and the young professionals in SUVs. The streets are full of stay-at-home mums with colourful prams, out-of work naturopaths with dirty bras, English tourists, Israeli backpackers, grumpy old men and hyperactive children.

For Sam, this place is a suburban hell, a bottomless pit of baggy tracksuit pants and unkempt hairdos that invariably smell of lavender oil and sweaty armpits. For Mama, this place is an urban nightmare, a concrete jungle with too much noise and too many accents, and she'd never set foot here again if it weren't for the fact that all her friends and family still live here.

My grandmother always greets me at her apartment with a goulash and a Monologue. Both have a similar effect on me: they fill me immediately with that warm, familiar taste of family, then leave me feeling irritated and uncomfortable for the rest of the day. I never learn. I always enjoy them greedily, completely in denial of the heaviness that inevitably follows.

"Hi my Lily," *kiss kiss*. She answers the door in a semi-transparent leopard print shirt, navy blue tracksuit pants and rollers in her hair. I can feel her crimson lipstick smear all over my cheeks. "Come in, daahrlink. You look terrible."

This is what's called a Jewish compliment.

"Thanks, Anyu," I reply.

My grandmother's name is Agi, but I've always called her Anyu, even though it means *mother* in Hungarian, not *grandmother*. Both my parents used that word when I was little. At first I thought it was her name, and later that it meant *grandmother*, and when I eventually learned the truth, it was too late. Anyu had stuck. It's the only part of my father's life that remains part of my every day. My mother, too, still calls her Anyu, though always through gritted teeth.

I head straight for the faux-wood table in the small dining area adjacent to the kitchen. The medium-brown shag-pile carpet makes the space seem even smaller than it is, its hairy fingers showing every wayward crumb and every granule of dust since the last half-hearted attempt at a vacuum by the "simple Filipino girl who hasn't stolen anything yet". That's Anyu being compassionate and understanding.

By the wall opposite the kitchen, a dark, wooden sideboard holds a messy patchwork of everyday things and obscure bits and pieces placed slowly one by one over the years, never to be thought about again: piles of half-opened bills and notices, car keys, colourful glass ashtrays, three fake Lalique statuettes of cats on an off-white crocheted doily, a set of blackened silver candlesticks, and a crystal decanter full of whisky next to three unmatched glasses. The table is set for one: a basket of rye bread with caraway seeds, a plate of roughly sliced pickled cucumbers, a large, steaming bowl of hearty beef and potato goulash soup and a plastic cup of soda water.

Anyu shuffles into the lime-green Formica kitchen to continue her pottering as I sit down. The sliding door separating the kitchen and the dining room is half open, and I can see her intermittently as she bustles to and fro.

But I have no problem hearing her.

I'm ready for it: today it's Monologue Number 43.

"It makes me awfully mad …," she begins.

My grandmother's monologues come in all shapes and sizes. There's the gentle but patronising lament on the plight of the peasant; the fiery rant about right-wing politics; the romantic and nostalgic account of Budapest in the 1920s; and the passionately paranoid tirades on world anti-Semitism. Then there's the lecture about living in a country whose kind but simple butchers give the best part of the meat to the dogs and the sermon on the absence of God during the war. And there are my favourites about how the Chinese and old men wearing hats are genetically pre-wired to be dangerous drivers, and how nothing is more barbaric than piercings, tattoos and chipped nail polish. The monologues are so well rehearsed and vary so little from recital to recital, that I sometimes find myself mouthing along to the words like I do with an old song. I'm not always in the mood for a monologue. Sometimes I can feel one about to break as it hangs heavy in the atmosphere and sometimes it comes out of a clear blue sky. Sometimes I find myself listening to one as if for the very first time, and sometimes I feel so lonely that I simply long for the comfort of her words.

Her monologues remind me of that famous joke about the old Jew who moves to a retirement home in Miami to start a new life. He is taken by a new acquaintance down to lunch where the gang meets daily. They are all sitting around chatting, when one of the group yells out "43!" which is met with roaring laughter. Another screams out "27!" Again, the place explodes. "What's going on?" asks the newcomer. "Well," the other explains, "we've all been together so long that we know every joke and every anecdote. So why bother repeating them? We just number them." The newcomer, eager to fit in, takes a deep breath, clears his throat, and goes for it. "32!" he says. Silence. When the chatter finally resumes, he turns to his friend. "What did I do wrong?" he asks. "Well," says the friend, "it's the *way* you tell it." And no one can tell a monologue quite like Anyu.

"... but whatever we do," she continues, "we must never let them think they are the powerful ones. For years we had them fooled and then came those bloody feminists who tried to be more and more like the men and you know what? Well, they become as stupid as the men in the end. Tell me, daahrlink, who said that women never had any power? We have always controlled men ... until these idiots came and tried to be like them ... it's your generation, Lily ..."

My mother is allergic to Anyu's monologues, in particular this one that ends with the bit about me being single and alone at twenty-two. By the second sentence, Mama is always up and out the door. My grandmother has been worried about my prospects since I graduated from high school. It's okay, she once explained to me, not to be a virgin when you get married, but it's not right for everyone to know it. My mother says she'd never let me get married so young, no matter what Anyu thinks. Neither has ever asked me what I think.

"... and we can't blame them either, poor daahrlinks. They are only simple creatures. They are made like that. You see, they are wired in such a way that there is only enough blood to go up or down, but not both ways at the same time. And then come all these women who couldn't find themselves a man, claiming that we need to have power over ourselves first. *Vot* rubbish! I'll show them power. All they need is an hour at my hairdresser's and a splash of red lipstick. Now that's power! Imagine, daahrlink, when I was a young girl, I had legs ... oh, all the way up to my armpits, and they queued around the block for just one dance ..."

Mama's told me all about my grandmother's legs, those same legs, she said, that just couldn't stay closed and got everyone into trouble.

"... when I was your age, daahrlink, things were different ..."

All of a sudden, I hear a scuffle at the door and smell a familiar, pungent concoction of perfume and cigarette smoke. Saved by the bell: rummy night.

"Ah, so they haven't forgotten me, the *kurvák!*" Anyu mutters, scrambling to undo the last of her hair rollers.

Dotsi, Zsuzsi and Punci are my grandmother's best friends and worst enemies. They come over faithfully every Thursday night at eight-fifteen on the dot for cards, whisky, chit-chat and the occasional scandal or two. Anyu calls them *kurvák*, or whores, but that's just her way of being affectionate. I call them *néni*, or auntie, even though we are not related at all. In Hungary, children always call older people in their lives *uncle* or *auntie* as a sign of respect, but they may as well be my real aunties. Apart from Mama and Anyu, I have no other family in Sydney. Both my mother and father were only children and Mama's parents passed away before I was born. There's a second cousin of Anyu's in America and Mama's great-uncle who never made it out of Hungary. I think Mama has a reasonably close relative who married a Russian soldier and moved to rural Poland, but no one talks about her anymore. The rest of my grandparents' family members never made it back from the war.

Anyu and the aunties are like real family. They are always arguing, but I can never entirely figure out what they are fighting about since they all talk at the same time. Regardless of the topic, they never agree. From the trivial, like money and men, to the more important, like money and men, I don't think they have ever suffered a harmonious conversation. They are so quick to disagree with each other that they'd rather contradict themselves than accidentally be caught with the same opinion.

But when it comes to an outsider, *any* outsider, they stick together like glue.

They are colourful creatures, with big hair, big diamonds and big boobs. Dotsi, the naïve and gullible one, has tattooed eyebrows and lives with the constant embarrassment of Irritable Bowel Syndrome. It can come at any time, *but when you've got to go, you've got to go.* She has a beautiful penthouse apartment with harbour views, but is, I'm told, too stupid to appreciate it. Zsuzsi, my favourite of the three, has flaming red hair and a temper to match. She always wears oversized sunglasses, day or night, and lives with the nuisance of an over-educated, over-liberal, WASP-y daughter-in-law and the shame of a homosexual grandson, although at least he is a doctor and has a good-looking boyfriend, which is more than Anyu can say about me. Punci, the envy of her generation, is the only one to live with a man. Always referred to by Punci and the gang as *The Special Friend*, he has managed to make it to the fabulous age of ninety-four with all his own teeth. He still plays tennis every Wednesday morning at the club and walks the two and a half kilometres down to the beach and back every morning come rain, hail or shine. He speaks seven languages fluently and still drives himself to the opera.

I turn to see them jostling and elbowing their way through the front door with arms flailing and air kisses all over the place. Dotsi's necklace gets caught on the balustrade. Punci drops her purse, knocking heads with Zsuzsi as they lose their footing on their way to the floor. It's like *The Three Stooges* in sequins.

I don't have time to laugh. Instead, the dance of disentanglement that follows has me and Anyu retreating to the sanctuary of her kitchen doorway.

"Idiot," says Zsuzsi. "A simple staircase she can't even climb without breaking all of our necks!"

"Come on Zsuzsi now, move that big arse of yours before you really hurt someone. And get rid of those glasses, would you? *Really,* I can't imagine how you made it up these bloody stairs ..." It isn't always Punci's fancy to protect Dotsi, but she often takes advantage of Zsuzsi's outbursts to slip into the role of defender, whoever the victim may happen to be.

"Well quite frankly, Punci daahrlink, thanks to our baby buffoon over there, I almost didn't ..."

"Baby buffoon? My dear, will you look in the mirror for just a minute? Dotsi, daahrlink, here, let me see, let me help ... what in God's name have you done to yourself?"

"Never mind what she's done to *us* ..."

"It wasn't my fault. My beads ..."

"*My* beads, you mean, which by now are probably tangled to oblivion. Let me remind you, Dotsi daahrlink, who gave you those beads in the first place ..."

"*Jaj!* You're pulling my hair!" Dotsi is now on all fours, and Anyu can't bear it any longer. She struts out of the kitchen and I fantasise for a moment that she's going to shut the front door and leave us in peace, but instead she grabs a pair of scissors from the counter top, mumbling to herself something about peasants, and I brace myself for the carnage.

"Precisely what I'm saying," Punci says, snatching the scissors from my grandmother. "If you weren't so smart about lending *her*, out of all people, your favourite beads, or should I say ex-beads, then we wouldn't be in this mess ..." *Snip.*

Everyone is safely inside the apartment, and I start to help Anyu clear away my plates and fit the green felt cloth over the table. My idea is to discreetly slink out the door without being noticed, but I know deep down that there is no getting out of here alive. I can see the wheels turning behind those hideous hairdos.

"You look too skinny, Lily daahrlink."

Too late. Punci starts the onslaught. "Doesn't she look too skinny, Zsuzsi? Agi, why aren't you feeding her?"

"What on earth do you mean?" Zsuzsi says. "Don't you know there's no such thing as too rich or too skinny? Or is it too pretty? Never mind ... You're okay, aren't you, Lily? Come on, leave her alone, girls." But the relief is only momentary. She suddenly turns my way, licking her lips, her eyes inflamed. "So tell me, come on, how did it go with the Muchovsky boy?" She sings *Much-ov-sky*, rocking her shoulders to the beat of each syllable.

"Muchovsky? You promised you'd tell her about Daniel Leventhal. You know, Helen's grandson." Punci always has better ideas.

"Leventhal? Don't you worry about him, Punci daahrlink, *he* found someone last week." Zsuzsi turns my way. "So tell me, was he nice? I told you he was nice!" She emphasises the last word with an affectionate tap on my shoulder, almost knocking me to the ground.

"Daniel Leventhal found someone? What a shame ..." Punci mumbles.

"I didn't call him," I say, without looking up. Of course he found someone. They always find someone sooner or later.

"I wonder who?" Punci scratches her head.

"You see, Lily, that's why you're in this situation. I can't do everything!" Followed by something in Hungarian.

"Who what?" Dotsi joins in. She's confused.

"Who did he find?"

"How should I know!" Zsuzsi now turns to Anyu. "She bloody asks me *who*. What am I, God? Can't you do something, Agi? Tell her to call the Muchovsky kid."

Anyu looks at me with longing eyes. She knows there is no way I will call him. I have never met him, but I already know the type: a good, solid job, maybe even a Master's degree. Plays some instrument like a dream and lost quite a lot of weight recently, or was it hair? Just out of a long relationship and bitter break-up with a non-Jewish girl from the office who was pretty but, as predicted, *simple*. And of course, we have so much in common because we are both single.

I pretend to rearrange the contents of my handbag as the four of them sit down to deal the first hand. I have to get out of here. I can stomach a little monologue, but a real live ensemble is too much for tonight.

"You're not leaving yet, are you, Lily?" says Punci. "Dotsi may need some help!" She laughs heartily and the barrage continues from all directions, this time in Hungarian, as Dotsi scurries urgently down the hallway to the toilet.

Anyu accompanies me to the doorway with a take-home pack of a week's supply of goulash and rye bread. I wave a broad goodbye in their general direction, dreaming of the day I'll be able to join in the banter in their own tongue, beat them at their own game. Eva will teach me a little something worthwhile: scathing but elegant, razor-sharp but cool. Knock their socks off. Imagine, if only they knew what I have up my sleeve. If only they knew my source. I can't wait till Saturday and my first Hungarian lesson.

"Forget the Muchovsky kid, daahrlink," my grandmother whispers at the door, just out of earshot. "His grandmother cheats at rummy. Romanian peasant stock. Trust me on this one. This Zsuzsi always thinks she knows everything."

I kiss her goodbye and leave her to her band of cronies. She won't be lonely tonight, but I feel sad for this once beautiful woman who reluctantly traded Old World elegance for sensible underwear and comfortable pants. Sometimes I catch glimpses of her former, lively self, but mostly I see this once prominent member of society relegated to the position of the irritating grandmother who nags and cooks too much. She spends her days attending the funerals of people she hated and her evenings at the rummy table with other bitter, fading souls. She's forever waiting for that miserable, monthly government cheque and for her *daahrlink* Lily to get on with it and live a happy life for her.

I step outside into the humid night, throw her leftovers into the rubbish bin on the corner, light a cigarette and start climbing the familiar hill towards the cliffs and home.

I guess when my grandmother sees me, she feels sad too. They say getting old is depressing, but it's better than the alternative. She must know that, just like my Papa, I might not make it that far.

Chapter Four

I have the whole day off. The whole day, that is, except for an early brunch with my mother at the Tea Gardens in Watson's Bay. This is Mama's idea of refinement: a salad sandwich on multigrain bread followed by Devonshire tea prepared painfully slowly from scratch by a brother-sister team whose family has owned this house for a million years. She'll make a point of asking for extra milk with her tea, of noting how the scones and cream are a luxury her hips can't really afford, and of casually mentioning the fact that she herself was born right here in Sydney. We'll spend the hour arguing about what we're wearing, what we're reading, what the Prime Minister should and shouldn't be doing, and then she'll empty out a purse full of silver and spend the next ten minutes excruciatingly assembling the total of the bill from ten and twenty cent coins. I'll head back home drained, hungry and irritated with no energy left to paint.

I'm working on a set of portraits of women. Their faces have been haunting my thoughts now for what feels like an eternity, but it's only in the last few weeks, since I quit my medical course, that I've had the chance to start bringing them to life on canvas. Most are still rough sketches with smatterings of colour, and two of them are still just eyes. I always start with the eyes: the centre, the window. My inspiration comes from those two little sparks. If the eyes don't work, the rest of the face will never see the light of day. I've been practising, playing with colour and depth and highlights. Now I look at an eye and see the person, not the vitreous, sclera, cornea and how they all relate to the optic nerve. Gone are the days of learning a person by parts.

This morning I feel like painting, like taking bits and pieces from the world of the real and rearranging them on paper to please my imagination. I'm not bound to anyone's vision of how things are but mine. I can take an eyebrow from here, a wrinkle from there, and create the look of how I'd like things to be. Mostly I paint the women of my family how I see them, not necessarily how they look. I paint my mother and my grandmother, I even paint myself – but I am not happy with those. The times I try to faithfully reproduce what I know, I am left dissatisfied. It is never enough.

My bedroom wall is plastered with eyes – scraps of photos, magazine cuttings and sketches: the beautiful, the interesting, the plain, the absurd, images I've liked and images I've hated, techniques I've mastered and those I've yet to explore. They are all there, staring at me while I paint and while I sleep. They make me feel less lonely. But they see all. Sam says it's creepy, but I don't think so. I like their company. They just watch; there's no advice, no opinions, no judgement.

The telephone rings. I can't find the phone. I scramble out from behind the easel and almost knock my head on the side of the internal archway separating my bedroom and the kitchen. It's just two rooms, my flat: a decent-sized bedroom with a huge window looking out onto Blair Street and a combined kitchen/dining/living/entertaining room. From up here on the third floor you can see the line of red-brick apartment buildings go on forever and the all-day traffic jam at the roundabout outside the butcher. The kitchen is big enough for a table and a washing machine, and the cabinets hold all my cooking stuff with room to spare for my paints and brushes. The floor is faux-timber and the walls are painted pale yellow but it's in pretty good condition for the measly three hundred and fifty dollars a week I pay for it. It is still North Bondi.

The phone keeps ringing. I finally find it. It's under my pillow.

"What's up?" I say.

It's Sam.

"I need you," he says. He is huffing and puffing and I wonder what inanity he has turned into the crisis of the century this time: his favourite café took the bread-and-butter pudding off the menu or Stephanie from *The Bold and the Beautiful* found out the man she thought was her real father was in fact her brother. Maybe Britney Spears is back in rehab.

"Don't be a bitch," he says. "I've had a fucking accident."

"Fuck."

"I know."

"Are you okay?"

"I'm fine."

"What about Jackson?" Sam has names for all his important tools. His Jeep is Jackson, his phone is Monkey, his penis is Phoenix.

"Oh, he's fine. A little scratch on the bumper. Nothing serious."

"That's a relief."

Silence. I hear a faint rustling, a click, and then a deep exhale.

"Sam?"

"I don't think anyone saw me. But I can't be sure."

"Sam – Sam, don't tell me … Oh my God, what happened?"

"Don't worry, nothing bad. It wasn't my fault. I had a hideous migraine."

"Well?"

"He had it coming."

"Who?"

"The guy! I don't know who! I just know he had it coming."

"What happened, Sam? What did you do?"

"I was parking in the lane in Darlinghurst, you know the one, the tiny lane where I always park off Darlinghurst Road. He was in the way, an ugly blue station-wagon. Not a big deal. I had a headache and I couldn't really concentrate. It was just a little tail light, that's all. The guy must have had it coming. I mean, it must have been karma."

"What?"

"Karma. I was just delivering his karma. Not my fault."

"Are you nuts?"

"Jesus, Lily, why are you in such a fucking bad mood all of a sudden?"

"I guess you didn't leave your number."

"It wasn't my fault, Lily. I mean, *don't shoot the messenger* and all that. I told you it was karma. God knows what the other guy actually did."

I pause for a minute. I don't think I have an appropriate response.

"Are you okay?" I say, eventually.

"I'm a mess. I can't face work. I'm calling in sick."

I invite him to come with me to Watson's Bay for scones and cream with my mother. I feel he needs something sweet to get him through the rest of the day, and I need a buffer against the advice I'm sure Mama has prepared to pile on me so she can get through her day.

"Pick me up in fifteen minutes," I say.

When Sam arrives, we check out the damage. Jackson looks completely fine. The hairline scratch on the bumper isn't obvious even when he points it out to me. Sam, on the other hand, *is* a mess.

"You haven't been home yet, have you?" He is still wearing his party clothes: a tight black T-shirt and even tighter black jeans. His suit, business shirt and purple tie are hanging in the back seat. "Give me the keys," I say. "I'm not in the mood for dodgems today."

In the car on the way to brunch we talk about guys. Sam tells me how he spent the night dancing with pretty strangers, but didn't get lucky with any particular one. We pass through the leafy Rose Bay streets. It's another glorious spring day in Sydney. Mercifully, the temperature dropped ten degrees overnight, and the cool, crisp air carries hints of sea salt and diesel fuel. The footpaths are peppered with squashed petunias and the purple confetti of jacaranda petals.

"I still had a good night," he explains. "What about you?"

"I thought it'd be a quiet one, but Jeremy called up at midnight."

"Jeremy? Oh Lily, no, not again." Jeremy and I are each other's backup plan. Whenever either one of us is bored or lonely we call the other for an easy lay. It's not a particularly passionate affair, but it's reliable. And it's all we both have right now.

"He's not that bad," I say.

"He's a dag."

"He's around."

"He's boring."

"He calls."

Sam and I are the only ones of our friends who are still single. We always joke that we have each other, but it's not really that funny. Even if Sam wasn't gay, we'd probably kill each other within a week. Monogamy is Sam's idea of a nightmare, but I guess I'm open to the idea. I'm still not sure what it is I want more, the boyfriend or the peace having a boyfriend will bring me: no more anxious monologues from Anyu, no more random set-ups from Punci and the gang, no more pathetic grooming advice from my girlfriends. They say it's all about love, but one thing I know is that a steady relationship would be a gift for those who love me the most: Sam, who loves the drama; Mama, who wishes for me the relationship she never had; and Anyu, who simply can't stand the shame.

We're almost there. They are digging up the road again on the S-bends leading down to the water. Five fluorescent-clad workers hover around a fractured hole, smoking cigarettes and talking on their phones, as one lone man jackhammers away at the bitumen. Sam motions for me to slow down so we can catch a glimpse of their gleaming, sweaty bodies. He sticks his fading chewing gum briefly on his index finger and lets out a strident wolf whistle, met equally vigorously by whoops and jeers from the troops. I quickly check the rear view mirror to make sure they're not following us with a sledgehammer. Sam smiles. He's feeling better. But I'm worrying about whether or not we'll find parking and how we can avoid the hordes of toddlers and geriatrics in the park on their precious day out and the busloads of Japanese tourists who will cram up the boardwalk in front of the café with their ever so polite murmuring and shuffling, blocking the view of the city skyline and the only reason to sit at that café in the first place.

As we get closer, I catch Sam mouthing a silent prayer to the God of Parking.

"Pray with me," he says, reaching for my hand.

"You know I don't believe in Him," I say.

I slow down and pull up in front of the white, knee-high wicker fence bordering the Tea Gardens. I scan the lawn while Sam looks ahead for a parking miracle. Mama is already there, her nose buried in the *Sydney Morning Herald*. She is wobbling on the rickety wrought-iron seat whose legs sink unevenly into the sparsely covered lawn. The café is uncharacteristically quiet. An elderly couple sips tea from paper cups near the fishpond. A skinny, rat-like dog noses around in the flowerbed. A bored waiter slowly wraps cutlery in serviettes by the counter. A car pulls out of a space right in front of us.

Sam grins.

"Screw you," I say.

Mama is excited to see us. She has news.

"Did you read about the monstrosity they want to build over at Darling Harbour? That place is getting uglier by the day."

I didn't read anything. I haven't read the paper for years, instead trusting Mama to wade through the news for me and filter out the important from the trivial. Sam's ready for a discussion; he loves any kind of drama, but she's not really interested in talking more about it.

"Aren't you kids working today?"

"Yeah," I say.

"I'm not in the mood," Sam says.

"What time do you start?" Mama asks.

"Oh, I'm not going to the gallery. I'm working at home."

"You mean painting?" she says. It is unfathomable to Mama that I dropped out of university to paint. "Oh Lily, if it's painting that you really want to do, well, nothing is wrong with that – you have plenty of time on the weekend for colouring in! But giving away your hard-earned place in medicine to draw pictures all day, well that's insanity." She turns to Sam. "Even *he* has a respectable job, right Sam?"

A respectable job for a *poof*, she means. A project manager, he sits in front of a buzzing computer screen all day and then has to drink and snort himself to oblivion each night so he can muster up enough strength to do it all over again the next day.

"You know I would have given anything to have gone to university. You don't know how lucky you are." Mama is the most educated person in her family even though she left her home economics high school when she wasn't quite fifteen. "Us girls weren't even expected to get our Leaving Certificate, darling. What for? It wouldn't be long before we'd find ourselves husbands and in the meantime, we had better earn our keep." It wasn't that Mama was stupid. Not at all. That was the problem. If she had been, there wouldn't have been a story. It's that she knew exactly what she was missing out on. "You see, Sam, you probably don't know this about me, but when Lily was a little girl, I went back to night school to finish high school, but then her father got sick again and it was all over. I had no help. We couldn't afford it. I had to go back to work and keep us going."

Sam nods understandingly. "Well, I think she's talented. Have you seen what she's done lately? What about talent?"

"What about talent? I'll tell you about talent. *Talent schmalent.* If it were all about talent, then I wouldn't bat an eyelid. But darling, it's a business. And a bad one at that. She'll never make a cent, that is, until she dies, so she'll be working at that silly little gallery for the next million years."

"She's gonna make you proud one day, Judy," Sam says. I'm glad he's here. I'm a ball of fire in front of the canvas, but I can never put two words together in front of my family.

"Yeah," I say.

"Proud? I was proud the day she was born. I was proud when she was dux of her class. I was proud when she got into medicine. I'll be proud again when she's a doctor." For weeks now Mama hasn't been able to face her friends. For what? To chat with Susan (whose son just got into Harvard Business School) or Cathy (whose twin girls will be the youngest barristers in Sydney)? It has become unbearable for her. Even Elizabeth's boy has a PhD. *How's Lily doing in her studies? When is she due to finish? When will she be a doctor?* They used to ask. And now they've found out I've dropped out, they ask again. Only louder.

It is hard for Mama. She has her private disappointment and her public disgrace.

And then she has Anyu.

According to Anyu, my failure, like our financial situation and my father's death, is Mama's fault. So was last weekend's bad weather, the traffic jam this morning and the fall of Rome. That's what happens, Anyu says, when you marry peasants. I know Monologue Number 14 by heart: *Peasants. Jewish peasants. That's what they were. You know, there were a lot of them in Hungary. Butchers. Tailors. Shopkeepers. Couldn't read or write, didn't know Nietzsche from their neighbour. And every now and then, one or two of them had the luck to make it big. Not your Mama's parents, of course. Don't be silly. But you know the Berger family from next door to the Lowensteins? Like them. Struck gold making belts. Can't read or write. His father was a schlepper for a tailor in Budapest, but when they came here, they made a fortune from little strips of leather. Well, everyone needs to hold their pants up, no? Good for them, I say, lucky break! But peasants nonetheless.*

Mama's father was a baker's assistant, a far cry from the professors and doctors littering my father's pedigree.

"Come on, Judy," Sam tells her. "Where's your sense of romance?"

"You think I don't know about romance? You think I don't know about art? I'm not an idiot. I've been taking Lily to galleries since she was a baby." Mama loves the idea, in principle at least, of someone being a painter. There is something chic, something civilised, about being an artist, and in that affected, small–l liberal way of hers she fancies herself a bit of a patron of the arts, a member of the avant-garde. But while it's terrific for others to live that kind of life, who would wish it on their own child? "Do you know what it takes to be a success? You think it's about hanging around, smoking cigarettes, arguing politics and painting pictures? Come on, kids, don't be so bloody naïve. Without an education, a woman is nothing. Trust me. You're going to marry the first no-hoper who walks through the door and all of a sudden, your dreams are gone. And then when the kids are all grown up and out of the house, when the husband is gone, what have you got? Hey? What have you got?"

"Nothing."

Nothing.

Just like her.

The food arrives and Mama spends the next few minutes complaining to the waiter about the scones, which are too hot, and the tea, which is too cold.

"Sorry," I tell him, "we're Hungarian."

Sam throws him a knowing wink.

I've found my voice.

"I took Anyu to Frankie's funeral," I say.

"I know. I know. I just hope she bloody behaved herself. You're a saint, Lily, did you know that? A saint. I'm sorry I didn't come with you. I couldn't, you know, you understand?"

"Sure."

"He was a bastard," she says from a mouthful of crumbling scone.

"I know."

"I bet Anyu was *awfully mad!* Who else was there?"

"Everyone."

"Mmm."

Sam excuses himself. Out of the corner of my eye I catch him on his way to the bathroom, leaning on the counter talking to the waiter.

I take a deep breath. I reach for a cigarette. I change my mind. Not now. Just say it. Another deep breath.

"Mama ..."

"Yes."

"Mama, well …"

"Yes, Lily, what?"

"Umm, Mama …"

"For God's sake, what is it, Lily?"

She picks up her newspaper and flicks through the sports pages.

"Never mind," I say.

I reach for another cigarette. I see Sam flirting with the waiter. He looks across to me and winks. He gives me courage.

"Eva was there," I finally tell her.

"Who?"

"You know. *Eva.* I think she used to be Anyu's friend. You know. But Anyu got really upset and we left."

"God, it must have been hot out there. Can you believe the air-conditioner stopped working Wednesday morning? Can you imagine the heat in the office without air-conditioning? I should have called the bloody union. That's what I should have done!"

"She recognised me, you know, after all these years."

Sam sashays back to the table waving a phone number on the back of an order form. He sits down triumphantly.

"No, wait," Mama continues, mainly towards Sam. "I should have gone to the funeral! That's what I should have done. It would have been cooler than that bloody furnace of an office, you know. But Anyu, oh Lily, I can just imagine how Anyu must have been in a shocker of a mood in that heat."

"I'm sort of … you know … kind of interested, you know … I'm sort of curious about Eva …"

"I probably should have sent Mrs Symonds a note. She probably thinks I'm a terrible person. But what was I going to say? Huh? *Oh, I'm sorry your bastard of a husband finally dropped dead.* No, it's better this way. I'm sick of bullshit. I'm sick of all these charades."

"And then, you know, as fate would have it, we … we sort of bumped into her at Dr Horvath's surgery."

Sam joins in. "Imagine, Judy, not for fifteen years, and then Lily bumps into her twice in one day! I think it's a sign." He smiles.

"A sign? A *sign?* You know what it's a sign of?" Mama puts down her cup of tea and throws her serviette on the table. "It's a sign of you being an idiot! You want to talk about fate? I'll tell you about fate! It's nonsense. Bloody nonsense. I don't want to hear about it. Lily, you're starting to sound like your father. You've been spending too much time with your grandmonster. You kids are going backwards, you know that, back to the dark ages. Why would anyone want to go back to the Old World? What the hell is wrong with you people?"

I smile. I know how Mama thinks. It's ideas like fate that made her decide never to teach me Hungarian. *The bullshit stops here*, she always says. But things are more complicated than that. You can't just cover up centuries of paranoia and superstition with a university degree, a different language and a new country, even one tucked away at the end of the world. The truth is this: bullshit runs in families, like curly hair or big noses. For some, it may be a recessive gene, but I feel the Hungarian-ness in my blood and I need someone to decode it for me before it becomes too toxic.

Mama suddenly gathers up her purse and keys. She glances quickly at her watch and stands up. She mumbles something about having to go and turns away.

"And stay away from that bitch Eva," she says, already halfway to the gate. "She's bad news."

Too late, I think. My fate is already sealed. Tomorrow is Saturday, the day I am to meet Eva at eleven am in a café in Double Bay for my very first Hungarian lesson.

Chapter Five

She's not here. I'm ten minutes late and she's not here.

I panic.

Maybe Mama was right. Maybe Eva is bad news. What on earth am I doing here? I can just hear Eva's voice as she booms over the telephone line to her own Dotsis and Puncis, laughing out loud about *that skinny, sickly granddaughter of Agi who is still single and, imagine daahrlink, comes to me to learn Hungarian because her own mother simply forgot.*

I check my phone. There is a voicemail from Dr Horvath's receptionist reminding me of my new appointment time and a cryptic text from Sam: *don't do anything I wouldn't do ;)*

I shouldn't have come so late. I spent an irritating morning working on a portrait of Anyu that looked at me accusingly. It got worse and worse with every layer of paint. It was the eyes. Anyu was watching me.

I take a deep breath. I settle into a booth in a far corner of the café and I wait. I think back to my last words with Eva.

"Come to the café on Saturday, daahrlink. I'll be there at eleven."

She didn't have to explain. I knew exactly which café she meant. It used to be *the* place to be seen in Double Bay: the place for Continental delicacies with a Hungarian accent, the place of my childhood. The Oktogon.

I haven't been here in more than fifteen years. Zany Gypsy music spills out from behind the bar. It's the soundtrack of my childhood: slow, repetitive whining that gradually builds up into a heated frenzy and when it finally hits that crescendo, there's only momentary relief. I wait for it to start all over again.

It's a bit early in the morning for frantic violins, but I smile. I'm home.

I look around. The place is empty. The smell of simmering *bableves*, bean soup, seeps in from the kitchen doorway and suddenly I'm six years old again. I remember long afternoons in one of these dark booths by a mirrored wall, sweating on sticky, burgundy vinyl benches. I remember the smell of fried onions and the sound of bickering in a disorienting blend of English and Hungarian. I remember the little tears in the seats that opened up under pressure, revealing a yellowy, spongy mattress that crumbled in your fingers and stuck under your nails. There was the fat delivery boy from the pastry shop. There were never-ending bowls of creamed spinach and the smell of cinnamon on my plum dumplings. I remember feeling at home.

I also remember when Mama told me that we would not be going back there anymore. I didn't ask why. There was no point. I knew the answer already: *Don't be an idiot, Lily.*

But that was more than fifteen years ago. I'm an adult now. I can have coffee wherever I like.

I think.

"I'll see you there, daahrlink, don't be late," Eva had warned me as she tumbled out of Sam's Jeep. Brilliant, I thought. We'll be safe there. I knew it would be the one place neither Mama nor Anyu would ever set foot, the one place their friends would never go, the ultimate safe haven. Still, I choose the booth furthest from the street front and sit with my back to the window.

You just never know.

I order a black coffee from an earnest-looking waiter with a sexy just-got-out-of-bed hairstyle. My fourth coffee for the day. He smiles sweetly as he rushes by. I wonder where he's going in such a hurry. Apart from a young Asian couple hovering dreamily over a giant bowl of rainbow ice-cream and a middle-aged woman agonising over the cake display, the place is empty.

The Oktogon isn't what it used to be. The room looks neglected. Lonely, limp carnations rest on every table beside unlit candles in petite glass bottles. Faded burgundy drapes frame dull mirrored walls. A heap of coffee-table-book-sized menus in tattered vinyl covers lies in a leaning tower beside the bar. A row of identical, bronze, semi-naked ladies with feathered headdresses lines the wall stretching all the way to the front door. One leans casually over my head balancing an orb in her outstretched palm. But there's nothing enchanting about her: the unlit bulb is mottled and discoloured and the end of her perky nose is chipped.

The waiter notices me from the other side of the empty room; he smiles again, scratches his head, buzzes around in an awkward semi-pirouette and then scurries off excitedly through the swinging doors to the kitchen. The Asian couple leave quietly and their leftovers sit on the table melting into a brown mess. What's happened to my Oktogon? Where is the bustle and commotion, the prancing and gossiping? I remember constantly wrinkling up my nose at the strong perfumes and waiting *ages* in the queue to the toilet. I remember fancy outfits, glamorous women applying lipstick in front of the mirror, and the incessant *ka-ching* of the register. Now all I see are leftovers. The Oktogon is no longer Old World. It's just plain old.

The entire Double Bay, or as we like to say, *Double Pay*, isn't what it used to be. Though it may still be home to the chic designer boutiques and

Viennese-style coffee houses that originally gave it its reputation for glamour and wealth, there's a palpable change on the streets. New money. Young money. The sunglasses are still big, the accents still strong, the perfume still potent, but these are no longer my people. The accent has changed. It is an accent fed on different flavours, different guilt trips, different tales of hardship and escape on their way to the Lucky Country. Gone are the elegant women in Chanel leaving three-hour salon appointments with big hair, carefully balancing their handbags on outstretched freshly painted nails; gone are the parties of suntanned, open-shirted gentlemen with heavy gold chains sipping cappuccinos at roadside tables. Instead there are groups of Asian university students sharing frozen yoghurt sundaes on plastic furniture and handsome, young, Armenian accountants at American coffee chains ordering double caramel decaf mochaccinos with soy milk.

It used to be that everyone knew me in Double Bay. I couldn't take three steps without someone pinching my cheeks or thrusting some sweets in my hand. They'd lean forward, bend down, throw me a token *how's school?* and then turn to Mama or Anyu without waiting for a reply and start talking in Hungarian. I'd squash ants in the cracks on the footpath with my sandals or nibble on the chocolate croissant I'd been handed until it would be time to go the next three steps. But that was many years ago.

As soon as I was old enough to stay home by myself, I rarely chose to accompany Mama or Anyu and their friends on their window-shopping coffee-house-stopping Double Bay circuits. When I eventually started going out with friends and boys unchaperoned, I preferred the anonymous, urban streets of Darlinghurst, Sydney's more hip, less up-market version of a café-boutique neighbourhood or the trendy Danks Street, where my gallery is. It was there that I had my first taste of freedom. The sound of sirens, the smell of bus fumes, the feel of grit and grime under my fingernails, the sight of facial piercings, purple hair, random graffiti. There I could wander all day without bumping into a single familiar face.

I never imagined how lonely that would feel here in Double Bay.

"What a surprise. I didn't think you'd come." A throaty voice comes out of nowhere, tired, jaded. I can't tell whether she's pleased or irritated.

"Eva?"

"Change places with me, will you, daahrlink? I have to keep my eye on them." I move to the other side of the booth, my inner thigh smack bang on top of one of those bristly cuts in the vinyl, my face exposed, directly opposite the front door. "Is that all you're having? Nixon, Nixon daahrlink," she sits down with a thump and calls over the waiter. "Bring us a nice piece of cake will you? The big one, daahrlink. Oh, don't look so worried, Lily. It's not for you." She slaps his bottom as he zooms away, then bellows after him. "And get me a coffee, daahrlink, would you?" *Vood you?*

"Sugar today?" he calls back.

"Five sugars! But don't stir … you know I don't like it sweet." She coughs up half her lungs and then whispers in my direction. *"He's gorgeous, you know, but so simple …"*

We watch him fumble over the cake display and we wait. He finally arrives with a generous portion of Black Forest cake, mounds of fresh cream atop a mountain of chocolate sponge littered with ruby-red cherries and snowflakes of icing.

I feel sick. Anyu is going to kill me.

"See ya, ladies," he announces, and then something in Hungarian. Eva responds, but I just stare at him. Something's not right. He's too young and too handsome to be speaking Hungarian. Only old people speak Hungarian.

Eva changes to English. "Meet my niece Lily. This is Nixon, daahrlink. Isn't he gorgeous?" I manage a half-smile. Niece? "Well we are sort of related, by marriage anyway."

So she is family. That answers my first question.

"See ya, Lily," he says, smiling. Is he saying goodbye? What do I say?

"Lily wants to learn Hungarian, don't you, daahrlink?"

I cringe.

But she's right. We are not here for fun. I take out a small exercise book and a pencil. I scribble a quick title: *Hungarian Lessons, November 2009.* Ready for action. Business only. I may be her niece, but this is no social call. I want that to be clear.

I conscientiously write down "see ya" on the first page.

"It's with a 'z'. S-Z-I-A. *Szia.*" Nixon reaches across the table to point out my mistake. "*Szia.* 'Sz' always sounds like an 's' in Hungarian. Our 's' is pronounced 'sh', and our …" I tune out. Eva's right. He *is* gorgeous. Clear, hazel eyes look straight into mine, as if without a care in the world. He has a handsome, boyish face with a sprinkling of freckles on his cheeks and two adorable little dimples framing a soft mouth. There's something earnest about him. (Or is it *simple?*) There's no design about his messy hair, no pretence in his voice, no hidden melodrama in his wrinkled brow. Anyu will definitely hate him.

"… so you see once you know how a letter is pronounced, it never changes, never ever. It's easy as pizza pie!" The waiter Eva calls Nixon has just given me my first Hungarian lesson: *Hungarian is actually easy to learn.*

"What does it mean, then?" I ask. "What's *szia?*"

Eva manages an opinion in between a mouthful of cream and a hearty cough. "Don't worry too much about *szia*, daahrlink. That's not what you're here for. Only real Hungarians say *szia*. We don't talk like that."

We means Jews, or Hungarian Jews who, according to my family, are not really Hungarian at all. Jews are different. They look different, speak differently, dress differently, value their family differently. Jews are educated differently, gamble differently, drink and beat up their wives differently. All this is fine until a non-Jewish Hungarian says anything about us being different. I wonder whether Nixon is Jewish. I wonder whether he is offended, if he understands.

But he doesn't bat an eyelid. "You know what *szervusz* means, don't you?"

"Sure," I say. *Szervusz* means both hello and goodbye. It is one of the few words of Hungarian I already know, together with *bazd meg az anyád* (fuck your mother) and *nem akarok fürödni* (I don't want a bath). Invaluable phrases indeed, but they only take you so far in a conversation.

"Well *szervusz* is old fashioned now. Hungarians have replaced it with *szia*," Nixon continues. "And it's not even true Hungarian word." Eva rolls her eyes. "Lots of people use it, don't they, Eva *néni?* Austrians, Germans … It comes from the Latin: *servus humillimus, I am your most humble servant.*"

I smile. I can't imagine the Hungarians I know being anyone's humble anything.

"And *szia* is so Hungarian then?" Eva asks. "Nixon daahrlink, stop putting propaganda into a little girl's head. Such a proud Hungarian, he hasn't told you where *szia* comes from, has he? Did you ever play poker, Lily?"

I nod.

"The only English these Hungarians remember comes from their beloved card games – *I see ya 250 forints, and I raise ya another 500.* Don't let them tell you how humble they are, Lily, don't fall for it."

"Yes," Nixon says, earnestly. "It does come from English, or probably *American.*" I watch his eyes light up. *America!* "It's from see ya later. It means the same as *szervusz*. Hello and goodbye." His entire body straightens up with pride. "Only more modern, of course."

"*Vonderful!*" Eva says. She licks her fork. "Go get me another piece of cake, would you? Lily's not hungry. I'm eating here for two." She then turns to me as he diligently dashes away. "What?" she says. *Vot?* "He needs something to do."

I watch him at the counter. He carefully prepares the cake, stopping every so often to throw a comment back towards the kitchen. He gets more and more distracted until he finally gives up on Eva's order and disappears through the swinging doors behind him.

"Nixon's a funny name," I say to Eva. I'm not so interested in our lessons anymore.

Eva sighs. "I know. I know. Not everyone is like us," she whispers. "Yes, everyone dreamed of escaping, but not everyone had the balls to leave in fifty-six like us. And when it was too late, it was just too late."

Hungarians talk about "fifty-six" like everyone else knows what they're talking about. It was the year of the Hungarian Revolution. Hurting from years of harsh Stalinist rule, the Hungarians staged a revolution which was quickly quashed by Soviet tanks. In those few short, chaotic weeks during which the borders were open, over a quarter of a million Hungarians fled the country, among them Eva, Anyu and my father. Those who got out quickly were the lucky ones. The West, deep in anti-Communist sentiment, opened its borders, its hearts and its wallets, and these refugees could literally go wherever they wished. But for those left behind, there was no more chance to escape. The Iron Curtain fell again, heavier than ever before, and it would be another forty years before Hungarians were allowed to leave. But it didn't stop the population from dreaming.

"They dreamed of America, they did. So when Nixon was born, they gave him a name that would help him in the big, wide world. But imagine, I'll let him tell you one day what it was like to grow up in state-run socialist youth groups with a name like *Nixon*." She stops momentarily for another coughing fit. "Between you and me, daahrlink, his parents were peasants. I mean, it's obvious, isn't it? Why not call him Pierre or something more intelligent if they wanted him to leave Hungary one day?"

I laugh. Anyu and her friends are the same. For their generation of women, no one is more sophisticated or refined than the French. No one more complicated or elegant. And as for Americans, no one is more crass.

"And they didn't even realise, you see, that Nixon is a family name."

I know this about Hungarians. They always say the last name first. It's Horvath Georgie, Freedman Eva, Nixon Richard. "So it's Nixon with a bloody 'X'. Come daahrlink, let me show you the Hungarian letters." She snatches the exercise book from my hands and takes over. She writes down the alphabet. "They are a little bit different to what you are used to, you know. But you'll be happy in the end. Once you know how they are pronounced, they'll never change on you. Ever."

I listen to her deep, scratchy voice go through the sounds, and watch her long, red claws point one by one to the elegantly scrawled letters on the page. I diligently repeat after her: *ahh, beh, tzeh* ... I catch a glimpse of Nixon at the bar. He really is cute. He is excited and animated, arms all over the place, talking to a big man in a bloodstained white apron who, if not for his jovial cheeks and lively eyes, looks more like an axe murderer than anyone I'd imagine seeing in a Double Bay café. I wonder if they're talking about me.

"Concentrate, Lily!" Eva snaps. "Come, repeat after me."

I don't know what I am expecting from my first Hungarian lesson, but sitting here repeating isolated, meaningless sounds one after the other isn't part of it. I know I won't leave the café this afternoon able to speak Hungarian, equipped with a new understanding of my personal history and cultural identity. But there is something surreal about my quest. I am, after all, learning the unlearnable. And Eva's not helping.

She senses my frustration. "Lily, come on! You are the one who wants to learn Hungarian. I know this already!"

But I can't help myself. "I want to learn sentences. This is boring!" I'm a little shocked that I actually said it, but it's the truth.

Eva isn't shocked at all. "Now come on, daahrlink, you're just being like your grandmother now. Don't be ridiculous. Hungarian is, after all, impossible to learn!" She coughs and reaches for her unlit cigarette. "Think you know best? You have to trust me, Lily. We can do this, but you have to let me do things my way. Okay?"

I nod. *My vay.*

"Jesus," she says. "What on earth has she done to you, you poor thing? I didn't really imagine she would fuck you up so badly."

Three tables arrive at the same time for lunch and Eva gets up to seat them. I pack my stuff and leave the café hungry and exhausted. I sit in my car and stare at the crisp exercise book. *Hungarian Lessons, November 2009.* I think about my outburst and the cute Hungarian waiter called Nixon. Eva gave me some homework and we arranged to meet again next Saturday morning, although, to be honest, I'm not so sure I'll be there.

But then there is Nixon. Maybe this whole thing isn't such a bad idea after all.

I open the first page and practise the alphabet. *Ahh, beh, tzeh* ... I go through the entire alphabet, and then again. I shake my head.

Typical.

There is no X.

Chapter Six

The phone wakes me at midday.

"Lily, it's me. Where on earth are you? I've been calling for over an hour."

Me who? I sit up to look out the window. It's raining again.

"Lily? Honey? It's Camilla! Are you all right?"

"I ... I'm ... I've just been ..."

"Never mind. I need you. Jacqueline called in sick and I need someone here to help set up for this afternoon. The Big A is coming! Can you get in here?"

I waver. It's my day off. I want to spend the day on Anyu's portrait. I'm grumpy. It's raining.

"Umm, let's see. Hold on a minute." I press the mute button and throw the phone down on the bed. I already know I'll help her out. I'm too curious to meet the Big A. But it's good for her to sweat. I go to the toilet, brush my teeth, and turn on the coffee machine. I can hear Camilla's muffled pleas from within the bedspread. I choose an outfit she'll probably hate and finally pick up the phone.

"Okay, I'll be there," I say, putting the phone down before she has time to hang up without saying thank you.

The bus is almost empty when I get on at Bondi Junction. An elderly woman with empty shopping bags on her lap grapples with her mobile phone and a teenage boy with industrial-sized earphones nods emphatically to the beat.

"Vun ticket to Crown Street," I say, almost in a whisper, as if that's the way I always talk, and find a seat by the window. The traffic is stop-go-stop-go all the way down Oxford Street and I watch people in their cars talk to themselves and pick their noses like they are all alone in their bathrooms.

Vot idiots, I think to myself.

It's been almost a week since my first Hungarian lesson and I've been reluctantly working on the homework Eva gave me.

"For one week, speak only with a Hungarian accent," she said to me.

"You've got to be kidding!" I said.

Why wouldn't anyone take me seriously?

She laughed. "Isn't that *vonderful,* daahrlink … I'll teach you how to speak English with a Hungarian accent." But she wasn't joking. "*Vell,*" she continued, looking straight at me with big eyes. "Do you want to learn Hungarian or not? Do you trust me or not?"

I don't trust her. But she's all I've got.

"You think it is easy talking like this?" Eva, like Anyu, sounds like she just stepped off the boat. And it's only been fifty-two years! But apart from the occasional mistake that I'd classify more as charming than grammatical, her English, unlike Anyu's, is quite respectable.

So I go along with it. How hard can it be? The Hungarian accent is the music of my childhood. I can recognise Hungarians speaking English from the very first sentence. It's not their morbid cynicism or their unmitigated disdain of whatever the other is saying that gives them away: it's their sound. It's not simply pronouncing '*w*'s like '*v*'s and '*th*'s like '*z*'s; it's all in the melody. In Hungarian, the stress of every word is always on the first syllable. It's IMportant to UNderstand BEfore you BEgin any CONversation. Think of a steam train chugging up the hill. Chugga–Chugga–Chugga … It's as though they need to give every single word a little push at the beginning just to help it out. They have no sensitivities around how word stress may change the meaning of a word, so they can't hear that REcord (the vinyl type) and reCORD (to write down) are two completely different words. It's REcord *all ze vay …*

After I left Eva at the Oktogon, I practised talking to myself in the rear view mirror of the car.

It was quite fun.

Vot's for dinner, daahrlink …

Vell, you know, she likes to talk a lot, but it doesn't mean she knows everysink …

Bloody bus drivers! Move out of ze vay already …

Now zis is somesink I can do. I'm not an idiot …

But it had been all academic until I was suddenly faced with the cheerful, obliging smile of the shop assistant in front of the acrylic paint display at the new art supply shop on Bondi Road.

I froze. I've bought paints a thousand times, but never as a foreigner. I opened my mouth but nothing came out. I wanted to put on the accent, but I didn't want him to think I was stupid. I thought about turning around and coming back when this ridiculous game was over, but I was in the middle of Anyu's portrait, and had run out of blue. So instead I smiled, tilting my head just slightly to the left, batting my eyelids furiously. Just like I've seen Anyu do when she's with my friend Sam.

"Vell …" I stammered.

He raised his eyebrows, waiting.

I wanted to know whether the Chromacryl Cobalt Blue came in the new two-litre bottles. But how do you say Chromacryl Cobalt Blue with a Hungarian accent? Hungarians don't say Chromacryl Cobalt Blue. How idiotic, I thought to myself. I'm not a bloody refo. I was born here for God's sake.

I tried to keep calm. All I could think about was how crazy this whole thing was.

"I vood like … vell … you know …" I looked around the shop hoping no one I knew was in here. "Um, vood you have ze two litres *Chrom*acryl? You know *Chrom*acryl Cobalt Blue? In ze bottle?" I finally said, looking at his shoes.

He wasn't fazed a bit. He smiled, then answered me straight away. It took me a moment to realise I couldn't understand a word.

He looked at me.

I looked at him.

He looked at me again.

"So sorry, daahrlink, I don't speak *Hun*garian!" I said in a panic as I fled the shop empty handed.

Now it's almost a week later and I'm exhausted. I have spent countless happy hours talking to myself in front of the mirror, but every now and then I have to venture out into the real world. No one understands a word I say (except the baker and the late shift attendant at the petrol station, both of whom have turned out to be Hungarian). Sam thinks I'm on drugs, which pleases him immensely. The lady at the pharmacy started talking more slowly and loudly, using broader and broader hand movements. Camilla won't let me answer the phone anymore after I accidentally blurted out a grandiose "no vorries, daarhlink" to a customer. And I've spent the week working on my portrait of Anyu in the wrong shade of blue. I don't know how I managed to steer clear of my mother this week; she would have positively killed me. And now I'm on the way to meet the next big thing in the Australian art world.

The bus turns off Oxford Street and heads down Crown Street through Surry Hills. Shiny glass skyscrapers and vast, brightly lit chain stores gradually give way to narrow colourful terrace houses and one-off designer boutiques. *You know, daahrlink, ver even a look costs you an arm and a leg.* There are still glimpses down dead-end side streets of the cheap fashion wholesalers and housing commission apartment blocks that once gave this part of inner Sydney its sleazy character, but the main road is now bustling with homewares and gift shops, fluorescent 24-hour convenience stores, and cafés selling organic, conflict-free coffee beans. *Vot bullshit! I never heard such nonsense in all my life.*

I see Crown Street before me, but all I hear is Anyu.

The street narrows to a single lane as we enter the residential zone. Three more blocks and we are there. I have to clear my head, prepare myself. I can't walk in there with a Hungarian accent. Besides, Camilla's instructions were clear: *do not open your mouth under any circumstances.*

I put away my phone – I am sick of those medical websites with explicit pictures of lupus symptoms. Instead I take out a copy of the marketing material Camilla designed: a shiny, double-sided, postcard-sized flyer with a landscape print of the artist's most expensive oeuvre on one side and his bio and postage stamp-sized photo on the other. A few short paragraphs capture his world.

> Roger "Sunny" Anmatjirra was born some time in the forties in the Utopia region of the Northern Territory, two hundred and fifty kilometres northeast of Alice Springs.
>
> He has a large, artistic family and is part of the Anmatyerre people. He is the half-brother of internationally renowned Australian Aboriginal desert artist Bindi Pultara Freeman.
>
> Sunny spent most of his life as a stockman and only started to paint acrylic on canvas at the age of sixty-five. He has custodial rights to the crocodile dreaming.
>
> Sunny's style has developed rapidly over the last couple of years. He has progressed from a very traditional, literal, dotted form to the more abstract, modern character he so wonderfully exhibits today, earning him the much deserved title of Australia's newest rising star of the art world.

Camilla did a wonderful job on the visuals: deep rust-coloured font with black trim on an ochre/burnt orange background, sponged for a rustic effect. You could almost taste the red desert dust on your scorched lips. The story, though short and probably not too inaccurate, is certainly compelling enough for the lion's share of our audience: armchair art critics, moderately wealthy collectors, accidental European tourists, and WASP-y housewives. But I can't help wondering why she didn't print my version (which reads better in a Hungarian accent):

> Roger "Sunny" A, who can't remember when he was born, has done all right for a demographic whose average life expectancy is 20 years less than its white counterparts. He was born in the middle of nowhere and never learnt to read or write (which really means he is one of the lucky ones because

he escaped being part of the Stolen Generation). He was taught to paint acrylic on canvas by a greedy agent who makes a fortune carpet bagging and exploiting elderly artists in sweatshops, but is guilt-free because he tells himself he is making their lives better than the miserable, petrol-fumed nightmare they were in before and they don't know what's good for them anyway.

He used to paint traditional stories of the crocodile dreaming for his people, but the acrylic medium made him nervous because of its permanence and pervasiveness, so he started experimenting with more abstract forms so as to obscure the secrets of his people from the every man. He turned out to be spectacularly talented and stands to make his agent a great fortune in the near future.

I arrive at the gallery just past two in the afternoon. Cold, minimalist font greets me as usual at the glass door: *Camilla McInhereney, Contemporary Australian Art. Wednesday to Sunday. 11am to 6pm.* A tradesman pushes past me as I step inside. The gallery is closed today, but the room is a frenzy of activity. They are setting up a retrospective of another world-famous Aboriginal artist. To get the community "in the mood" explained Camilla to her backers.

Two handymen are putting up new curtains along the back window. Another measures an area of wall with aggressive, exaggerated strokes. An electrician sits beside the front desk atop a mound of tangled cables and a window cleaner polishes the glass room divider with a toxic-smelling spray. Whoever said art galleries were temples of serenity? *Zis is culture?*

I hear Camilla before I see her. She is clinking and clanging around the corner, snapping at anyone in her way.

"Tony, honey, what a mess! What a disastrous mess! And Jim, do watch your step …" Her middle finger, nervously playing with her necklaces, gets caught in a sophisticated knot. There's a brief moment of panic as she shakes her hand into even more of a bind and then relief. "Can you believe it?" she continues, to no one in particular, about nothing in particular.

Trotting along beside her, a short red-haired man mumbles into a Dictaphone as he tries to keep up with her interminable strides. That must be Jim, Big A's agent. I've not seen him before, only heard his voice on the phone. I sigh. His boyish looks don't match his deep, macho voice. But the Big A doesn't disappoint. He is exactly how I imagined: two dark eyes staring from a face almost completely covered with thick, tangled, white hair. He sits quietly on a metal chair in the centre of the room.

"Oh Jim, turn that thing off, for goodness sake. That thing is driving me crazy. Can't you write notes or just *remember?* I know, I know," she adds, without waiting for a response, waving her hand in reluctant acknowledgement. "It's dyslexia, right? Or is it dysfunction? Ha!"

Then she sees me.

"Oh Lily, you've arrived! What a relief! She's here!" She runs up to me. "I am absolutely dying for a coffee."

Camilla can't say I'm not good at my job. I memorise the order effortlessly: two flat whites (one with no froth, the other with one sugar), a skim cappuccino, three long blacks, and *Jim, what will Sunny have? Let's get him a flat white. Can't go wrong with that.*

Sunny doesn't complain. He smiles sweetly from under his weather-beaten Akubra.

The rest of the afternoon is lost in a blur of random commands and coffee runs. *And zis is vy you qvit medical school?* I scurry about trying either to keep up or to get out of the way. And invariably, it's the wrong one at the time. Camilla flaps about, stopping every now and then to pout into the mirror above the front desk, her high-heel boots bang bang banging on the bamboo floor like a military band in full swing. She is happy to discuss things all day long but, in the end, it's her way or the highway. Jim looks like a "good bloke" – comfortable clothes and a big smile – but he is really the male version of Camilla: he dots all his i's and crosses his t's. He's an ambassador of culture and a patron of the arts, but all I see are dollar signs in his eyes, like a cartoon: *ka-ching!* It's a kind of controlled warfare. Neither wants to upset the other, but they disagree about everything: the order of the canvases, the lighting, the price list, the description tags. Even Sunny's upcoming cataract surgery is a topic for dispute.

"What a crazy idea to time the surgery with a Sydney debut!" says Camilla. "Surely that wasn't your idea, Jim!"

"Come on, Camilla. He's here, isn't he? When's the next time you think he'll be down in the big smoke?"

"Fly him down a month later! Surely it's not out of the question."

"Oh, he'll be right."

I turn to Sunny. Still, he sits quietly. I can't help admiring the way he manages to stay so calm in the eye of such a storm. Every now and then I approach to hand him another coffee or pastry from the hamper; he smiles kindly and then continues to eat. Something in me feels compelled to feed him.

"I think you're bloody crazy," Camilla tells Jim after much reflection. They are now standing right in front of us.

"What are you saying?" asks Jim. "Are you saying he shouldn't have the operation?"

"I'm just saying: maybe you should think about it."

"It's bloody cataracts, Camilla. He needs it."

"Well, have you thought about what's-his-name? You know the guy … water lilies and all that?"

"What?"

"Have you thought about what's-his-name? Isn't that why his work was so brilliant? It was his cataracts that fucked up the way he saw the world …"

"Who the hell is what's-his-name?"

I put my hand up. "You mean Monet?"

"Yeah," says Camilla, without looking over. "Exactly. I mean Monet. Cataracts only made the world more beautiful to him."

"Are you out of your mind? We gotta fix him!"

"You don't *gotta* do anything, my dear. I'm just saying: think about it."

"But he'll go blind!"

"You don't know that … and anyway, he may go blind just from the operation. I mean there are risks in every procedure, Jim. Have you thought about the risks?" asks Camilla.

"Have you thought about what you are saying?" asks Jim.

I smile at Big A and hand him a croissant. He nods politely and takes a bite.

"Have you thought things through?" asks Camilla.

"Have you lost your mind?" asks Jim.

I wait for the next obvious question: *Have you ever asked him?*

But it never comes.

Instead, they move on to the next important discussion topic on today's agenda: what are they going to hang in the foyer? They are now huddled over a floorplan.

"Camilla, we should move *Crocodile Dreaming IV* from the entrance. It's not his best work. We want to overwhelm them!"

"We want to tell a story, Jim, and it can't start in the middle. We need to give the viewer a sense of continuity, a sense of progress, to show where he's come from and where he's going."

"I think we should hit 'em with *Croc Dreaming VIII*. Hit 'em with a bang! Knock their socks off right from the get go."

I wonder which one Sunny prefers to place at the front door. I'm itching to ask him. I wonder which is *his* favourite. I scan his face for a clue, but it's impenetrable. I look at him and it occurs to me that he may not even have a favourite. I love *Crocodile Dreaming X*: a masterpiece, an enormous, roaring canvas which, in my opinion, rivals any Rothko or Still I've seen. Thick layers of huge, blurred patches of colour and light. When I stand before it, I feel limitless, free, like I'm flying.

But no one's asking me, either.

Camilla and Jim continue their inimical tango.

"Oh Jim, I forgot to tell you … the posters arrive tomorrow. I hope you don't mind that I changed the title of the exhibition. I decided on *Secrets*. That works."

"You did what? *Secrets?* What's so good about *Secrets?*"

"Everyone loves *Secrets,* Jim."

"No one likes *Secrets*, Camilla! Sunny doesn't have secrets! He doesn't like 'em. They make him crazy!"

"Of course he does! What a thing to say. Secrets are exciting. Secrets are what Sunny paints, what he tells, what he keeps, what he leaves for you to imagine. Secrets are important, Jim. Trust me."

Sunny bites into another croissant. I wonder what secrets he is keeping. I smile. I feel like I am at a family dinner: Anyu and Mama, reluctant partners, arguing with insincere courtesy over what Lily wants. Everyone knows better than Lily what Lily wants.

All that's missing is a big bowl of goulash and heated sentences that suddenly change into Hungarian just as they become interesting.

But Lily's a big girl now. Lily can have secrets, too.

Imagine the excitement! Lily learning Hungarian from that no-good *kurva!* Don't even say her name! Why would she trust her? And why would anyone want to learn Hungarian? Anyway, it's impossible to learn!

It's not that I like having secrets. It's just for their own good. Just to protect them. They would be devastated if they thought Eva could hurt me. But when I eventually speak Hungarian, they will be so proud.

Imagine: the moment after which all would be forgiven. I have pictured it countless times during the last week. There are many versions: the public one, the private one, the romantic comedy one, and the family sitcom one. It's always a beautiful scene. Sometimes it includes tears of joy; other times, bouts of uncontrollable laughter. But there's always the same ending (which is in the style of a 1950s black and white film): Anyu, filmed with a soft focus, looking young and glamorous again, with pale, velvety skin and dark, watery eyes, stares up at me from behind her kitchen stove. Gracefully, she stirs a steaming pot of goulash. In fluent Hungarian, I tell her how wonderful she is. First, her eyes grow wide with surprise and wonderment. Then, she squints slightly in disbelief, only to finally explode with pride and admiration. *My Lily!* There's a warm, powerful embrace. And then: *The End.*

But by the time I arrive home late from the gallery, I'm sick with guilt. I run straight to the bathroom sink and unload what can only be described as a Jackson Pollock masterpiece.

It's already dark outside. This is when a loneliness usually sets in, when not even the respite from the chaos of the day can comfort me. It's just me, my yellow walls, my unfinished canvases, and the guilt. Others feel the loneliness in my apartment, too. It hangs heavy in the air, its stench soaked into the curtains, the carpet, the walls. Sam calls my room *The Isolation Ward*.

Ze I-solation Vord.

I can still smell Jeremy on my sheets from the night before. Whoever thought that one day I'd be fucking with a Hungarian accent? But Jeremy never makes me any less lonely. He only fills the place with noise. Again, he was up with the sun and gone before I awoke. Anyu says it's simply the fate of women in my family to find men who don't last. Papa didn't live past the age of forty and Mama's father's heart didn't last the long boat trip to the New World. Anyu's husbands (there have only been three if you don't count the one who died of a heart attack on top of a prostitute only four hours into their marriage) stuck around only just long enough to be the subject of another scathing monologue. Jeremy, like the others, simply can't defeat the Curse.

Ha! *Ze Curse.*

Mama doesn't believe in curses. She says Anyu's *an idiot* and tells me to stay away from Hungarians.

I do think about it, but I don't call Jeremy tonight. Not even his noise can fill the void.

So I paint into the night. *Into ze night.* Anyu's face slowly fills the canvas. Another layer and she's gone again. I paint and paint until I can no longer stand upright. Finally, I lie naked and exhausted in the early dawn light, a distorted Lucian Freud figure sprawled over my bedcover. My mind wanders in and out of Eva and Guilt and Anyu and *Ze Curse*.

The phone wakes me violently. It's morning. What time is it? Have I missed the Hungarian lesson? No! I can still make it if I leave now. I don't remember drifting off ... but I do remember deciding not to set my alarm. I remember thinking whether or not I should turn up to meet Eva this morning. I decided to leave it up to fate. If I happened to wake up, I would go to my Hungarian lesson. Otherwise, the game was over.

I pick up the phone. It's Anyu. This morning it's Monologue Number 72, the one about how crazy it is to live in a country where one needs to put the air-conditioning on already at seven in the morning. I tune out. I've been up all night finishing her portrait. It has been so hard to get it right and last night, after a week of talking to myself with v's as w's and of course, *daahrlink*, with stress on the first syllable of every word, I finally found myself in that special place. Anyu keeps talking and talking. I sit up in bed and as I focus my sleepy eyes on the finished image on the easel by the window, I smile. It is perfect. It's that something in the eyes. She stares at me from the canvas with scorn and pride. That's Anyu. But there's something more there, something I've captured this time that I've never managed to before. There's an uncertainty, a slight glint that gives her away: this time I've caught her unguarded. That singular combination of contempt and vulnerability that is my grandmother. There it is. I have painted Anyu with a Hungarian accent.

Chapter Seven

The main drag in Double Bay is eerily quiet this morning. It's too early for the boutiques to open and too late for the pre-work coffee scene. Only Pixie's, would-be hairstylist to the stars, shows any sign of life. Emaciated women with big hair hustle back and forth through the open French doors. Through the plate glass window Hollywood-style make-up lights sparkle in a neat row. The potent, chemical smell of peroxide seeps out onto the sidewalk. I pause for a moment to glance at my reflection in the window and run my fingers through my hair. A few wayward curls bounce back into my eyes. Sam's right – I could probably do with a couple of summer highlights or at least a trim. But not here. At Pixie's it's a week's wages just for a wash and blow dry. Wait! Is that who I think it is? I notice Dotsi, Anyu's friend, with her head stuck in one of those cocoon-style heaters and I quickly turn away. I can't afford to be seen here, not on this side of the street anyway. It's too close to the Oktogon. She would surely ask questions.

I continue hastily down Knox Street, past Sammy's and the florist, all the way past the Oktogon until my heart finally stops pounding and I catch my breath. She couldn't have seen me, I tell myself. She's a bird-brain at the best of times and anyway, between the hot curlers and the schmutz magazine and the hustle and bustle of the women in there, surely she couldn't have taken in the sight of little Lily out on the street so early in the morning.

I stop at the shoe shop at the end of the road to gather my thoughts, pretending to browse next season's fashions. I look left. Look right. Look left again. The coast is clear.

A huge white Mercedes rolls leisurely in my direction. A moment of panic: this time I'm caught! I try to catch a hint of recognition through the tinted windows and past the large sunglasses while at the same time hiding my own face from the driver. Zsuzsi has a white Merc. So does Punci's son, Paul. Either one would mean the end of my charade. The car slows down almost to a halt right in front of the Oktogon. I hold my breath. I may still be far enough away to escape suspicion. And then suddenly it's okay. It veers away in a casual three point turn. I'm safe.

My only chance is to make a quick beeline for the Oktogon. At least there I'll be completely secure. Neither Anyu nor any of her cronies would dare be seen there. This is deep inside enemy territory. This is Eva's domain. I don't know exactly how it happened, but I imagine Anyu and Eva carved up Double Bay the way the Allies divided up Berlin after the war: you have the East; we'll take the North! The Wall runs from the florist next to the Oktogon, over the pedestrian crossing on Knox Street, to the taxi stand outside the Cosmopolitan. The Red Zone includes the butcher, the dry cleaners, and all the designer boutiques until the jewellers next to the shoe shop just before the intersection with Bay Street.

I hold my breath; I can do it. I put my head down, take the plunge, and for the second time in a week, I disappear through the doors of the Oktogon and cross over to the other side.

It's just on nine-thirty in the morning. I want to walk straight through to where Eva and I sat last time, right at the back near the kitchen door, but there's already a large man in a chef's tunic sitting there amidst a pile of un-folded cloth serviettes. He is conscientiously working on a plate of paprika chicken. My stomach turns. I look around for Eva. She's not here. I wonder if the young Hungarian waiter from last time is here, the one with the ridicu-lous name and the handsome, earnest look. Nixon. I quickly fix my hair. I should have worn my red top, the one that Sam says makes my tits look bigger.

I check again. All I see is the fat chef. He beckons to me mid-mouthful with a huge, clumsy hand. He tops up his almost empty glass of white wine and wipes the pink sauce from his lips with the sleeve of his not-so-white-anymore tunic. Still with a full mouth, he stands up, bows flamboyantly, and introduces himself as Peter *bácsi. Uncle Peter.*

"Please, Lily, come. Sit. How delightful for Peter *bácsi* to have the pleasure of finishing his meal with a beautiful young lady." *Belch.*

Probably in his late sixties, with slightly graying blond hair and an open round face, Peter has the friendly sort of look of a Diego Rivera peasant: fat, soft, simple. Everything about him is big: sausage fingers, swollen lips, thick neck, broad shoulders. Even the pores on the end of his nose seem worthy of being categorised as separate facial features. He has a deep, masculine voice and that certain confidence I've seldom seen in a Hungarian man. It's clear this man is healthy and happy! The Hungarian men in my world are not so wholesome. They're a little watery, kind of tired and frail. It is the Mama that you ask to open the lid of a stubborn jar or to climb the ladder to change the light bulb. It's the Mama who controls the remote and always drives the car. The Mama is always right. The Mama is who you ask for permission. The Mama is who you fear. Men are important too. Every Mama needs a man or two, but there is nothing like the comfort of being smothered by those enormous soft bosoms. In every Hungarian family I know, there stands a woman of Stalinist proportions, a complex and often unpredictable character who generates by demand copious amounts of love, fear, and reverence, who is unreasonable as often as fair, generous as often as cold. I wonder how Peter *bácsi* would fare against the wrath of an Eva or an Anyu.

"You know, daahrlink," he continues after a few minutes of awkward silence. "You should eat something. You're too skinny!" He throws back the last drop in his glass and grimaces soulfully at the empty bottle between us. "Too skinny like your father," he adds, looking away. He says father like it has three syllables. *Faa-aa-zer.* He stretches out his sausage hands, reaches behind the bar for a new bottle, and pours himself a new glass of wine. How does he know about my father? "Anyway," he says, taking another sip with closed eyes. "It's wonderful, daahrlink, that you are learning Hungarian. But you know, of course, it's impossible to learn."

I wonder if this is something one learns at school, part of the curriculum for every young Hungarian boy and girl: Literature, History, Geography, and How Hungarian Is Impossible To Learn.

"You know it's different from any other language. Imagine!" He straightens up his back, now sitting tall and proud. "But it's the prettiest of them all!" He smacks his lips together and kisses his fingertips in delight. His fingernails are long and thick, the cuticles discoloured with specks of white powder. "And the poetry! And the music! Let me play you something, daahrlink." He bounces up with a sudden burst of boyish energy and charges over to a cabinet behind the bar, almost bumping into Nixon who has meanwhile meandered in through the swinging kitchen doors.

He's here!

Nixon, noticing Peter lunging towards the bar, tries to stop him from getting through. Peter pleads briefly with him in Hungarian and Nixon reluctantly steps aside. But he doesn't take his eyes off him for a moment. As music starts from the speakers, Peter turns back towards the table and Nixon relaxes. He looks relieved Peter didn't get up for another bottle of wine, but then winces when he sees the new bottle already on the table.

Peter sways to the music and conducts with a fork in one hand and a half-eaten slice of bread in the other. Nixon cringes. DA dum … DA dum … DA dum …

I know this tune, but I can't think where I've heard it. Was it from that TV ad, the one with the cars dancing in sync on a race track? Or is it the one with the little girl sneaking into the pantry after dark? Or maybe it's from the Bugs Bunny cartoon? Slow, exaggerated, shifty footsteps: DA dum … DA dum … DA dum … gradually getting faster and bolder, building up to a frenzied, passionate commotion. The opening bars of Liszt's famous Hungarian Rhapsody No. 2 sound like a Hungarian sentence. TRAlala TRAlala TRAlala, not tra LALA. Even here, the accent is on the first note of each bar. I have been practising my Hungarian accent all week. I am hearing it everywhere.

Nixon turns to me as if noticing me for the first time. He blushes.

"It's Lily, right?" He asks. He doesn't wait for an answer. He remembers me! "Would you like coffee?"

"Sure, thanks," I say.

"We say *köszönöm. Egy kávé.*"

"Okay, *köszönöm*," I mumble. Now I'm blushing. He remembers me!

"Would you like something else? Something like cake?" He winks.

"I'm not hungry," I tell him.

"*Nem vagyok éhes.* Try it – *Nem vagyok éhes.*"

I try to repeat it, but to my ears it sounds more like "*Bla bla bla.*"

He smiles. "Good enough! Coffee coming right up!"

Finally a show of support. Someone who thinks it is possible to learn Hungarian.

Peter's eyes are closed and he continues conducting the symphony.

Nixon returns a minute later with the coffee and an idea.

"What about Spanish?" he asks.

"Excuse me?" I say.

"I said Spanish," he explains. "Did you know over four hundred million people in the world speak Spanish? It would be much more useful to you than Hungarian."

"Spanish is good," Peter agrees. "Why not Spanish?"

I look around for Eva. Where the hell is Eva?

"Or Chinese," Nixon says. "Now there's the future! Learn Chinese and the world is your pearl!" His face lights up: what a brilliant idea! "You know in life we have to stay on the lookout for future trends," he explains. "Stay one step ahead. That's what my parents taught me. You know, chance favours the prepared mind. We have to act while the iron is hot. We have to pounce while the cat's away." He pauses for a moment and frowns, a little overwhelmed by his intermingled proverbs and takes a deep breath. "Anyway," he continues, "China is clearly the future and we all need to somehow get on bandwagon." He says *bandvagon*. His fervour is endearing, but also ridiculous.

I try to smile.

Peter nods, then hiccups.

Nixon continues, "My parents taught me you can never be too prepared in life." I try to imagine his parents, those cultural prophets who elected to stay in Communist Hungary and call their son Nixon to prepare him for the future. I wonder if they know he is waiting tables in a run-down bistro at the end of the world where the name Nixon is synonymous with fraud. A few cleaning ladies speak Spanish and the only Chinese in Double Bay is Beef in Black Bean Sauce. No wonder he is obsessed with predicting the future.

Nixon doesn't skip a beat. "Imagine: one billion of them just waiting to explode. One billion mouths to feed, two billion feet to shoe, three billion meals per day ... The possibilities are endless." He leans over the table and reaches for the pile of serviettes. I feel his face brush past mine and for a moment I catch the sweet smell of his aftershave. He smiles at me, then starts folding.

"Ha!" Peter cries out as if he has suddenly woken from a sleep. "China schmina! You guys want to talk about great civilisations? Well then let Peter *bácsi* tell you all about the Hungarians!" He stands up, knocking over Nixon's pile of neatly folded serviettes and puts a hand on his heart. "Can you imagine, kids, that a little country of only ten million people produces so much talent?"

Here it goes. I know this one. The one about how only a few million Hungarians make a disproportionate impact on the world.

"Do you know," Peter continues, "just how many Nobel Prize Laureates were Hungarian?"

I shake my head. I look around for Eva. Where is she? Nixon shrugs his shoulders *I don't know*, good naturedly picks up the pile of messy serviettes and starts over with the folding.

"I tell you ... lots!" Peter *bácsi* scratches his head like the answer is somewhere in there just below the surface. "Eighteen. Eighteen Nobel Prizes. Imagine! Unheard of! China, schmina ... I'll show you the future. Kids, I bet you never knew that the electric train and the helicopter were invented by Hungarians."

I look at my watch. This is crazy. Surely Eva will arrive any minute? Or is she having second thoughts about me? I turn to Nixon hoping to find some support. He smiles at me and winks, but this is no show of support. Slowly his eyes widen and he seems to forget himself in a moment of excitement. "And Peter *bácsi*," he says, "Don't forget computer! We invented computer as well!"

"You see, Lily!" Peter says. "Peter *bácsi* knows what he's talking about!" He suddenly reaches over and snatches a pen from Nixon's apron pocket. He holds it high in the air, like a gold medal. "You kids know who invented the ballpoint pen? Biro Laszlo! You know my uncle went to school with him in Budapest. A bit of a clown, but what an invention! So simple! A classic!"

He pauses for a sip of wine. "And the hydrogen bomb! Well, perhaps not so simple, but Teller, a Hungarian, was the father of the hydrogen bomb! Ha!"

I hear her before I see her. Suddenly she is coughing over my shoulder and then sits with a thump on the bench next to me. She hits the conversation like a freight train. Where did she come from?

"Now that's something to really be proud of, daahrlinks! Wonderful!" She is almost singing. *Vunderful!* She grabs hold of Peter's wine glass, but he is holding it tightly in his sausage fingers. Time freezes. Their eyes lock in a silent battle. "Did you know," Eva continues, without letting go of the wine glass or Peter's gaze, "Did you know that Peter's hero here, Edward Teller, was also the crazy lunatic who inspired the movie *Dr Strangelove?*" Peter's grip loosens; he gives up. Eva wins. "Don't you listen to Hungarian men, Lily. The have a way of, *vell*, they never know what the hell they are talking about."

She gets up, takes the wine back to the bar, and turns to the three of us at the table. "Peter daahrlink, the potatoes are almost ready. See if you can make it to lunch, huh? And Nixon, sweetheart, make him another strong coffee, will you? A double! Lunch starts in an hour and a half."

Peter and Nixon, heads down conceding defeat, scuttle off in opposite directions to carry out their orders.

"That Peter is going to kill me one day!" she sighs. "You know, don't be angry, daahrlink. Peter isn't stupid altogether. He just gets a little over-excited every now and then." She sits next to me coughing heartily for what seems like an eternity, then sighs again. "He can't be trusted for a single second, Lily, but no one, daahrlink, and I mean *no one* makes a fried calf's liver quite like him."

I take out my exercise book and open to our last page of work. It looks like a mindless scribble of random letters and words. I turn to a new, clean page.

"I'm ready," I say.

Suddenly, Peter pops his head through the swinging kitchen doors. "What about Mr Rubik? Ha! You know the Rubik's Cube, Lily? Another Hungarian for you!"

Eva doesn't even turn around. The effort is too much. "She knows the Rubik's Cube, daahrlink. It's driven her crazy for years, just like you are driving me crazy right now! The potatoes, Peter! Are you trying to kill me here?"

"Just one more word: Harry Houdini and Uri Geller! Ha!" He winks at me and disappears into the kitchen before Eva has a chance to open her mouth.

"They were all Hungarians?" I ask her. I guess I am a little impressed. All these people?

Nixon, cleaning glasses at the bar with his head cocked to one side for maximum eavesdropping ability, smells the bait and quickly runs over to our table. "Would you like hear more? We invented the vinyl record, the carburettor, and you know what else? The famous Model-T Ford! I can go on, you know: the transformer, the telephone exchange ..." He scratches his head. "There's more, I think. Sh, let me think."

I try to remember the famous Australians I learnt about at school. I guess all nationalities have this kind of a list. So there was Ned Kelly, the notorious bush ranger who, notwithstanding his brutal crimes, became a folk hero; Bob Hawke, the former Prime Minister who was more famous for his world record at beer sculling and crying when his daughter had a drug problem than anything he ever achieved in politics; and then there was the actor Mel Gibson who started out as a heartthrob and ended up an aggressive religious fanatic. Other icons included cricket stars and a horse. I don't feel equipped to compete here.

Nixon suddenly remembers. "You know the Pulitzer Prize? Hungarian! Ha!"

Eva looks at me, eyes half closed, eyebrows raised, as if the effort of this next comment is just too much. "Lily daahrlink, that's all very well, but what they don't tell you about is the other nine point nine nine million bigots and liars and wife beaters and alcoholics and Communists."

"Eva *néni*," Nixon says, a little taken aback. "How can you say that?"

"You're right," she says, pointing to his chest. "I forgot to mention the anti-Semites and the fascists and the hypocrites!"

"But you must admit," Nixon says, "we do have special talent for business and money. Think about George Soros."

Peter's head pokes through the door. "And we have Frank Lowy!"

"We?" She laughs. "*Veee?* We can't even save the potatoes from burning on the stove, let alone save ourselves a fortune! Don't be ridiculous, please, you're embarrassing me."

But Peter isn't finished. "It's the same population as Belgium. Or Chad. How many inventions can the Chadians claim, huh? How many famous Chadese do you know? I mean, I can go on if you like – Tony Curtis: Hungarian. Zsa Zsa Gabor: Hungarian."

"You mean Hollywood's most expensive whore! Charming, daahrlink, wonderful."

I laugh.

Nixon takes this as a sign of encouragement. "Did you know that Drew Barrymore had a Hungarian mother?"

Eva has an answer to everything. "So now it's enough for your mother-in-law's neighbour's dog to be Hungarian! Imagine! When you're famous and successful, when it suits you, it's good to remember you are Hungarian, right? But when things go wrong, don't worry, daahrlink, the truth is really not too hard to find – it's easy to trace back to the fact that the father was really half Czech!" Eva pauses to cough. She puts a serviette to her mouth and then inspects it before putting it back down next to my coffee. "Oh daahrlink, you can't bullshit a bullshit artist," she says. "Let me ask you something: how many of these proud Hungarians actually live in Hungary? Hey? How many of these Hungarians actually call Hungary home?"

Silence. Peter's head disappears back into the kitchen and Nixon looks at his shoes. He fumbles for another serviette to fold.

Finally, Nixon speaks. "That's not the point, Eva."

But I already see the point. I know the game from Mama's arguments with Anyu. It's easy to get caught up in the nostalgia and rhetoric, to take delight (and even pride) in a quirky, original language, and to bask in the glory of outstanding countrymen – as long as you don't take the whole thing too seriously. What they are forgetting to tell you, of course, is how miserable their lives were in Hungary before they left, how they spent every waking moment scheming and plotting an escape, how trapped and harassed and oppressed they felt by everyday Hungarians, how betrayed they were by the passing fads of political extremes, how "out", wherever that may have been, was always a place of hope and freedom and always in their dreams.

According to my mother, nothing about Hungary was wonderful. Ironically, she never experienced it personally. Her parents found their way "out" before she was born. They were the real prophets; they caught a drift of the winds of change in the late 1930s and left before the war. Of course they couldn't have known exactly what was coming, but they knew the fear of sitting around the radio listening to news updates listing the latest restrictions on Jews. *It never ends well for the Jews*, her father told his wife. A colleague of his had recently emigrated to a faraway land called Australia where the sun was always shining and food grew on trees. So they packed up their life and made it out.

My father's version may have been different, but I don't know any of it from him. I only have Anyu for stories about my father.

"Don't listen to Anyu," my mother always said when I used to ask her what life was like in Hungary for my father. "She has such a good memory she even remembers things that never happened."

All Anyu likes to talk about is life in Hungary before the war, and then the repertoire jumps straight to her first few months in Australia. Monologue Number 27.

I know this one by heart:

When we arrived at the port in Fremantle, it was already 1957. We couldn't believe our eyes. It was like we had stepped off the boat and into the last century. Men were wearing tight grey flannel suits, you know, two sizes too small, and imagine daahrlink, double-breasted! With felt hats! Everyone wore hats, women too, with little veils like in my grandmother's day. The stockings had seams up the back! Well I thought we had landed in the Middle Ages. They looked like those Russian tourists we used to laugh at during the summertime, parading around Budapest in their great-uncle's hand-me-downs. It was embarrassing. And the trams! I didn't allow your father to ride them, you see, they were about to fall apart. But you know, I told myself, "Don't worry, daahrlink. This Fremantle, it is just a small town. Sydney is the big city and things will be different there." And they were! Well, it was more like turn of the century than a hundred years ago! Imagine! I spent the first six months trying to get the hell out of here. I begged them at the Jewish agency to get me out, but they just thought I was mad. I wrote to everyone I knew around the world to see if we could get sponsored. You needed a sponsor in those days, you see. My father had a cousin in Paris – but he didn't want to hear about desperate refugees hanging around his neck. I tried an elderly couple I knew in Cincinnati, but they never wrote back. We were stuck at the arsehole of the world.

So we lived in a two-room apartment in Coogee with another family of six. It was across the road from a cemetery which made your father very sad. He said, "This country is haunted by the ghosts of the black ones." He said to me, "Mama, you think we had it bad. No one talks about it, but look at the Schwartzes. Now they're really done for!" He was such a sensitive one, your father. God bless his soul.

We were poor, but you know, some people were nice to us. Like that Stern man, you know the one I mean, Zsuzsi's old bridge partner. He was a butcher and he used to save us the ends of the salami, the bit with the string tied on. He used to put them aside and I'd send your father there on Friday afternoons to pick them up. There was a nice Australian woman next door. Dot. Can you imagine a name like Dot? What sort of a name is Dot? She was rich. She had a television in her living room and sometimes she let your father stand at the back of the house, outside the window, and watch shows from her garden. Imagine, daahrlink, she had three ducks hanging on her wall. The duckers, we used to call them. She mowed the lawn every weekend. That was their weekend. She drank awful watered down tea with milk. Imagine! She went to the store in her hair-curlers. This is what they called civilisation!

According to Anyu, Budapest before the war was a buzzing metropolis. Life was hedonistic and decadent. It was all about opera and good coffee, fur coats and fittings with French couturiers, walks along The Corso followed by pancakes at The Gundel. Women had nannies and wet nurses; men had Swiss watches and mistresses. They were part of the European elite: educated, sophisticated, urbane.

I tell Eva that the only nightmare Anyu ever spoke about was arriving in Australia.

"It's easy to be proud of Hungary once you've made it out, Lily," she says. "And anyway, no one knows complaining like your grandmother. She's the world's biggest exaggerator."

Nixon suddenly jumps up with a start and races to the front door. An elderly couple saunters in from the street looking for a table. He tries to settle them at the front of the café, near the window, but they're not happy. They spend the next five minutes discussing where they'd like to sit. I hear them argue in Hungarian and I take a second look; I don't recognise them. I can't believe there are Hungarians in Double Bay I don't know.

I turn to Eva. "Why did you do it?" I ask. "Why did you leave Hungary?"

Eva notices the couple too. She waves, smiles, and nods her head in their direction.

"It was your grandmother's idea," she says, semi-distractedly. She mouths *how are you?* towards the old Hungarian woman.

"Anyu?" I think for a minute. It was Anyu's idea? Then I think about asking more. Eva is still mouthing pleasantries at the old couple across the restaurant. I close up the exercise book and wriggle my bottom on the seat. I try to settle in. And then I say it.

"Tell me what happened," I say. I'm a little startled about how easily these words come out, but then again this is not Anyu I'm talking to.

"Tell me," I say.

Eva is still nodding towards the couple, but her eyes move slowly back over to me and then roll as soon as the couple is out of sight. "Talk about stupid Hungarians," she whispers to me, and then her head flies back and she laughs an evil guttural laugh. I don't move. I can't move, as if any movement, even of the smallest, most insignificant type, would somehow give her permission to go on ignoring my question. *Tell me,* I plead silently. Eva stares at me for a minute and then nods.

"Okay," she says. "Okay."

She clears her throat and smiles. "You see something changed in Agi the night Lesley didn't come home. One night, your Papa just didn't come home." I hold my breath. I've never heard this one before. Eva coughs, then continues. "He was too young for girls, and of course, we didn't worry about crime; the only criminals in those days were the police. I was at home with her when he stumbled in at seven in the morning. I saw with my own eyes what those animals did to him. They must have picked him up from the hall where he used to meet up with other Jewish kids from the area. She comforted him, held him while he cried. Then she turned to me and said, 'Start packing.'

"Les screamed at her, 'Shut up, Anyu. Shut up. I don't want to hear it.' After his interrogation at the station, he didn't want to know about any real plans. So I told her, 'Don't put the boy in this situation.' But she wouldn't stop. And I didn't take her seriously, you see."

"What do you mean?" I ask.

"Agi was always talking about leaving. You see, it was only the ones who didn't talk about it who left," she says. "Like what happened to my brother-in-law: one day we were all huddled round the table discussing where we'd go if the borders were open. I said France, my sister said Israel. I think Agi said something about Canada. But my brother-in-law, he said *nowhere*. Nowhere! If the borders were open, he said, he wouldn't need to leave. Huh," Eva says. "Next day he was gone."

At that moment, Nixon comes over to our table with two coffees. Eva suddenly stops talking, sits up straight and smooths out her shirt. She knows not to talk about these things in front of other people. Nixon places the coffees on the table and quickly turns away. He somehow knows not to interrupt us.

"But you got out," I say when Nixon is out of range.

"Yes, we got out. We all got out. But not then. You have to remember, daahrlink. Bela was still in jail." Bela wasn't my grandfather; he was Anyu's second husband. He married Anyu in 1946 after it became clear that my grandfather wasn't coming back from the war. Bela never made it to Australia. He left Hungary with Anyu, but died in the refugee camp in Austria waiting to be resettled in the West. I heard somewhere that he was sentenced to five years in a jail on the outskirts of Budapest for "unCommunist activities" which basically meant selling imported watches on the black market. "But we didn't wait too long," Eva continues. "The Revolution started six weeks later and we knew it was then or never."

So far, my knowledge of the Hungarian Revolution feels like it comes straight from a textbook, not from my own grandmother's personal experience. In October 1956, thousands of students and intellectuals stormed the streets of Budapest and sent the country into a state of chaos for weeks. National institutions broke down, army personnel tore off their red stars, the borders were open, and hundreds of thousands of Hungarians crossed over into Austria. Then came the Russian tanks literally trampling everyone's hopes of a free Hungary.

"We heard the jails were open," Eva continues. "Ivan went to help Bela get back to Budapest. By the time they arrived back at the apartment, Bela's leg was badly broken, he was feverish. He wasn't well, that Bela. He had a very bad heart from a childhood illness, something like rheumatic fever I think."

"Who's Ivan?" I ask.

"You don't remember Ivan?" Eva sounds surprised. She starts coughing. "Ivan was my husband and ..." She stops mid-sentence and reaches for a drink. There's only the leftovers of Peter's breakfast wine. She finishes the glass and leans back for a moment. She bangs her chest with a white-knuckled fist and sighs. "Ivan was my husband."

"What happened next?"

"We started to make arrangements. Your grandmother did most of the talking, but she was worried about her mother. She was too old to come with us. We didn't know whether they would arrest her when they found out we'd gone. We didn't know whether anyone would dob us in, whether anyone would be chasing us, whether anyone would be shooting at us as we crossed the border. We didn't know much, but Agi knew that when she left Hungary, she would never see her mother again. A carton of American cigarettes and about a year's salary in cash got us a trip in a butcher's van out into the countryside near the Austrian border. We hid in a farmer's barn during the day with the help of my mother's diamond and ruby ring and then when night fell, we walked across the border to Austria. The Red Cross picked us up and took us to a refugee camp outside of Vienna. We were out.

"Yes, we were afraid to leave. We didn't know what the hell would happen. But let me tell you, Lily, believe me when I tell you this: we were even more afraid not to."

Two more couples arrive at the door waiting to be seated. Nixon is nowhere to be found. Eva gets up, irked, and shows them to a table. Nixon eventually comes out through the swinging doors of the kitchen and takes their order, but before Eva can sit back down at our table, a group of middle-aged women come in looking for a sunny table. I look at my watch. Lunch has started. I hear the banging of pots from behind me and the smell of garlic wafts in from the kitchen. I don't want to go home, but it's another twenty minutes of harried activity before I realise Eva's not coming back to talk anytime soon. I reach for my exercise book and decide to write down the words Nixon taught me at the beginning of the day. How was it again that you say *thank you* in Hungarian? How did you say *I'm not hungry?* I look down at my page and it's no longer empty. I don't remember anyone writing anything down, but there it is on the top of the page. In Eva's immaculate calligraphy-like scrawl are the following words: *"Hungarian Lesson Number Two: Don't let them bullshit you."*

Chapter Eight

It's exactly one week later. I'm sitting at our booth in the Oktogon, making myself comfortable.

"Eva's not here," Nixon says, arms flapping about, limping out of the kitchen in that excited way of his.

I've just had a near miss on the way to the café so I'm a little nervous. I was sprung in the side street across from the liquor store where I was parking my car. It could have been worse. It was only Sylvie and Rachel, two friends from school, but they caught me unaware. I was so shocked when I saw them walking towards me that I slammed the car door and dropped my keys over an open grate in the gutter. Then they had to watch me squat on the road and feed my hand through the slat into the murky drain below. Not my most elegant moment. I already know what they think at the best of times: they don't understand why I'm ruining my life by quitting my studies, why I'm wasting my time hanging out with the likes of Sam, why I would want to paint portraits rather than learn how to save someone's life. So I didn't tell them I was on my way to a Hungarian lesson with my grandmother's nemesis. Instead I pretended I was meeting my boyfriend for coffee – the life of an artist is decadent and sweet.

"Your boyfriend?" Rachel asked, flicking her golden locks to one side. She was wearing jeans that looked like they'd been painted on and three-inch heels. From down by the gutter she looked ten feet tall.

"You don't mean Sam, do you?" Sylvie added.

Both girls laughed out loud.

"Very funny," I said, scrambling to my feet and dusting off my obviously-way-too-baggy pants. "No, this guy is the real deal. He's Eastern European, terribly debonair. Hangs out all day in a coffee shop discussing art and philosophy. You'll meet him one day, I'm sure."

Rachel rolled her eyes.

"Call us when you're ready to come back to the real world," Sylvie said, calling over her shoulder as she walked away in step with Rachel, arm in arm.

I'm not sad we're no longer close friends. I used to miss hanging out with them every day on the library lawn at university but now I'm just relieved I don't have to try and keep up with them. It's not my world anymore; I am free.

At my booth in the Oktogon, Nixon is steadying himself on my table with a shaky arm and tells me again.

"Eva's not here," he says.

I take out my exercise book and a pen like I haven't heard a thing. I arrange the vase, sugar bowl, and salt and pepper shakers at the far right of the table near the wall and dust a few crumbs onto the floor.

"Oh," I say, mainly to myself.

"Eva's at doctor," he explains.

"Oh," I say, again.

But I don't move. Well, he is Eastern European. He does hang out at a coffee shop all day.

"It's okay," I say eventually. "I'll wait."

"*Vell ...*" Nixon looks around nervously. He glances behind him toward the kitchen door and then again down at his watch. He wipes a bead of sweat from his brow and then continues. "Not a good idea to wait. He's not coming back today."

"Who's not coming back?" I ask, confused.

"Eva. Eva's not coming back. Not good to wait."

I don't understand. Maybe not so debonair. But definitely Eastern European.

"I don't understand," I say. "We had a date. We have a lesson now."

"He gave me this to give to you," he says, unfolding a crumpled printed paper from his apron pocket. "Eva says sorry he is not having a lesson today."

"He or she?" I ask.

"What?" Nixon asks. *Vot?*

"Never mind."

I open the paper slowly. Nixon peers over his shoulder toward the front door, then back to the kitchen. The corners of the page are wet and slightly torn, but the words are still legible. I have a quick look.

And then I laugh out loud. Seriously? Indeed the words are legible, but also completely incomprehensible. It's an entire page of Hungarian words. There's no explanation, no translation. Just a jumble of SZs and GYs and umlauts and accents that's making me go cross-eyed.

"What's this?" I ask, waving the page at Nixon's face in an attempt to gain eye contact. "It looks all Greek to me."

"Not Greek," he says, earnestly. "Hungarian. Hungarian poem." He is still distracted, but stands strong and completes his message diligently. "Eva says to learn this. Eva says learn it all by heart."

I laugh.

He turns to me abruptly. "Not a funny poem," he says. "Sad poem. Sad Hungarian poem."

I look down at the indecipherable text and shrug. "Thanks," I say, smiling back up at Nixon. "I guess I will learn Sad Hungarian Poem by heart." I give him a playful wink but he is all work, no play.

"Good," Nixon says, nodding.

He waits, but I'm not going anywhere. I'm staying for my Hungarian lesson with or without Eva.

"Will you help me?" I ask, a long minute later, a little sheepishly because by now I've run out of moves.

"No good," he says, shaking his head toward the kitchen door, then back down at me. He is serious now. "I have problem."

I smile. There is something so sweet about the earnest young Hungarian waiter *with problem.*

"You have problem?" I tease.

"I have Peter problem," he says. And with that, he turns on his heels and walks through the swinging door to the kitchen.

My phone sings. A Lady Gaga ringtone special from Sam's favourite website. It's Camilla. I let it ring and look down at the page Eva so thoughtfully left for me. Eva could simply have called me and told me not to come. The café is now quiet save for the regular moaning of the swinging kitchen door and Lady Gaga blaring from the crappy iPhone speakers. The vibration makes the entire booth shake with the beat until Camilla finally gives up.

I decide to stay and learn the poem. This is my Hungarian lesson, after all. I look at the title: *Szomorú Vasárnap. s-z-o-m-o-r-u-v-a-r-s-a-r-n-a-p.* I've forgotten what sound the letters *sz* make. I check my exercise book. *Sz* is pronounced *s*. Great. What's *s* then? *S* is pronounced *sh*. Oh boy this is going to be fun. *s-z-o-m-o-r-u-v-a-r-s-a-r-n-a-p. s-z-o-m-o-r-u-v-a-r-s-a-r-n-a-p. s-z-o-m-o-r-u-v-a-r-s-a-r-n-a-p. She sells sea shells by the sea shore.* How am I ever going to learn Sad Hungarian Poem?

I look up. Two blonde, middle-aged women wander in from the street and find themselves a table by the window. They are both talking at the same time.

And so I said what did he say and she said he said no/ I mean I don't believe it/ can you believe it/ I mean he said no.

s-z-o-m-o-r-u-v-a-r-s-a-r-n-a-p.

Then what does she say/ she says what she always says/ you know what she's like/ of course I know what she's like/ I'm dying for a coffee/ I need a coffee.

The ladies stop suddenly to scan the café for someone to help them. No one's here. They look at me, look at each other, look at me again. I shrug. No one's coming. They discuss the situation and get up to leave.

What's Nixon doing?

I wait until the ladies are out of sight and creep over to the kitchen door. I can't hear a thing. I peer through the glass window, but I can't see Nixon. There are three large pots simmering on the stovetop and a pile of diced carrots sitting on a chopping board by the stove.

"Nixon?"

I wait, but there's no response.

"Nixon? It's Lily …" I edge open the door. It's noisy and hot and steamy, but there's no Nixon, no Peter. A thunderous roar blares incessantly from the extractor fan above the busy stove and the steam from one of the pots bounces its stainless steel lid up and down like an out-of-time tin drum. The oven timer on the opposite wall is beeping, and the fridge door, left wide open, is sounding a persistent alarm. Powerful heater lamps on the serving counter make the small entrance way unbearably hot. It smells wonderful, but I'm sweating and irritated before I even manage to get to the stove only three steps away. I close the fridge and take the lid off the clanging pot. I take a quick peek at the bubbling chicken soup. It looks delicious. I grab a spoon from the counter top and have a little taste. Now that's chicken soup! Just one more spoon. Delicious.

I continue to the back of the kitchen and turn the corner into a side alcove which must be the office.

And there they are.

Peter is sprawled out on the office chair fast asleep while Nixon, red-faced and trembling, is rummaging through Peter's pockets like a cat burglar. An almost empty bottle of vodka rests on the desk in front of them.

"Hi," I say, not knowing what else to say. It could have been "Oops, sorry" or even "What the fuck is going on?" but all that comes out is "Hi."

Nixon stops his searching and looks at me.

"Hi," I say again.

"I have Peter problem," Nixon says, quickly stepping away from Peter.

"I can see that," I say.

"Peter *bácsi*, Peter *bácsi*, wake up." He starts talking to him slowly, calmly. He puts both his hands on Peter's shoulders and shakes him gently. "Peter, please." Peter stirs. His eyes open briefly, then he burps and scratches his head. Nixon starts speaking Hungarian. I can't understand a word, but it's the sound of a Mama feigning patience, desperately pleading with her three-year-old troublemaker to behave in public. Peter opens his eyes again and shakes his head at Nixon.

"No good," he says in English, over and over again. "No good."

Nixon slumps down on the floor at the foot of Peter's chair. Defeated, exhausted, he is almost under the desk.

I walk over to them and kneel beside Peter.

"Peter *bácsi*," I say, gently.

Peter looks at me and smiles.

"Agi!" he says. "Oh Agi, help me."

"Not Agi," I tell him. "It's Lily! Agi's granddaughter."

"Oh Agi, I'm so sorry. Please don't tell Eva. I won't do it again. I promise."

"Peter *bácsi*, it's Lily. I'm not Agi."

"I didn't tell Eva about you. I promise it wasn't me. Don't be angry with me, Agi. Don't tell Eva this time."

I turn to Nixon who shrugs and points to the bottle of vodka above him. He makes a crazy sign with his fingers. When I turn back to Peter, he is snoring softly.

"What are you going to do?" I ask Nixon.

He shakes his head. His cheeks are rosy and he looks up at me like a child. I sit down on the floor next to him. The tiles are cold and uncomfortable, but it feels good sitting this close to Nixon. Our shoulders touch slightly and I can feel his warmth through his shirt. I edge a little closer. He doesn't pull back.

Peter murmurs and wiggles and tries to get comfortable on the seat. He turns on his side and the chair swivels around so he is facing away from us.

"He'll be sober before dinner," I reassure Nixon. "Don't worry. We need strong coffee and cold water. It's going to be okay. Why don't you go and serve customers and I'll wait here with Peter?"

"Dinner time is too late," says Nixon, almost heartbroken. "I need the money before dinner time."

"Money?" I ask. "What money?"

"The money Peter takes from Eva," he says. "I need the money to pay the butcher."

"So that's what you were looking for in Peter's pockets?" I ask.

Nixon nods.

"Peter stole money from Eva?"

"Peter stole money from Eva, *again*. Peter always steals money. Eva knows Peter steals the money, but today I need the money to pay the butcher. Eva is at the doctor and the butcher comes with our delivery soon. This happens every time. The butcher will be so angry and Eva will be angry too because the butcher will stop her account. I don't know what to do." Nixon starts getting agitated. He wriggles on the floor. He scratches the back of his head. He looks behind him. Then he gets up suddenly, as if getting up is something he can actually do, and bumps his head on the desk. "If the butcher is angry, then there'll be no more butcher and Eva will get angry too." He starts pacing up and down the small office with his hands on his head. Every now and then he gives Peter's chair a little kick.

I watch his histrionics with a secret smile. He is even cuter when he is frazzled.

"It's okay," I tell him. "We'll think of something."

"Nothing to think," he says. "I need the money. This butcher has best veal knuckle in Sydney. The only veal knuckle in Sydney. Eva needs veal knuckle. And I need the money."

I get up.

"We'll find the money," I say. "Come with me. We can do this." I take his hand and lead him back through the kitchen, through the swinging doors, and into the café. "Make Peter a coffee," I say. "A strong one." I stand next to Nixon at the bar.

"And me too," I say. "*Egy kávé.*"

Nixon smiles at me.

"Okay," he nods.

A sudden "excuse me" startles us from behind.

We turn around. A young man is sitting at a corner booth with two others, holding up his menu and pointing emphatically at the page.

"We're ready to order," he shouts.

I look around. Two more tables are full. Nixon looks at me in a panic.

I turn to him and put both my arms around his waist. My heart skips a beat. I can feel his breath on my face. Slowly, I untie his apron and slip it around my waist. I walk over to the table, take out the note pad from the front pocket, and smile sweetly.

"What can I get you gentlemen today?" I say.

***

By five-thirty, the café is quiet again. I sit back down at my booth, exhausted. I make a pretty bloody good little waitress, I tell myself. We had a major rush around four o'clock and every table was looked after without a hitch. Nixon held down the fort in the kitchen making orders for customers, feeding Peter strong coffee, and combing the place for the stolen butcher money which never turned up. When the butcher arrived with his delivery fifteen minutes ago, we managed to pay him from the afternoon's takings (including most of the tip jar) and so a serious veal knuckle emergency was averted by Nixon and me. *Hungarian Lesson Number Three: Everything's going to be okay.*

I take out my order pad and shout towards the kitchen. "One more order, Nixon!"

A sombre Peter stumbles out of the kitchen minutes later with my chicken soup. He slumps down on the bench opposite me, cradles his head in his hands, and moans. I eat greedily. I pick up the paper Eva left for me and give it to him, but before he gets a chance to read it, Nixon storms over and snatches it from Peter's hands.

"This is not for you," Nixon says. "It's not a good day for Peter *bácsi* to read *Gloomy Sunday*."

"For what?" I ask.

"*Szomorú Varsánap*," he says. "It's *Gloomy Sunday*."

"So that's how you pronounce it!" I laugh.

I pack the paper in my handbag and gather the rest of my things. Peter manages a vague smile, but still no words, and Nixon walks me to the front of the café.

"Thank you, Lily," he says at the doorway.

I want a kiss, but he turns away.

I walk back slowly to my car. I'm expected for dinner at Anyu's. I don't have the strength to do it alone. I almost turn back toward the café to invite Nixon to come with me when he finishes his shift, but I know that's just plain suicide. I can imagine how it would go: *Nixon, is it? Oh how lovely … Oh from the Oktogon … Oh with Eva … Oh with my Lily … Just one moment while I kill myself …*

I dial Sam's number.

I know it's not right to use a civilian as a human shield, but he'll get the chance to raid her costume jewellery and try on her fur coats. He loves that. We can then go to a club later in the evening where he'll get the chance to flirt and maybe even pick up someone. He loves that, too.

In the car, I tell him I met a boy.

"What's his name?" Sam asks.

"Nixon," I say.

"What?"

"I said Nixon."

"Oh, sorry," Sam says. "I thought you said Nixon."

I suddenly regret inviting him. He's in a bad mood again. He's only in a good mood once a week and you never know when it's going to hit. And besides, he's never happy when I meet someone. It always has to be about him.

"I really like him," I say, almost to myself.

"Well Rachel told me you met an elegant stranger who writes poetry. Jesus, Lily. A waiter? From Hungary? Called Nixon?"

Rachel and her big mouth.

"You'll see," I tell him. "This one's a keeper."

Humph.

We drive down Blair Street towards Anyu's building. The evening hustle has started and the streets of Bondi are abuzz with Friday night fever. Groups of religious Jews in black coats and hats march downhill towards the synagogue in the old Catholic school hall. It's over thirty degrees Celsius in the evening and they're dressed like it's January in Poland. Three buff gorillas with ear pieces and handguns guard the gates. "Idiots!" Sam sneers. I don't take it personally anymore. I think they're just as crazy as he does. A kamikaze skateboarder flies past our car at a million miles an hour. I have to swerve to miss him. "Idiot!" Sam sneers. As we park the car, an unaccompanied dog squats in front of Sam's door, leaves his load, and then ambles across the street.

"I fucking hate Bondi," he says, getting out of the car. "And anyway, Lily, what the fuck are you wearing?"

I look down and notice I'm still wearing Nixon's apron.

"Nothing," I say, untying the knot, scrunching it in a ball and throwing it in the back seat. "It's nothing." As it hits the seat, the order pad and pen fall to the floor. I reach back down to pick them up. There's something colourful in the apron pocket.

"What are you doing?" Sam shouts, impatiently. He is standing on the footpath concentrating on avoiding dog shit and broken beer bottles.

"Just a sec," I shout back. I reach deep into the apron and feel it. I know exactly what it is. "I'm coming," I say, shoving the wad of cash into my jeans pocket.

I walk into Anyu's building in a daze.

***

Anyu and Sam greet each other like long-lost lovers.

"Oh Sam, daahrlink, how wonderful you came to visit. I've missed you." They kiss and hug and hold hands. "You've brought my Lily with you. What a lovely surprise, kids." She must have forgotten our arrangement. Damn, I didn't have to come after all.

She looks me up and down with a puckered brow and then turns back to Sam. "When are you going to teach her to look like a woman, daahrlink?"

"Oh Anyoo," Sam says, "you know what she's like!" I look down at my baggy jeans and blue T-shirt. I don't think it's that bad. Sam takes hold of both Anyu's hands and takes a small step backwards. "You, on the other hand, look more beautiful than ever! What moisturiser are you using? You've lost ten years since I saw you last. If only I were a few years older ..."

Anyu blushes and waves away his remark with a shaky hand. "You are such a naughty boy!" She fixes her hair and welcomes us in. "Come and sit while I fix something for you." She turns and disappears through the kitchen door.

"Hi Anyu," I say, but she's already gone.

I sit down with Sam in the living room while Anyu scurries about in the kitchen. She is banging pots and pans and mumbling something about how although it is her greatest pleasure to see Sam, it would have been better if she had known we were coming beforehand, only, of course, for *our* benefit, you know, so she could have prepared a few things (meaning, of course, a three-course meal and a week's worth of leftovers). I try to explain to her that we did make the arrangement and that we are not hungry, but she won't hear any of it. I try to explain that Sam doesn't eat carbs, but she tells me she'll see if she has any pasta instead.

All of a sudden she is scampering down the hallway and emerges from her bedroom with her jewellery box.

"Samuel, my daahrlink, do I have a job for you!"

"Good-o!" Sam squeals, rubbing his palms together.

This is his idea of a good time: organising a heap of tangled earrings into some sort of meaningful order. He loves arranging them first into matching pairs, then according to colour. Daytime earrings on the left, night-time ones on the right. They are a garish, tacky, cheap-looking bunch. Clip-ons, of course, because Anyu thinks pierced ears are only for primitives. He always makes a start with genuine enthusiasm, but gives up three-quarters of the way through when he realises it's all too difficult. Obsessive compulsive disorder without the discipline, I always say.

I pick up a framed photograph of my father on the coffee table while Sam starts sorting through the earrings. My father stares out from within the blackened silver frame. He is standing at the famous Echo Point in the Blue Mountains. Behind him stand the spectacular and iconic Three Sisters, a formidable rock formation rising steeply from the olive green valley below.

I know that lookout point well and the vista is stunning, but the photo doesn't do it any justice; all that stand out are his eyes. Large, dark almonds, almost black, almost liquid, they seem to melt into the page. He is looking straight at the camera, but somehow, it doesn't quite feel like he is looking at you. His lips are smiling, but his eyes are sad. He was already sick; his eyes tell me so.

In the few childhood memories I replay over and over in my head, some are real and some are imaginary, and some are in between. And in them, Papa looks just like he does in this photo: his hair dark and wavy and tousled by that strong mountain breeze, his navy blue parka zipped up all the way to his chin. When I imagine him standing against the countertop in our kitchen or sitting casually at the card table in Anyu's living room, when I imagine him giving me a sweet kiss on the neck or lying in bed in the days before his death, I see that same blue parka, that same windswept hair, those same sad eyes.

I wonder how Anyu feels living with Papa's eyes looking out into her lounge room. What does she think as she dusts around the photo frame or brushes up against it on the way to the bathroom? I wonder how she feels casually placing the TV remote down next to her dead son.

I wonder; but we never talk about Papa.

Mama doesn't have any photos of him displayed around her place. It's as if she is still angry with him for dying on her. Maybe she wants to protect me. Maybe she just wants to irritate Anyu.

A waft of fried onions seeps in from underneath the kitchen door. I put down Papa's photo and brace myself for the nausea. Sam rolls his eyes at me.

"Smells good, Anyoo," Sam calls over his shoulder in Anyu's direction.

"Don't encourage her," I tell him.

"Oh daahrlink, it's nothing special," she shouts back, "just a little something. Of course, if I had known you were coming ..."

"We're not hungry, Anyu. Just come and sit with us," I say.

"Rice or noodles, daahrlink?" she asks.

"I said we're not eating!"

"Well?"

"That's not why we're here."

"I think it goes better with rice," she says.

"I'm not hungry," I reply, this time in Hungarian. My heart skips a beat. Will she notice? I bite my lip.

Sam looks at me like I'm crazy. "What are you doing?" he mouths.

"I didn't ask if you were hungry or not," comes the reply.

I get up, annoyed, and move over to the other side of Sam toward the bookshelf by the wall. Anyu's couch is lumpy and uncomfortable. The cushions are too soft and the frame is too hard. The fading green upholstery is falling apart. I brush past Sam as he thoughtfully fiddles with a pair of earrings.

"Okay then," I shout back. "Make it rice."

Sam sniggers.

"She didn't even notice," I tell him, slumping back down on the couch, nuzzling my hips in between Sam and the bookshelf.

"Ouch!" he cries. "Your butt is too bony! Hey, don't mess up my piles." He hovers protectively over the stash as I browse through a few magazines and books piled up next to me on the shelf.

"What do I have to do to make her notice?" I ask, picking up a random book. It's written in Hungarian. One day, I say to myself, and then again to the book. One day I'll be able to read you.

"Hey Lily," he says after a pause long enough to mean he thinks my question is rhetorical. "I need your help. Do you think they should be in the Emerald Section or the Diamante Section?" He hands me the two earrings. One is more offensive than the other. They are loud, flashy, garish pieces of junk.

I shrug, handing them back. "Where did you put them last time?" I ask.

"Last time they were in the Nightwear Section. Jesus, Lily, don't you care about anything?"

No, I don't. I'm not much into Anyu's type of jewellery. The only piece I wear is an old watch of hers from the thirties. It's nothing terribly fancy or chic, and though I do have to remember to wind it up every morning and take it off before I have a shower, it reminds me several times a day of who I am. It is, after all, one of the few concrete things I have of my family's life in Budapest. And it doesn't look half as cheap as those earrings.

Sam holds the earrings out at arm's length and tilts his head pensively. He thinks about it earnestly for a moment, then puts them in the Diamante Section. We both sigh with relief. I place the book back on the shelf and scan the area for something else to look at.

"You kids are so quiet!" Anyu shouts, pleased. She ducks her head around the sliding door for a quick peek. She has long been hoping Sam and I would become romantic. I think she knows he's gay, but she probably thinks he can be cured. *Just wear something fabulous, Lily,* I imagine her saying. *That will do it! When I was a young lady I wore slacks. Slacks! Imagine. I was a sensation in my time! And they used to queue up around the block for just one dance …*

I place one arm around Sam's shoulders and leave it there just long enough for Anyu to have noticed, then take it away and give him a friendly punch on the arm. He pokes out his tongue at me.

"Don't you encourage her," he scowls.

A fading green album catches my eye. I check to see Anyu is back behind the kitchen door before I take it down. Loosely held together at one end with a piece of string, it is coated with a thick layer of dust. I place it on the coffee table, pushing aside some of Sam's piles.

"Gross, Lily," he sniggers. "Get that disgusting thing away from here! Can't you bloody move over?"

As I hold up one corner and brush some of the dust in Sam's general direction, a bulging yellow envelope falls to our feet.

"You're fucking up my order, Lily!" he says. I bend over to pick it up. My hair gets caught in a clip. He mumbles something about what an idiot I am.

"Look at this," I tell him. "You have to come and look at this."

The envelope is stuffed with photos.

Sam's still mumbling. But I don't care. I am too excited.

I can't believe my eyes.

I look again.

Every photo is of Eva.

I go through the pile one by one: Eva in a swimming costume and bathing cap at a lake, Eva in an elegant suit and high heels smoking a cigarette at a train station, Eva in a fur collar at a card table. She was beautiful! There's a young, dreamy-eyed Eva staring into the distance wearing a large-brimmed hat; a skinny, thirty-something Eva with her head thrown back, laughing. I can't catch my breath.

I go through them again. Every single photo is of Eva! Though some are completely intact, the great majority of the fifty or so photos are ripped and not the usual tearing off of the corners by overhandling over time. These are man-made, deliberate tears. Some of the strips are almost cleanly severed, as if by a knife or a blunt pair of scissors, but most are torn by a clearly angry hand. There are remnants of other people's arms and hairdos around Eva's shoulders, fragments of limbs, ears, and coat sleeves.

I wonder why she never threw them out.

I imagine an angry, huffy Anyu fuming up the stairs, madly turning the pages of her albums for any sign of The Enemy and ripping her out melodramatically: out of lakeside holidays and birthday parties, out of embraces, out of memories, out of her life. I imagine her sitting here on this same couch with scissors and tissues, crying as she safely stored away her best friend in a yellow envelope.

For now, she must have thought.

I try to work out how long ago she must have done this. I don't know exactly when the *break-up* took place, nor whether the *tear-up* happened at the same time. I think I'm looking at that all too short period of time between my birth and my father's death, but I can't be sure. I look at the photos for clues. The last few shots were taken somewhere between flares and shoulder pads. I'm hopeless with fashion. I enlist Sam's help.

"What do you think?" I ask.

"I think you're annoying me," he says.

"It's her, Sam. It's Eva. She's here. Look at these outfits!"

He puts down an earring and leans over my lap at the photos. Suddenly he's interested.

"She's gorgeous, Lily!"

"Yeah, she really was," I say. "When do you think this one was taken?" I hand him the last photo in the series. Eva is smoking a cigarette, holding an ashtray in the other hand. She casually leans against what looks like a kitchen bench-top. She is smiling cheekily at something or someone on her left, but that half of the photo has been ripped off.

"Let's see," says Sam, snatching the photo from my hand, "a brown ribbed turtle neck with tan corduroys. It can't be much later than 1988. What a figure! Look at that ring! I bet you she has a jewellery collection or two."

I sigh. 1988. That's the year after I was born.

"I don't know," I say, snatching the photo back. "I'm not so sure you're right." I think of the way Eva dresses today and it gives me little confidence in assigning the picture an absolute date.

"Then why are you asking?" he says.

"I think that's our kitchen," I say. "I remember those blinds." I pick up the green album; I want to see the other halves. Surely they must have been put back.

"Come to the table, kids!" Anyu sings. She bounds into the room. I panic, throwing the album under the coffee table. "I hope you're hungry!" she says.

"Distract her," I mouth quickly to Sam as he gets up from the couch.

Sam sneers and gives me a look – *Jesus you're annoying* – but he is my best friend, after all. "Anyoo, can you show me where the bathroom is again, you gorgeous thing you?"

I know I only have two seconds as Anyu leads Sam down the hallway. I quickly gather all the photos of Eva and put them back in the yellow envelope. I pick up the green album and just as I'm about to put the envelope back, I change my mind and slip it into my handbag. I hide the album under the bookshelf so I can find it easily again next time. I'll bring back the envelope next time, I tell myself. Next time I'll bring it back.

Walking toward the table for dinner, Sam whispers in my ear.

"Lily," he says, "why don't you just simply *ask* Anyu about Eva?" He shrugs his shoulders melodramatically. "What's the big bloody deal?"

Is it me or is everyone around me completely crazy? Why on earth would I want to *ask* my grandmother something like that? I know exactly what she would do.

I look at him with exasperation and shake my head.

"Don't be an idiot," I say.

Chapter Nine

I'm driving to the gallery today which means another parking ticket. It's not my fault. The doctor said I had to get a blood test early in the morning before I had anything to eat or drink. Georgie said he could fit me in before his first patient.

"The results will be in tomorrow," he said, giving me a kiss on the cheek. "I'll call you."

The traffic on Bourke Street is flowing nicely. I light myself a cigarette. The window winder is stiff and my arm hurts. I'm sick of this bloody car.

I leave the window open when I get out at the gallery. Hopefully someone will steal it this time. I spot a group of Aboriginal men sitting on the front lawn of a dilapidated terrace house not far from my parking spot. Most are wearing footy jerseys or truckie singlets, smoking and laughing, possibly already drinking even though it's not even nine o'clock. *The bloody car's all yours,* I whisper, daring them to take it. I hear a wolf whistle but I don't turn around. But I do check that my skirt isn't caught in my undies.

Camilla is swearing at the computer when I arrive.

"Oh Lily," she says, getting up from the stool behind the front desk. "I need you to do the blog today."

I sit down. The computer is off.

"Here," she says, handing me a piece of paper. "Here's this week's entry."

I look at the page, then back up at Camilla.

"I thought you were going to do it on the computer this week," I say.

"I know," she says.

"So?" I ask, starting up the computer.

"What's the problem? Here's the computer. Here's what I wrote. Just type it up."

"It takes me two minutes to cut and paste it into the blog. Just type it in the first time."

She takes a sip of her coffee and turns to the mirror behind me. She smooths back her hair into an immaculate bun, raises herself up on her tippy toes, puts her hands on her waist, and pouts. She straightens up her bra, rearranges her cleavage, and falls back onto her heels with a frown.

"And take off that ridiculous band-aid," she says. "What are you? A five year old?"

I lay the page out in front of me and start typing. She'll never get it.

And I'll never get how she manages to run this successful gallery when she's still living in the last century.

She slumps down on the couch by the wall opposite me with a copy of the new *Vogue*. I peel off a corner of the band-aid on my arm. It's too sore to take off, so I leave it on and roll down my sleeve instead.

"Patricia Clarkson called me last night," she tells me, without looking up. "She wants me to do a couple of weeks for her in March. Do you think we can fit her in between the Germans and Greta Baker?"

Patricia Clarkson paints for the Australian Ballet. She does what are called performance portraits. She sets up an easel in one of the VIP boxes on opening night and slashes away madly at the canvas while the dancers are on stage. As soon as they finish the set, she puts the painting aside and *swears* she doesn't touch it again. She can paint up to twenty portraits in a single evening.

"I don't know," I say. "Let me check." I open the calendar and find March. "We've only got a week," I tell her. "That's not enough."

"Can't we shorten Baker's run?" She puts down the magazine. "Surely she won't mind."

Camilla knows Baker will mind. She also knows Baker will make her more money than Patricia, but none of that will stop her.

Camilla always dreamed of being a ballerina when she was young, but no one takes you seriously when you're fourteen years old and a double-D cup.

"I'll deal with it," she says with a frown.

I'd like to feel sorry for her, but it's hard to take her disappointment seriously with tits like that.

I put Patricia in the calendar for March and continue typing up Camilla's blog.

Camilla smiles and goes back to her magazine. "Good," she says, sinking back into the couch.

I type. Camilla reads. There's peace in the gallery.

For now.

I'm almost finished but I don't want this time to end. I have an idea. I quietly reach into my handbag and pull out Eva's Sad Hungarian Poem. Camilla doesn't stir; she's lost in her *Vogue*. I put the page with the poem on top of Camilla's blog and bring up Google Search. Camilla will never notice; the pages look almost identical.

I type in *Szomorú Varsánap*.

The Wikipedia article *Gloomy Sunday* comes up as the first result. I smile; that must be it. What did Nixon say again – that it wasn't a good day for Peter *bácsi* to read about a *Gloomy Sunday*?

I bring up the article.

> "Gloomy Sunday" is a song composed by Hungarian pianist and composer Rezső Seress and published in 1933 as "Vége a világnak" meaning "End of the World". Lyrics were written by László Jávor and in his version, the song was retitled "Szomorú Varsánap", meaning "Sad Sunday". The song was first recorded in Hungarian by Pál Kalmár in 1935. It became well known in much of the English speaking world after the release of the version by Billie Holiday in 1941.

Camilla looks up. "Still going?"

"Yes," I lie.

She shakes her head and stares at me menacingly.

"It takes ages when we do it this way," I tell her.

I switch screens back to the blog and continue typing until Camilla, satisfied, goes back to her article.

"I'm going to need another coffee soon, Lily," she says.

I switch back to Wikipedia.

> The song was composed by Resző Seress when he lived in Paris. The original music composition was a piano melody in C-minor ...

I scroll down a bit to see what else there is. I'm not so interested in technical bullshit. I want something juicy.

> ... the song was written at the time of the Great Depression and increasing fascist influence in the writer's native Hungary, although sources differ as to the degree to which his song was motivated by personal melancholy rather than concerns for the future of the world ...

I scroll down some more. I need something more about the lyrics, maybe there's a translation somewhere. Wait, this looks interesting.

> ... There have been several urban legends regarding the song over the years and radio networks purportedly banned the song mostly because it was allegedly connected with ...

"Lily," I hear. "It's coffee time. You can finish this later." Camilla is suddenly up and moving towards the desk.

I quickly close down the browser window and bring up the blog. I finish off the last line.

"Done," I say, closing the lid of the laptop. "I'll upload it when I get back with your coffee."

***

There are ten minutes to go. I finish at one today. Anyu is meeting me here for a quick lunch before I head back home to do some painting.

I call out to Camilla on my way up the stairs. "I'm just going to the loo. Back in a minute."

On my way back down, I see Anyu standing by the desk chatting to Camilla. She is perky and animated, almost flirting. I freeze. What the hell is she doing here so early? And what the hell is she telling Camilla? Last time I saw her this excited she was telling my neighbour what a difficult child I was. "What?" she said to me when I told her off. "I was just saying how much you've grown up!" Then there was the time I overheard her telling my high school maths tutor how relieved she was when I finally got my periods at fifteen and a half.

There's an awkward silence as I approach. I cringe.

Then Camilla speaks.

"What lovely cheekbones you have Mrs Fekete! Tell me, are you Slavic?"

I hold my breath. Oh no. Here we go.

"Slavic? No, daahrlink," Anyu says. "We are educated." She smiles. *Bloody Australian peasant.*

"Oh, I see," Camilla says. She smiles back. *Bloody wogs, the lot of you.*

I gather my bag and take Anyu by the arm. "Let's go," I tell her, pulling her towards the door.

"Lovely to meet you, Mrs Fekete!"

As we choose a table at the Danks Street Depot next door, Anyu is settling into Monologue Number 17.

"Those Schwartzes are painting a lot, aren't they, daahrlink? What the hell are they going to do with all that money? You know, your father, God bless his soul, he was such a sensitive one. He said this country is haunted by the ghosts of the black ones. He said to me, 'Anyu, you think we had it bad … '." I recite the last part together with her. "… no one talks about it, but look at the Schwartzes. Now they're really done for!"

"It's not quite like that any more, Anyu," I say. "Things are different now. The painter we are going to show in a couple of months is a genius. A true genius."

"Don't be ridiculous, Lily," she says. "They are like children. The government gives them paints so they stay out of trouble. But can you blame them? What else can they do?"

I shake my head. "You don't understand, Anyu." I look around for a waiter. "I only hope that I can paint like that one day."

Humph!

No one's coming, so I get up to grab a menu from the counter. I spot a friend of mine two tables away who works in the Korean art gallery next door. We chat for a minute about Big A's opening and how cute the new window cleaner is.

Anyu grabs the menu when I get back to the table. She's irritated.

"So tell me," I say. "How are you, Anyu?"

"Oh daahrlink, don't ask," she says.

I do ask.

"*Vell* … you know, when you get to my age nothing's so *vell* anymore."

"Come on, Anyu, you're not that old."

"I've seen enough," she says. "I've seen enough. You're still young. You have so much to see in your time. Tell me, Lily, when are you going to find yourself a man?"

"Anyu! Not again! Let's just have lunch."

"You know, whatever you do, you must never let them think they are the powerful ones. For years we had them fooled," she monologues, "… and then came those bloody feminists who tried to be more and more like the men and you know what?"

"They became as stupid as the men in the end?" I say only for the millionth time.

"Tell me, daahrlink," she continues without skipping a beat. "Who said that women never had any power? We have always controlled the men. It's your generation, Lily …"

She opens the menu and squints. "This thing just makes me awfully mad! How am I supposed to understand any of this?" She reads out loud.

> Rillettes made with Cornucopia Farm's Biodynamic Duck served with Cornichons and Toast
>
> Beetroots pickled in Red Wine and Red Wine Vinegar served with Shepherd's Avocado and Skordalia

"I know," I say. I'd also prefer Peter *bácsi*'s simple, wholesome chicken noodle soup, but I don't say that.

"What do you know?" she says. "It's your generation, Lily. It's why intelligent girls like you want to be more like Schwartzes. It's why I can't order a meal in a café anymore. It's why my beautiful granddaughter doesn't have a boyfriend, let alone a husband!" *Humph.*

"Well actually, Anyu …"

"Actually what?" she snaps. She says *vot* like she's spitting.

"Actually nothing," I say, changing my mind.

"I know what you wanted to say: actually you have Sam! He's lovely, daahrlink, but how can I say this? *Vell* … you know, let me explain … It's probably something I should have told you long ago but you are still so … you see Sam, he's not much of a man …"

"Anyu!" I can't believe she's talking about Sam.

"*Vell*, Lily, someone has to tell you one day," she says.

"Anyu, are you kidding me? I know Sam's gay!"

"You know?"

"Anyu! I'm not a baby."

"*Vell* it's just we love to tease each other, Sam and I, and I didn't want you to hang on to dear hope …"

"I'm not talking about Sam."

"You're not?"

"I'm talking about someone else!"

"Oh!" She sits up straight and puts down the menu. Her eyes narrow. "Someone else? There's someone else and you waited this long to say something?"

I shake my head.

"So tell me about this someone else, Lily … Who is this *somevun else?* Do I know him? Who are his parents? Do they play rummy?"

"Anyu!"

"So … ?"

"Well, firstly, nothing's actually happened yet," I say. I don't want her to get too excited. And she may as well know the truth straight from the start. "And I don't think you know him."

"Oh," she says.

"Or his parents," I add. "He's not …" I stop myself. Well, technically he *is*. But not *that* kind of Hungarian. I guess she doesn't have to know everything. Not just yet, anyway. "He's not … Jewish. He's not *unsere*," I say, instead. *One of us.*

"Oh," she says.

That's it? That's all? He's not Jewish and she just says "Oh?" I breathe a sigh of relief. This isn't going to be as bad as I thought. She's finally happy for me.

"He's very cute," I continue, smiling, "cute and a little naïve." I hear Anyu *humph*. "And he's a good boy, I think. He's nice and works hard … I really like him, but I just don't know."

"Oh," she says.

"I just don't know if he likes me," I say.

"Lily daahrlink, a woman always knows," she says without much expression and motions to the waiter. We order bio-organic lentil something or other with a sauce neither of us can pronounce. I feel good. This is going to be good.

"He has a little limp when he walks," I continue. "And when he gets excited, Anyu, you should see when he gets all excited and flustered! He does this sort of twirl, this kind of semi-pirouette. It's adorable."

"Oh," she says.

I go on. This is the best conversation we've had in years. "And he has interesting stories and anecdotes. I think you'll really like him, Anyu. I really like him, Anyu. And I think he likes me."

"Oh."

"So tell me, Anyu," I'm so excited I ask. "Tell me: what do you think?"

But I regret the words as soon as they come out.

Anyu stares at me for a moment, her eyes narrowing and squinting as if she's about to start a running race. Ready, Get set, Go …

"You know what I think, Lily? I think you quit medical school to look after primitive finger painters and now you are alone. Alone." She say *a-lo-one* like it has three syllables.

"But I don't understand. I just told you. I like him! I think he likes me!"

"Of course *he likes you*. They always like us. They are always nice when they want something and trust me, Lily, a man always wants something from a woman. I was young and beautiful once upon a time too, you know."

The food arrives, but I'm not hungry anymore. This is no longer a conversation about me and Nixon. I should have known. I never learn.

She slowly cuts off a piece of lentil patty with shaky hands and takes a bite. A blob of yoghurt sauce gathers in the corner of her mouth and she fumbles for a serviette. I pick mine up and hand it to her. She slowly wipes herself clean and takes a deep breath.

"Yes, I was young and beautiful once. And boy," she says, "was I a sensation!" She stares up at the corner of the ceiling for a brief moment and then remembers what she was saying. "What I'm trying to say, Lily, is that deep down ..." She burps. "Deep down they hate us."

"What?" I say.

"They always have, always will. It's hard to know what I mean when you are so very young, but it's how it is. When all is well, when times are good, there are never any problems. They can be cute and naïve. They can have interesting stories and work hard. But believe me, Lily, believe me when I say that when the shit hits the fan and trust me, it always does. When the shit hits the fan, deep down, you are, and always will be, a Jew." She takes another excruciatingly slow bite of lentils and I wait. I am so stupid. "Never forget it, Lily, because trust me, they never will. You know," she continues, "I was young and beautiful once upon a time."

"Once upon time? Once upon a time you lived at the other end of the world. It was another time. It was another planet ... This is Australia, Anyu! This is the twenty-first century! This is different!"

"That's exactly what I said then, Lily. I said this is Hungary. This is the 1930s. This is different."

"But aren't you happy for me? Isn't this what you always wanted? Aren't you excited for me?"

"Excited? I've had enough excitement for one lifetime."

I want to say something. Instead we finish our lunch in a tortured silence. I wait for more. I wait to hear more about all the "excitement for one lifetime" but it doesn't come.

On the way to the car, she finally explains in the only way she knows how. "You'll never understand, Lily," she says. She takes my arm. "Just trust me and stay away from this boy."

Oh, I understand all right. Anyu just doesn't want me to be happy because what will she talk about then?

I'm irritated because the shitty little car is still there. So are the same group of Aboriginal men sitting on the lawn doing nothing. *I left you the bloody window open! How much easier can I possibly make it for you?*

I peel off the parking ticket from the windscreen and get in. It must have rained while I was at work. The car seat is all wet.

Bloody Schwartzes.

"How much is the ticket?" she asks me.

"$62," I say.

"Bloody anti-Semites," she says.

***

It's midnight and I just can't paint anymore. Nothing has worked today. I stand in front of my easel defeated. The young woman looks blankly back at the room from the oversized canvas. She's bursting with colour and detail, but she doesn't have soul. Empty eyes stare at an indeterminate point somewhere over my head. Her individual features are petite and lovely, but together they do not make her beautiful. I throw down my paint brush and it hits the easel with a splash.

I take down the photo I pinned onto the wooden frame and wipe off a splatter of orange paint. I hold it close.

"Sorry, Eva," I tell her. "Tomorrow I will make you beautiful again."

I turn towards the mirror hanging on my open wardrobe and place the photo next to my face. My fingers cover the torn edge. I try to match her smile. Open-mouthed, she is actually laughing. I smooth my hair over to one side just like hers. I put one hand on my hip and endeavour a laugh. It doesn't come. I throw myself onto my bed and place her gently on the pillow next to mine. I turn towards her. "I bet you were never this lonely when you were twenty-two," I tell her.

Still she laughs.

I reach across for my phone on the bedside table and find Jeremy's number in the index. I look out the window. The rain has finally stopped. I know he'll come. He always does. I look back at Eva lying on my pillow. She is laughing at me. I laugh back. This time it's real.

"Fuck it," I say out loud, and hit the *delete contact* button on my phone. I reach for my jeans.

***

The streets are eerily quiet in Double Bay. I'm a little scared I've missed him. I stop the car behind a taxi across the road. The lights in the Oktogon are still on. The front door is half open and I see Peter *bácsi* waddle slowly to the street and light himself a cigarette. The chairs are stacked in the front corner and three garbage bins are lined up out front. A stray cat jumps onto the top of one of the bins and Peter *bácsi* goes to pat him.

Then I see him. Eyes down, he is hunched over a mop cleaning the floor. My heart skips a beat. He's still there.

The wind blows cigarette ash back onto the wet tiles inside leaving a grey watery streak like smudged charcoal on paper. I can't see Nixon's face anymore. He has turned the other way and is re-washing the sullied floor without a word.

Peter *bácsi* sees me first. He watches me deliberately as I get out of the car. He smiles at me as I approach and continues petting the cat. All is quiet. It is at once creepy and arousing; we both know why I am there.

When Nixon finally turns around, I am already standing at the door. We both freeze. I had it all worked out. Every detail of it, that is, until this very point. Peter flicks away his cigarette, salutes the two of us with a smile, crosses the road, and disappears into the night.

"Lily?" Nixon walks up to the door. "Well, you know, I'm just closing up." He doesn't smile. One hand on the broom, the other on the door handle, he balances on one foot as if ready to close the door at any moment. "Everyone's gone home," he says.

Suddenly I panic. He has a girlfriend. He thinks I'm fat. He's gay. I feel sick.

But then I see it. I don't know what it is: a twinkle in the eye, a slight opening of the lips, a wrinkle of the brow. Like Anyu says, *a woman always knows.*

I don't talk. I can't say a word. I step forward, head first, eyes closed, and kiss him square on the mouth. At once, he pulls back. *What's going on?* He takes a small step backwards, cocks his head to one side, and stares.

I hold my breath. I can't move. I can't breathe. A dog barks in the distance and a truck reverses with a painful beeping. I hear car wheels screech and a baby cry. I can hear the ticking of my watch. I open my mouth to talk, but he places his finger on my lips to stop me. He smells of smoke and disinfectant. I lower my eyes and turn to leave. And then it happens. Like Bogart to Bergman, he sweeps me in his arms and kisses me as if it were to be our last.

People talk of fireworks and lightning bolts, but I'm shaking too much to imagine anything of the sort. I hear the mop handle land with a clang on the tiles and feel him lift me off my feet. Suddenly he is carrying me to the kitchen. I can smell fried onion and Eva's *Poison*. I feel drunk. He places me gently on the floor. The tiles are cold and still a little wet; his skin is warm and sweaty. The oven's soft glow warms my legs. He protects my head with a strong hand. He holds me as if I'll break in two. He kisses me from head to toe. He is tender and calm. He is strong and hard. He wants me. I close my eyes and let myself go. "Lily," he whispers. "Lily, I want you."

***

Back at my apartment, Nixon oohs and ahhs over my unfinished canvases. He touches the eyes on the wall and stares back at them with a confidence

I've never found. He picks up a paint brush and swirls it in a cup of murky water. He puts his face close to the mouth of a portrait and studies the brush strokes with a curious eye. He is an excited child. His sense of awe delights me and I watch from the window sill as he plays. I am happy.

I show him around my canvases. I introduce him to Anyu and Mama. I show him the portrait of Zsuzsi as a young woman and then another one of her in her seventies. "You'd like Zsuzsi *néni*," I tell him. "She has a big heart."

He picks up a portrait of a child, a young girl in braids holding a doll. "*De édes!*" he says. "You were very sweet."

"That's Anyu," I say. "My father's mother. Here's what she looks like now." I hand him Anyu and he studies her face.

"Oh," he says, putting down the canvas. "That's Anyu. She is a ... How do you say it? *De érdekes* this one."

"Interesting," I tell him. "*De érdekes.*"

Interesting indeed.

I smile. Introducing him to the family is not as hard as I thought it would be.

"But these are my favourites," he says, pointing to a series of self-portraits I have resting behind the curtain. How did he find those?

"Oh, they're nothing," I say, sliding them one by one under the bed and out of sight.

"This one is nice." He holds up a portrait of me looking back over my shoulder. "You look so scared, so unsure. But your eyes are still happy. Your mouth sort of curls up at the edges. You are beautiful," he says, touching my cheek.

I kiss him.

"I guess a picture paints a million things," he says, wisely.

He can't stop talking. And I can't believe my luck. Only a few moments before, we had left the Oktogon arm in arm as if we had done it a thousand times before. In the car, he told me how he was once in love with his fourth class teacher and that his Budapest football club is on a winning streak. He teaches me to say *kiss me* and *I play the violin* in Hungarian. He tells me the story of the Hun migration to Hungary in the fifth century. He is still talking even as we collapse in each other's arms on my unmade bed. He talks even as I fall into a deep, sweet coma. A complete surrender.

I awake with a start. I look at the clock. 5:07. Where am I? The room is warm. I have been sweating. The thick smell of sleep hovers above the bed. All is black save a dramatic shaft of light coming in from the street lamp outside the naked window, a classic chiaroscuro from the heavens. God is watching. And next to me, the bed is empty.

I want to cry. The family curse is too strong for even this one. I reach across to the packet of cigarettes on my bedside table. Where has my lighter gone? I find Eva's half-torn photo hiding in the sheets and toss it on the floor. Both Anyu and Mama were right not to trust Eva.

But then I jump. There he is, an illuminated Caravaggio, naked chest coming out of the shadows. He walks out of the bathroom door, at once frightening and beautiful. Every fibre of his skin seems in hyper focus. His chest and shoulders, freckled and covered in sparse, wiry hairs. He smiles at me and I fall back on the soft pillow. I watch him. I follow the ripple and flow of his boyish arms until they are around me again, and without a sound he nuzzles his face into the small of my neck; within seconds I feel the rhythmic swell of his sleep.

But I can't sleep anymore. I am deliciously exhausted and at peace. Then the sulfur-crested cockatoos in the big fig trees across the road start their ritual squawking earlier than usual and the ruckus steals the stillness from my grip. Nixon stirs, mumbles, and rolls away from me. In a second, I lose my cool.

"I'm sick," I whisper, a little too loud and a little too soft. "I'm sick and the doctors just don't know how much longer."

He doesn't move. I don't know whether or not he heard me. I don't even know if I wanted him to hear.

Chapter Ten

It rings and rings and rings. And then it stops. Nixon moans and rolls over. He nestles his face into my neck and mumbles Hungarian nothings in my ear. I don't understand and I don't care. His breath is warm and he's here. He's still here.

It rings again. Nixon buries his face in the pillow. I want the ringing to stop.

"Hello?" I say. The phone feels strange in my hand. I open my eyes. Oh no.

"Lily daahrlink," a voice says. "It's Eva *néni*."

I sit up suddenly. Oh no.

"Lily daahrlink, can you tell Nixon to wake up already! He's half an hour late for work."

I panic. Shit. Nixon. Work. Eva *néni*. Eva *néni?* I look down at the phone. It's not my phone!

I manage a few awkward syllables and cover the mouthpiece. I nudge Nixon out of his sleep. "Nixon, it's Eva *néni*. You're late for work!"

Nixon rubs his eyes. He sits up slowly. I watch the words compute. Eva *néni*. Late for work. Where am I? The wheels start turning. It takes forever.

And then he's got it.

He jumps out of bed and starts fluttering around the room. He waves his arms about and runs in a circle. He finally finds his underwear under the easel.

Eva's voice bellows from underneath the palm of my hand. "And Lily daahrlink," she says. I put the phone to my ear.

"Yes," I say.

"Happy birthday, daahrlink," she says.

I smile.

Nixon grabs the phone from my hand, places it between his ear and his shoulder, and starts babbling away in Hungarian. He hops around the room in a tizzy. He gathers his things, starts dressing, keeps talking. He even manages an awkward pirouette or two. He runs to the door, remembers something, and comes back to the bed. I can hear Eva carrying on through the phone. He kisses me on the lips and whispers: *I'll call you.*

"Go!" I whisper back, and watch him limp out the door.

"Aaaah!" I scream. I throw the covers over my head and kick my legs into the air. I want to disappear into the earth. I want to jump for joy.

Happy birthday indeed.

***

It's six-thirty the same evening and I'm sitting on a stool in Mama's kitchen covered head to toe in flour. We are making lángos, a Hungarian speciality of deep-fried flat bread. We have spent the last hour slaving over several kilos of dough which needs to be mixed and rolled and kneaded to perfection before being cut into flat, round pieces and thrown into hot oil until they turn golden brown. Then you take a clove of garlic, slice it open, and while the lángos is still hot, you rub it with garlic, and smother it with salt and sour cream. It is both utterly disgusting and totally delicious.

When I moved out of home after school, Mama moved into a small flat in Woollahra. It pleases her to live in such an affluent, WASP-y area but all she can afford is one dark bedroom and a tiny living room with damp walls and paint peeling off the ceiling from the upstairs neighbour's bathroom whose landlord hasn't yet located the leak. There's no parking spot, the Moreton Bay Fig tree out the front blocks out any natural light, and the hallway is cluttered with boxes of books that can't be unpacked because there is no room for bookshelves. The kitchen is semi-decent, although Mama doesn't cook so much. But tonight is special. Tonight is Hannukah.

This year my birthday falls on the first night of Hannukah. Anyu thought we could celebrate with the Jewish tradition of eating something fried to commemorate Hannukah's miracle of the oil. Two thousand years ago, the Jews led a successful revolt against the Greeks, I think, and freed the Temple in Jerusalem. But when the time came to light the candelabra, they found only a small jug of oil which would burn for only one day. That's when God came down and made that little jug of oil last eight days. It was a miracle.

"It'll be a miracle if your grandmother makes it in time," Mama mumbles. "That's the Hannukah miracle I'm hoping for."

I take a piece of dough and squash it in my fingers. It feels warm and sticky.

"Don't be like that, Mama," I say. "It's my birthday after all."

"So why are we celebrating something that happened a million years ago, in a country a million miles away, to a people we call our own, but who were filthy, uneducated peasants! How any modern person can take any of this stuff seriously completely baffles me. Baffles me!"

Neither Mama nor I have much of a connection to Judaism. Hannukah is the only festival we celebrate because it's always around my birthday. There are other Jewish things we keep: a copy of *Portnoy's Complaint* on my bookshelf, a silver Star of David necklace from Anyu's trip to Israel, an old family recipe for Matzo Ball Soup for cold winter nights. Anyu would love us to be more involved, but she gave up nagging Mama about keeping Sabbath and the festivals after Mama took her to a synagogue with a woman rabbi.

"But Mama," I tell her. "I love lángos!"

She rolls her eyes and pours herself a glass of wine. She looks down at her watch and groans.

"It's peasant food," she says.

We are waiting for Anyu to arrive before we start the frying. Lángos has to be eaten immediately, otherwise it goes greasy and soggy. It's never good cold. I also invited Sam to join us. He's the honorary male at the table for all our celebrations. Maybe next year Nixon can come too. I laugh. That'll be the day.

Mama readjusts the heat under the fry pan. "What a ridiculous bloody idea this was anyway," she says. "If I leave the gas on, the oil will burn. But if I turn it off now, Anyu's going to complain it's not hot enough. I can't win. She kills me!"

"It's not a competition, Mama," I say.

"And if she doesn't kill me," she continues, "the bloody cholesterol will!"

I smooth out a ball of dough with the rolling pin and put it aside. I take a pinch of flour, sprinkle it on the counter top, cut off a new piece, and start again. Mama cringes as specks of flour fall to the floor. She squeezes out a sponge from the sink and bends down to wipe the tiles at my feet.

I take a breath.

"I met someone, Mama," I say. I smile. I think back to last night: Nixon's childlike excitement over my canvases, his crazy stream-of-consciousness babble, his casual philosophising about how a picture paints a million things. And I think back to this morning: he was still there when I woke up. *I met someone.*

"Uh-huh," she says without looking up. "Not another artist, I hope!" She says *artist* like she's saying *murderer*.

I shake my head. "No, Mama, he's not an artist."

"Good," she says.

"He's a waiter!" I say, smiling.

That'll teach her.

She stops her cleaning and looks up at me from the floor.

I continue, "And it doesn't bother you that he's not *unsere*, does it? You're not prejudiced and close-minded like Anyu, are you? When I told Anyu about him, she lectured me about non-Jews and how they hate us. I know you're not like that. I know you're smarter than that."

"What?" She moves to stand up and bangs her head on the counter top. She holds her head and throws the sponge back in the sink. She puts both hands on her hips.

"You told Anyu before me?"

"Oh," I say. I didn't really mean to offend her. Not in that way, anyway.

"Well," I tell her. "Not in that much detail."

That seems to calm her down. She smooths her hair back and takes a deep breath.

"Well, you know Anyu," Mama says. "She's just a bitter woman."

"I see," I say.

I know all about bitter women.

Mama continues, "She was once engaged to a Catholic boy and it didn't end so well. Don't listen to Anyu," she says, rubbing the back of her head with a tea towel. "And don't you go rushing into anything, either."

"Anyu?" I can't believe what I'm hearing. "Anyu engaged to a non-Jewish guy?"

Mama clears her throat and pulls up a stool next to mine. "Okay, okay. I'll tell you what happened," she says, almost reading my mind. "You may as well hear it from me because God knows how she'll make it sound." She cuts off a piece of dough and starts kneading. "It was before the war. Things were different then. Anyu couldn't study medicine because she was a Jew. Her father was already a doctor, you know, a big shot at the hospital. Anyu fell in love with a junior obstetrician, a student of her father's. He wasn't Jewish, of course, but that didn't bother anyone at the time. Anyway, the Hungarian government passed anti-Jewish laws restricting the number of Jewish professionals and even though her father was a senior professor and very well known, he was black-listed and lost his position."

I've never heard this story before.

Mama continues, "So one day, the police come to his office door without any warning. She was there that day. She was meeting her friend. She saw the whole thing: the shame, the public fall from grace. She watched as her father was humiliated in front of his colleagues. She watched as the police man-handled him forcefully from the building. She watched all the other doctors watch the entire show without a single word. And then she watched her fiancé discreetly move his things into her father's office."

I lower my eyes. It's an awful story. Why does Anyu monologue when she has real stories to tell?

"But this is not your story, Lily," Mama says. "This is not about the hatred of one non-Jewish boy. This is about the hatred of an entire people. Of an entire system. Of an entire era. It's our responsibility to not let this hatred live on." Mama puts aside her perfectly rounded piece of dough. She cuts off another piece as if moving on automatic pilot and starts kneading. She kneads and kneads and then she stops suddenly and throws the piece into the rubbish bin behind her. She gets up from the stool. She points to the candelabra I brought from Anyu's place to light the Hannukah candles tonight. "Anyu lights this bloody thing every year to bring back all the misery and hatred of another time. We can remember it, Lily, for her sake and for others, but we don't have to keep it going. The misery stops here, I say. The bullshit stops here. This is not Budapest. This is not the 1930s. You can't hold onto the actions of one non-Jewish boy brought up in a world of prejudice and hatred and assume it holds true for everyone today."

"Poor Anyu," I say. "No wonder she was so upset."

"Let's not get carried away, Lily," Mama says. "We are not like her. We don't judge all non-Jews by this one arsehole's behaviour, do we? Hell, we don't want all the non-Jews of the world judging us because of Anyu's behaviour now, do we?"

"What behaviour?" I say.

But she doesn't hear me. The doorbell has rung and she has gone to open the front door for Anyu.

"*Szervusz*, Judy," Anyu says and comes straight to the counter to kiss me. "How is my birthday girl, huh?"

"Hi Anyu," I say, holding her hand.

Anyu inspects the kitchen and turns to Mama. "The oil is not hot enough, Judy."

Mama explodes. "For God's sake, Anyu, you just walked in the door."

"I don't know why your mother is always so awfully mad with me," Anyu says. "It's not my fault the oil is not hot enough. The lángos will be inedible."

I laugh. "Come on, let's light the candles."

Anyu takes out two thin candles from a plastic bag and sets them in their place in the candelabra. She pulls out a lace scarf, her Sabbath scarf, and places it on her head. I stand next to her. She lights the first candle, holds it in the air and recites the blessing. "*Baruch atah adonai eloheinu melech haolam …*" Mama sits on the stool behind us scowling and folds her arms. She rolls her eyes. "*… asher kidishanu bemitzvotav vetzivanu lehadlik ner Shel Hannukah.*"

"Amen," I say.

Anyu takes the lit candle and with it, lights the second one which stands in its place on the candelabra. She turns to kiss me warmly on the cheek. "Happy Hannukah," she says, softly, and turns to Mama. "You too, Judy."

Mama rolls her eyes. "You know what I think of this whole thing, Anyu."

Anyu ignores her. She picks up the candelabra and walks across the room to the window beside the table. She places it on the window frame and then walks back to the stove.

Mama gets up. "We're not leaving it there, Anyu. The curtains are going to catch fire!"

"But that's the tradition, Judy. We leave the candles at the window sill so everyone knows we are celebrating Hannukah."

"Not in my house, Anyu! Burn down your own apartment if you like, but I like my house to still be standing!"

The two of them elbow each other on their way to the window. Mama gets there first and Anyu, stuck behind the table, starts whining. "An old woman can't have a little happiness on her granddaughter's birthday?"

Mama, both hands already on the candelabra, lets off a huge sigh and gives in. She ties back the curtains to protect them from the flames. Her shoulders drop. "Happy now?"

Anyu nods. "I am," she says and walks back to the stove, smiling. She turns up the heat under the fry pan and looks over to inspect the dough. "All right, all right," she mumbles, "not bad. Not bad."

And suddenly there's peace in the land.

We discuss whether or not we should wait for Sam.

"Did he say he was coming straight from work?" Mama asks.

"I think he said something about a quick drink," I say. "Let's just start. He won't mind."

Mama gently nudges Anyu out from in front of the stove, picks up a piece of flattened dough, and places it in the pan. It sizzles, but not like it should. Anyu leaves the room in a huff. We hear her rummaging around conspicuously in the living room. Mama mouths *ignore her* and continues cooking. I prepare a plate lined with kitchen paper for the ready pieces of lángos and start peeling the garlic. The smell is intoxicating. I hope I don't see Nixon later. He won't come anywhere near me!

All of a sudden, Anyu walks back into the kitchen. She's still in a huff. Or is it again?

"What the hell is this?" She is holding up a piece of paper. It looks like Camilla's blog.

"That's from my work!" I say. "That's from my boss!"

Anyu looks down at the page and frowns. "Not this," she growls, peeling the page away. There's another page underneath it. "I mean this!"

She holds up the Sad Hungarian Poem.

"Anyu!" I shout. "That's mine!"

"What the hell are you doing with this, Lily?" Anyu hisses. "Tell me: who gave it to you? Was it you, Judy?"

Mama shakes her head. "What is it?"

I snatch the page from out of Anyu hands. "What are you doing looking in my handbag, Anyu?" I scream.

"I asked you who gave it to you?"

"What's going on?" Mama says.

"That's my private stuff, Anyu," I say.

"I was looking for your parking ticket," Anyu says. "I wanted to take care of it for you on your birthday. But then I find this!"

A piece of lángos starts burning in the pan. Mama swears and fumbles for the kitchen tongs.

"It's just a poem," I say, folding it in half and putting it in my jeans pocket. "None of your business." I can't tell her about Eva. Not now. Not like this.

Suddenly, the phone rings. I check the screen. It's Dr Horvath. He must be ringing with the results of my blood test. Anyu turns to Mama and starts speaking in Hungarian.

"I have to get this," I say, and run out of the room.

I take a deep breath.

"Hello," I say.

"Lily darling," he says, "It's Georgie. I've got your results. There's no change from the last time. Come in tomorrow, will you, and we can talk about it then. I just wanted to let you know now."

"Thanks," I say and hang up. I sit down for a moment on the couch and breathe. *No change from the last time.* I decide not to say anything to Anyu and Mama. They don't need to know anything just yet.

Mama and Anyu walk into the room together arm in arm. Their solidarity is unnerving.

Mama sits down next to me and places a hand on my shoulder. "Where did you get this from, darling? You can tell me." She is calm and speaks slowly and carefully. Her composure makes me uncomfortable, but I am not giving in. I will not tell them where I got it. I will not give myself away. I will not give in!

I shake my head. I don't say a word.

"It's just we want to help you," Mama says.

Help me? What are they talking about?

The phone rings again. Maybe the doctor forgot to tell me something. I check the number. It's from a blocked caller. I don't usually answer if I don't know who it's from, but I need to get out of this ridiculous conversation. And anyway, what if it's Nixon?

"Lily?" It's a woman's voice.

"Speaking," I say.

"This is Catherine Stewart," she says, "Samuel's mother."

My heart skips a beat.

"Catherine," I say. "Is everything okay?" I stand up from the couch and wave away Anyu and Mama's urgent vibes. I turn my back to them. I have only spoken to Sam's mum once, by accident, when Sam and I bumped into her at a restaurant. Sam doesn't even speak to her himself. Why is she calling me? How did she get my number?

"I'm afraid not, Lily. I'm calling you from down at St Vincent's Hospital. Look there's no easy way to say this. Samuel has had an overdose. They're not quite sure what it was. They are saying something about a bad pill. I know he would want you here," she says.

I feel sick. "Overdose?" I say. I cover the receiver and turn to Mama and Anyu. "Sam's in trouble," I whisper. They scamper to my side to listen in.

"It looks like an accident, Lily, but things are not so clear yet. You may be able to help. You know Samuel and I haven't been … you know …" her voice breaks. "Can you come down here?"

"Sure," I say, collapsing back down on the couch. Mama and Anyu rattle in Hungarian over the top of my head. I'm in shock. I can't breathe. Sam's in hospital? Oh my God.

"Was it Sam, Lily?" Mama asks after a while. She waves away Anyu's commentary. "Did Sam give this to you?"

I don't answer. I can't answer. I try to collect my thoughts.

An overdose. A bad pill. I have to go.

I grab my bag from the floor and push past my mother and grandmother. They follow me down the corridor as I move towards the front door.

Mama is screaming after me. "Was it Sam?"

I turn around to her. "Leave me alone. Enough about this bloody Sad Hungarian Poem!" I shout. "Sam's in hospital and you're still talking about the fucking poem!"

"Lily stop," Mama screams. "It's not just a poem." Anyu comes to my side and holds my arm. The three of us hover in the tiny hallway by the front door. "It's the suicide song," she says. "It's the famous Hungarian suicide song. *Gloomy Sunday,* the song that makes people kill themselves."

I can't think. A suicide song. What the fuck?

"I think Sam was trying to tell you something," Mama whispers. "A cry for help."

Anyu nods at Mama. "We were upset, Lily, because we thought it was yours," Anyu says.

What's going on? Eva gave me a song that makes you kill yourself?

"It's not Sam's. It *is* mine," I say. I am confused and angry. "And for your information, Sam didn't commit suicide! Sam can't even read Hungarian! What is wrong with you people? It was a bad pill. It was an accident!" Now I am screaming.

"Lily, darling," Mama whispers, placing a hand on my shoulder. "That's what everyone always says."

"Get away from me!" I yell, pushing away her arm. I open the front door and run down the front steps to the street. "You just don't understand! Neither of you understands! Leave me alone!"

I jump in the car and head straight for St Vincent's.

***

I park illegally outside the Emergency Department and run in through the automatic doors. Everything is a blur. I don't even remember driving here. I look around the room. Colours and sounds swirl into a disorienting haze. Women in blue rush around me. Babies scream. An old man moans. A woman with blood on her face pushes past me. I look for Catherine. I don't even remember what she looks like. A teenage boy coughs in my face and two policemen march through me. I try to concentrate. A middle-aged lady is standing at a doorway. She talks on the phone. She twirls a string of pearls in her hand. Our eyes meet and she waves. That's her.

I go to walk towards her and that's when a strong hand touches my shoulder and stops me a few metres from Catherine.

"Lily, what are you doing here?"

I look behind me.

It's Nixon.

"Nixon?"

"Lily, are you okay?"

I shake my head. "What are you doing here?" I say.

"I just dropped off Eva *néni*. She has a late appointment in the other building. I'm walking to my car."

"Eva *néni*?" I ask. "Eva *néni* is in hospital?"

"She's fine," he says, smiling. "It's just her regular appointment at the clinic. They were running late. That's why we're still here. Tell me," he takes hold of my hand. "Are you okay?"

Catherine starts walking towards us. I can't think. I can't talk. I throw my arms around Nixon and burst into tears. I feel so relieved. So confused. So scared. I don't know what's going on.

"No," I sob. "No, no, no, I'm not okay." I look into his eyes. He looks back with concern and … and something else.

"Stay with me, Nixon," I say. "I need you. Can you stay with me?"

Nixon nods and holds me close.

"I'll be your knight in a shiny suit," he whispers.

I don't know whether to laugh or cry.

"Hold me," I say. "Don't leave me."

Catherine is almost by my side. I can see her clearly now. Her hair is dishevelled and her mascara smudged. She is holding a monogrammed handkerchief and there are tears in her eyes. She takes my hand.

"Lily," she cries. "He has woken up. Sam's woken up!" She takes my arm. "They say he's going to be okay," she says.

Chapter Eleven

It's been a busy month. Anyu was caught shoplifting again at Woolworths on the main road. They didn't call the police this time. They took pity on her because of her age, but she was banned for life. So now I have to pick up her groceries every second day and listen to what anti-Semites they are. Peter *bácsi* had the hiccups for three days in a row without a break and was in such agony that he eventually wound up in hospital heavily sedated. Then there has been the usual last-minute crises that come with every gallery opening: the caterers went bust three days ago and the council blocked the footpath outside the gallery for "emergency unscheduled roadworks". But by and large, the plans for Big A's exhibition are on track. Big A's cataract surgery went well and he is coming out of hospital this afternoon just in time for the opening.

As for Sam, they kept him in hospital overnight and then released him the next morning with a pamphlet on the dangers of ecstasy and an invitation to a Narcotics Anonymous meeting at the church down on Darlinghurst Road. Not that any of it has had much of an effect on him.

I've been happy. Nixon stays with me all night and leaves early in the morning for work. I spend the early part of the day painting. It's been a hot January. The warm salty air blows in from the cliffs at the top of my street and I strip down to my underwear and just paint. The sweet smell of the oil paints fills my little room. The streets are quiet. I live on coffee and cigarettes. I am in my own world.

But it only lasts until about lunchtime when it all gets to be too much. Scent turns into stench, warmth to sweltering heat, solitude to loneliness. I have to get out.

That's when I go to meet Eva.

***

The morning of the opening Sam is pacing up and down outside my front door with wide eyes and a big grin. His pupils are completely dilated and he is chewing incessantly on a piece of gum.

"Jesus, Sam," I say. "It's eleven in the fucking morning!"

"Come on, Lily, let's go out," he says. He wiggles his hips and grabs my hands. "Get dressed! I'm in a great mood."

"Sam!" I say. "You almost died!"

"Don't be boring, Lily," he says. "I'm totally fine. Look at me!" He turns around with both arms high in the air. He pulls out another piece of gum. "Want one?" he says.

I shake my head. He does look okay considering what he's been through. I had the scare of my life, but all he seems to have taken away from the hospital was a mild sore throat from when they pumped his stomach and proof that his mother loves him.

"Get dressed!" he sings.

"I am dressed!" I say.

"Then let's go!" he says, looking me up and down with a scowl.

I shake my head again. "I've got a Hungarian lesson," I tell him. "I'm meeting Eva this morning."

"Again?" He stops moving for a moment and drops his shoulders. "Boring …" he sings.

"I love it," I say.

"Lily, when are you going to give the whole thing a rest? You've been there every day this week."

"I'm making good progress, Sam. I'm kind of on a roll. I'm going to learn this stupid language if it kills me," I say.

Sam laughs. "It's all about the boy, isn't it?" I smile. I can't help myself. I haven't stopped smiling for four weeks straight. "What's his name, again? Oh, Mr President," he does his best Marilyn Monroe. "I love you, Mr President."

"It's Nixon," I tell him. "And no, it's not all about the boy. I want to learn Hungarian," I say.

"Well, you know, when your mother and Anyoo find out about your Hungarian lessons, it had better be all about the boy, Lily."

"Don't worry," I say. "No one's going to find out." I turn to grab my bag and close the door behind me. I start walking down to the street. "And anyway," I continue, "I don't know how good a cover story Nixon would make." Both of my little secret affairs are dangerous liaisons.

We walk to my car.

"I've got to go, Sam," I tell him. "Eva doesn't like it when I'm late." I open the car door. "Should I pick you up for tonight?"

"Tonight?" Sam scratches his head.

"The opening, remember? It's Big A's opening night. It will be huge," I tell him. I'm excited.

Sam covers his face with his hands in mock despair. "Oh shit, sorry, Lily. I totally forgot. I've got that thing."

"What thing? Sam, this is my big night! You said you'd be there."

"Sorry, Lily, I can't make it."

"What bloody thing? You never have *things*."

"Um ..." he says. He starts biting his fingernails. "You won't be alone will you?"

No, I won't be alone. When I bumped into Nixon at the hospital a month ago, I asked him to stay with me and he has kept his word. *My knight in a shiny suit*. We have been inseparable ever since. I guess he has sort of informally moved in – last week he went back to his apartment for an hour and came back with five boxes of stuff, his father's violin, and his pillow. Yes, Nixon will be with me tonight. But that's not the point.

I don't answer Sam. He promised he would be there. He never has *things*.

"Lily, wait!" I hear as I start up the engine. "Don't be like that ..."

I can't listen to the rest. I leave Sam standing on the footpath with his fingers in his mouth. I'm not interested in a reply. And anyway, it drives Eva crazy when I'm late.

Everything drives Eva crazy. Her favourite topic of conversation is Things That Drive Me Crazy. From the quiet couple upstairs to the woman next door who won't shut up. From the way Peter *bácsi* overcooks the beef to the way he undercooks the potatoes. She hates the weather girl on TV with uneven boobs and the regular guy at table 43 with the ridiculous toupee who always spills his coffee. There are fake tans, real tattoos, G-strings sticking out of low-cut jeans, doof-doof music blasting from car windows, too much sunshine, too little sunshine, our Hungarian lessons, Nixon and our relationship. Especially Nixon and our relationship. It's as if she takes it personally. She cringes at his cheeky glances from behind the coffee machine, our sneaky kisses between orders, the protracted goodbyes in the afternoons.

Nixon and I drive her crazy. I think that's why Eva suggested we go for walks in the park instead of sitting in the café. It's as if she simply can't stand the sight of the two of us together.

I don't mind our walks. The green, open fields of Double Bay Park are our new classroom. We tell each other stories, both true and imagined. We learn old Hungarian nursery rhymes and practise thorny tongue twisters. We conjugate verbs and make up funny dialogues. Many of the phrases she teaches me trigger a part of my brain that has heard it all before. I am beginning to speak Hungarian.

I am learning more than I ever imagined. It's on these walks, promenading arm in arm with Eva, that I learn the most about the language, the most about my family, the most about me.

***

Eva can't walk and talk at the same time. Mid-sentence, she suddenly stops as if the multi-tasking is simply too much. Today I'm especially impatient. She stops in the middle of Bay Street to finish her sentence. I continue crossing the road towards the park.

"I'm talking, Lily, where are you going?" she says.

"For a walk, Eva, with you. Isn't that what we're doing? Walking?"

"Don't be an idiot."

Bay Street just isn't safe. Anyone can walk down Bay Street on their way home from the bridge club or from a day of shopping. The park is sheltered by enormous fig trees, and by the fact that Anyu hates greenery. Here children from the public school across the road play soccer, and middle-aged mums with their personal trainers do push-ups on the muddy grass. Occasionally a group of yoga gurus practises by the water's edge. The likelihood of running into an elderly Hungarian in the park who might tell Anyu about Eva and me is low.

So I can't stop until I'm inside the park. I simply can't take the risk of being spotted.

Eva catches up to me.

"You look terrible in black, Lily," she says. I notice that she has no trouble walking and insulting at the same time. "You'll never find a man wearing black, Lily," she continues. "Why on earth do you want to look like an Italian widow at your age?"

"I've already got a man, Eva *néni*," I say.

Humph.

I could be talking to Anyu.

Except that with Eva, I actually hear things for the first time.

We walk. We are halfway around a circuit of the playing field when we are ready to start the lesson. Sometimes we can go twice around the entire park before we are both over the initial feeling of resentment towards one another that we seem to stir up every time we meet up.

"I have another little word, Eva *néni*," I say, feeling better about things. I'm excited. It's on these walks that Eva teaches me all those little words that aren't in the dictionary, words that aren't in poems or texts, words

Hungarians just *know*. My favourite is the little *na!* that seems to appear so often at the beginning of a Hungarian's sentence, even when speaking English. *Na!* as in *here it is, you idiot* or *I told you so!* The same *na!* can mean *what the hell?* (when there's suddenly a blackout) or *what are you doing here?* (when you bump into someone in the street) or even a simple *really?* (when you hear something for the first time).

Today I ask her what *jaj* means. It's pronounced *yoy* and is almost as pervasive as *na*.

"*Jaj* doesn't mean anything," she says, prepared to end the conversation right then and there.

But I don't despair. This is how every Hungarian lesson starts.

"But I have a hundred examples!" I say. "*Jaj* as in *oh! how beautiful*, or *oh my God I can't believe you said that. Jaj* sounds like *oh no, I've run out of cigarettes* or *you've got to be out of your mind* or *I can't believe my best friend is fucking my husband.* I'm sure they're only very subtle differences. I want some Hungarian *jaj*'s. Like the *jaj* of *that's amazing news, I'm so proud of you* or *come on, if you do that I'll kill myself.* Give me some examples."

Eva laughs. She reaches out and takes my hand. She slips her arm through mine and we walk in step. "Well," she says, "let's see. There's *jaj Istenem!* (oh my God), *jaj de édes!* (oh how sweet), *jaj de jó!* (oh how wonderful)." She uses her whole body to translate. "And you can't forget *jaj de csúnya!* (oh how ugly)."

I smile. I have heard these expressions millions of times. I have probably used them millions of times. I've had no idea what they mean.

Well, that's not entirely true. I thought I knew, but I was wrong.

"I thought they were rude, you know, like swear words." I tell her.

"Which idiot told you that?" she replied.

"No one."

"Then how the hell do you come up with swear words?"

"I don't know," I say. I shrug and think about it for a minute. "No one tells me anything," I say, "so I just make it up."

"A genius!" Eva says.

We walk a few steps before she continues.

"Don't be such an idiot," she adds.

This time it's me who stops.

"You don't have to be so harsh," I say, turning towards her.

She continues walking, pulling me along with a strong arm. "Who's harsh? It's not my fault you're an idiot," she explains.

"Well, that's probably why I don't ask! If no one tells me anything, and if every time I ask a question I get called an idiot, then it's easier to just make it up. You don't have to be so mean."

Eva laughs. "Why is everyone so bloody sensitive these days?" She stops under the shade of a big fig tree and starts coughing. We sit down on the wooden bench by the water's edge while she catches her breath. A pigeon lands on the seat between us and she shoos it away with pointy nails. "I can't say anything anymore! You act like an idiot and then I'm the bad guy? What's wrong with you people?"

She coughs again.

I don't know who "you people" are but I don't want to be lumped in with *them*. I don't deserve to be called an idiot. I just want to learn Hungarian. I just want to be taught all the things no one tells me, all the things I am afraid to ask, all the things I was forced to make up.

We sit in silence for a minute. It feels like an hour. Eva takes out a handkerchief to wipe her brow. Her hand trembles. Her lips quiver. She looks old. I remember I'm not here to be angry. I'm not here to be dutiful. She is not Anyu. She is not my family. Or is she?

I decide on the spot that it's time.

"So how exactly are we related?" I ask, quickly, before I have time to change my mind. I am stuttering. But it's okay. She's not Anyu.

"Related …" She looks straight at me. I'm ready for the answer, whatever it is. "What on earth makes you think we are related?" she says. "What sort of an idiot are you?"

I take a deep breath. *I can do this.*

"There you go making things up again," she says.

I look at her face. She isn't angry. She isn't upset. She is neither shocked nor disappointed. This is just her. But I'm not giving up. This is what I'm here for. I don't want to make it up anymore.

"Tell me," I whisper. "Tell me how you know Anyu."

I can't look at her.

"Well really," she says. "It's not such a secret." She smiles. "*Anymore.*" She turns to me and grabs my arm just above the elbow. I feel her nails digging into my skin.

"I remember the day as if it were yesterday," she says. "It was the worst day of my life. I saw lots of trouble in my time, you know, but you probably wouldn't understand. Things are so different now, so much easier. You people don't know what trouble is."

Here we go again. Here it comes: the one about how my generation is so spoilt and so ungrateful. We don't even know the meaning of suffering, let alone the appropriate amount of recognition and requital that that allowance comes with. But I have heard that one a thousand times. I know what's coming, the whole story, even how it ends. I know what I am supposed to feel and how I will never understand. But I'm not asking about *that* story. I want the other one: the one about how two young, beautiful women met in a changing world, in a Budapest on the brink of transformation, in a life on the verge of revolution; how two young Hungarian Jews built a friendship so strong and intimate that they felt safe crossing the world together like a family; and how, in a land on the other side of the world, on the other side of *their* world, it could all come crashing down; how one of these women could be so bitter that she'd meticulously go through her entire photo album and tear the other woman out of her life. I want to know how after a long life of change and uncertainty, littered with war and revolution and immigration, the day Eva met Anyu could be the worst day of her life. That's the one I want to hear.

"Well imagine, daahrlink. You can't even imagine what it was like at the time. It was so very difficult to be a woman in those days. Now there are so many things one can do, you know."

She gets up and starts walking again, her eyes looking straight ahead, without a word. When we reach the open fields, she grabs my hand and entwines her fingers in mine in a way she has never done before. Ahead, there's a group of schoolgirls in the middle of a sweaty hockey game, squealing and squawking at each other, their pony tails bobbing up and down as they run. I wonder if they realise how lucky they are to be women today.

Eva waits until we pass the furthest goal post near Ocean Avenue before she continues. My palms start to sweat in hers and I desperately want to let go.

"Well it isn't a very nice story, daahrlink." She stops in the middle of the park. "But you will probably find it funny, you know. I guess it *is* funny, now."

She's about to tell me everything and all I can think of is my sweaty fingers. Can I let go and pretend to scratch my nose? Fix my hair? Will she be offended? I wiggle my fingers and feel her chunky diamond ring knocking against my knuckles, but I don't let go.

"You see, well, it happened like this: I was lying there on the bed in her father's house. You know, your great-grandfather, daahrlink. I was lying there half bleeding to death and this young woman suddenly barges into the room. She takes one look at me and do you know the only thing she comes up with? She tells me a dirty joke! The most offensive one I had ever heard.

I tell you, I laughed my head off." Eva smiles. "Imagine, Lily, that was your Anyu. A dirty joke, she told, a bloody joke."

I don't think I've ever heard Eva call her Anyu before.

She starts walking again, letting go of my hand to pull out another cigarette from her silver case. She tosses her current, unlit one on the ground, and steps on it dramatically with the toe of her shoe, digging into the dirt as if she were putting it out.

"But she made me forget, she did. Forget the pain, forget the fear, forget the baby. Well, I remember I liked her straight away."

I want to say something, but nothing comes out.

"Don't look so shocked, Lily. It happened to us too, you know. But things were different then. You think that things are complicated for your generation, and I really don't envy you, you know, with all those horrible diseases from Africa and the queers ... well it was really another thirty years before we had the pill and it was too late for me then. That's what we were worried about in my day, Lily. Pregnancy was a real problem. A killer."

"An abortion?" I manage only a whisper.

"Oh come on, Lily. That's nothing. I had four of them! All at Agi's father's house. And you know, I kept going back and back and back until my insides were so cut up that it stopped being a problem anymore." Eva put her hand on her stomach. "But that first time, I remember that first time. Well I was so very young, you know, so very frightened. But you don't want to know the details."

The details? That's all I want! That's what I'm here for. That's what it is all about. I smile. Finally she understands.

"How old were you?" I ask. I try to picture Eva scared. I can't imagine what that would look like. I can't imagine how that could happen. I didn't know she could tell the difference between an opinion and an emotion.

"Old? Well, daahrlink, I was sixteen years young. How do you call it? Sweet sixteen!" She sings the word *sweet*. *Sve-ee-eet*. She continues, "I couldn't have the child, you understand. Well, I was still one myself, after all. A girlfriend's neighbour heard of someone who could take care of it hush hush. You know, no hospitals, no parents, no police. Just cash, daahrlink. All you needed was a bottle of brandy, clean towels, and lots and lots of cash. Half a year's salary, imagine! 'Tell no one,' the woman told me, 'no one can know. Otherwise we will all be in trouble.' But Ivan knew, of course, well how could I hide it from him? But he couldn't come with me. This was women's business. He was kind to me, then, you know. Ivan understood. He wanted it taken care of as much as me, you see. He didn't want a child. *I never want children*, he always said. Ha! What a joke that is! What a joke!"

We continue along the edge of the park, near the playground, and on towards the water. The tide is low and smelly and Eva crinkles up her nose against the sulfurous air. I have never heard her talk about Ivan so nicely before. Ivan the husband, Ivan the business partner, Ivan the father of all her unborn children. I know he died around the same time I was born. I often wondered about their relationship since, though she spoke of him rarely, it was usually full of mockery and scorn. *Ivan the Terrible*, I thought, and I imagined a big, ugly giant with pointy teeth and bloodshot eyes.

I'm not sure whether Eva's sour expression is from the ocean or the memories. I pick up a fallen frangipani flower from the wet grass and play with it in my fingers until it withers away to nothing. My hands are still stained from the morning's painting session. I hold my hand up to my nose to mask the stench of the sea. The sweet smells of frangipani and oil paint comfort me.

"You see," she says, "well you know, doctors who did abortions earned a lot of money in those days. It was a big deal. If you were caught, you'd go to jail for a long time. Lots of money, they earned," she continues. "Ha!" She looks away and shakes her head. She turns suddenly and leads me back toward the playing field. Something in her mood has shifted. "Well I guess your family always had a thing for money, didn't they?"

Suddenly the old Eva is back, her fleeting vulnerability just a temporary bug in the system. I'm almost relieved. I don't know the scared Eva, the affectionate, nostalgic Eva. I only know the sharp one. That's my Eva.

And of course she thinks we've always had a thing for money. It's easy for her to say ... she's rich! I have never been to Eva's place, but I know from Nixon she lives in a penthouse in Darling Point with a three-hundred-and-sixty-degree view of the harbour and a swimming pool on the roof. Yes, it's easy for her to talk about money! It's funny how it's always the ones with money who feel like they need to judge us. Our family always did have a thing for money, it's true, but that's because we didn't have any! Anyu left everything behind when we came here and she never managed to get it back. Eva could talk, but she wouldn't know what it was like watching friends get driven to school in BMWs, go skiing in Aspen, have televisions and phones and stereos in their own bedrooms, their wardrobes filled to the brim with designer jeans. She wouldn't know what it was like to live in a rented apartment with no air-conditioning, to wear hand-me-downs from the nosy but well-meaning neighbours and acquaintances. Of course my family always had a thing for money. Easy for her to say.

I light myself a cigarette and calm down. I don't know how much of what I've been thinking has come out aloud.

Eva continues without skipping a beat. "Mind you, Lily daahrlink, he was a good-looking man, your *dédnagypapa*, and very gentle he was. A real *mensch*. And his wife. *Jaj!* Mad as a three-dollar bill, I tell you. Mrs Wyner was what you kids call a real weirdo!" She says *veerdo*. I laugh out loud.

I know all about Anyu's crazy mother. Anyu won't talk about it, of course, but Mama always litters her insults of Anyu with snippets of anecdotes about this mythical, deranged character. *You think your Anyu's crazy, ha! You ain't seen nothing yet, my dear.* I used to love hearing about it all, how she would never touch her food, even eating bread with a knife and fork, how she'd insist the maid wear gloves while making her bed and, my favourite, how she organised all her books in alphabetical order, not according to the author, nor the title, but rather by the first letter of the first word of the text. But Anyu was ashamed, said Mama, not because of her mother's lunatic behaviour, but because of where she came from.

Mrs Wyner, as it turns out, was the product of an incestuous affair between two first cousins who had been brought up as siblings. Like everything in my family, it sounds convoluted at first, but ends up being another simple story of generations of secrets and lies. My great-grandmother's mother was only three months old when she was orphaned. Her aunt, who already had a young boy, took in the little baby and raised her as her own. There was always a special bond between the two young kids, and when they found out the truth from their mother's will, that they were actually cousins and not brother and sister, they consummated their love and ran away to Budapest to start a new life as husband and wife.

It's funny how some family stories are recounted so regularly and in such explicit, vivid detail while others are omitted with almost the same rigour. Why did I know so much about my great-great-grandparents' uncomfortable tale of incest and their obsessive compulsive child but I had never heard once about how my Anyu was fond of telling inappropriately dirty jokes to strange young abortion patients half bleeding to death in her father's spare room?

Suddenly I'm being led back to the café by Eva. But I don't mind. I'm exhausted, too. Eva is quietly chuckling to herself, mumbling this, that and the other, gesturing both with her hands and her immaculately pencilled-in eyebrows. "Dirty jokes, she told me! Well, you know, ha! Would you believe it? What would you know ... well, imagine, daahrlink!"

Eva stops in front of the café. She takes out her lipstick and uses her reflection in the window to reapply her red colour.

"It's YOU, Lily daahrlink. I'm laughing at you!" she clarifies, taking a small break between the upper and lower lips. "You used to be so funny."

I smile. "Me? Funny?"

"Oh yes, daahrlink, you had us all hysterical. I remember it well – that skinny little girl sitting like Lady Muck on three cushions at the head the of the table. You were very clever, daahrlink, waiting till everyone was quiet and then you'd start: *Listen to this! One sperm said to the other, where's the egg? And the other answered, it's a long way off … we only just got to the stomach!* You were very cute, you know."

"What do you mean? I told dirty jokes …" I try to do the maths, "… as a *three*-year-old?"

"Did you tell dirty jokes! And then everyone would stop what they were doing and clap! And your Anyu, well, of course she would beam. She was so proud of you. And then she'd say something like, *Oh Lily daahrlink, where on earth did you hear such a thing?* Well, where do you think you heard such things? Come on …"

I smile, imagining myself as that skinny little girl with a big, filthy mouth. I have never heard anything like it!

"You'd stand on your chair in the middle of dinner and say *FUCK* and then wait quietly until there was an applause. No one could imagine such garbage coming out of such innocence. I remember." She smacks her lips together with a loud smooch and glowers at the bemused customers sitting directly in front of her on the other side of the window.

"Boy do I remember," she continues. She turns to enter the café and I start to follow her. I see Nixon scurrying through the swinging kitchen door at the back of the room. Suddenly, Eva stops and bars my way to the doorway with an outstretched arm. "Enough, Lily daahrlink," she tells me, "enough bloody Hungarian lesson for one day."

And with another smack of her lips she disappears through the café doors leaving me standing outside the Oktogon Café in the middle of Double Bay in broad daylight.

***

Mary, Dr Horvath's secretary, is not exactly being rude, but even from the other end of the line I can sense her already thinly constructed composure deteriorating by the second. I can almost hear her eyes rolling.

"Lily darling, what do you want me to tell you?"

"Tell me, Mary. What else did the results say?" I'm sitting in heavy Bondi Junction afternoon traffic behind a cavalcade of school mums in their oversized SUVs vying for access to the parking lot of the Westfield Shopping Centre.

"Listen, you know I can't read this stuff. George said to tell you that everything is fine. Everything's just like last time. There's no need to worry."

"But the antinuclear antibody count? You said they looked elevated." I toot the horn for no good reason other than to make some noise. It doesn't get me any further along Edgecliff Road, but it does make me feel better, even if only for a few moments.

"Lily, what do I know? He said it was what is to be expected. It's marginal, that's what he said, marginally high is all." She takes a deep breath. "Everything is just fine," she repeats.

"That's what he always says," I tell her. "That's what he always tells you to tell me. Can't I have a quick word with him?"

"He's in with a patient. I think it's important."

"This is important!" I say. Important! Ha! More important than the daughter of a dead friend who came out fifty-two years ago on the same boat as you to Australia? More important than *me?*

"Listen, what do you want me to do? I can fit you in at four-fifteen if you promise to be on time. Is that what you'd like?"

That's in half an hour. I could probably make it. I think about it for a minute and then shake my head. It will have to wait. I'm already late for the gallery. "I can't do it, Mary. I have a big day at work. Thanks anyway."

I think I hear her say something, but it's too late. I hang up the phone and throw it on the passenger seat beside me. It bounces awkwardly off my handbag and lands in the narrow gap between the seat and the far door.

"Shit!" I lean as far as I can to the left, but it's out of reach. Then, without thinking too much about the oncoming traffic and the woman walking her dog across the road between cars at a standstill, I grab the wheel with both hands and make an abrupt u-turn over a blind median strip. As I'm straightening out, I hear tyres squeal and horns toot, but I'm moving now and that's all that matters. It's in the wrong direction, but at least I'm moving.

***

I'm late. Big A's opening starts in just over two hours. Camilla will soon be busy with pre-sale buyers and she'll need me there to conduct the new caterers and the cleaners, line up the sell sheets, set up the playlist on the iPod, direct the photographer, and brief the PR woman. She'll need me to babysit Sunny and make sure his agent handles the customers instead of the cocktail waitresses. Camilla needs me and I'm not there.

It's quite a good run down Crown Street. Suddenly my phone rings. I can't reach it. I can't stop now; I'm almost there. It rings out. I take a deep breath. What if it's Georgie calling me back? What if it's Georgie realising how important *this* patient is? I thump my fist on my chest. *This* patient is important too.

It rings again. I have to get it! I stop the car in a bus stop outside the Surry Hills Shopping Centre on Baptist Street. I reach it just in time.

"Lily! For heaven's sake!"

Oh no, it's Camilla.

"Lily," she says. "Why can't you answer your phone for *heaven's sake?* It's an emergency. I need you here now." A bus pulls in behind me and beeps. *Beep beep.* I check my rear vision mirror. The driver is mouthing something like *move your fucking car,* giving me the finger. He inches the bus closer and closer to the back of my car until I can no longer reverse to get out of the way.

"Just a sec, Camilla," I say. "I'm almost there."

The bus driver keeps beeping and swearing in my rear vision mirror. It's a Mexican stand-off. I can't move until he gives me room to reverse. He can't move until I get out of the way. I try to ignore him and concentrate on Camilla's hysterical pleas to get my arse into the gallery this very instant. I think I'm going to go mad.

"Lily, I need you now," I hear Camilla say. "Sunny's gone blind."

Chapter Twelve

"Are the glasses to be placed in rows of five or ten?"

"Where are the mains? We need to turn the juice off for a few minutes."

"Up here, Lily! How's the angle of this light from here?"

"Close the bloody door!"

"Can we meet the artist now?"

I catch my breath. Camilla is nowhere to be seen. The room is swarming with bodies darting this way and that. Waitresses in fancy black vests and bow ties arrange tables in all the wrong places. An electrician up on a ladder blocks the middle of the room. Two journalists and our PR girl race around in circles. A cleaner vacuums the entrance hall. A strong hand pushes my ankle out of the way. I look down. The handyman fixes a loose floorboard under my feet without looking up.

Camilla storms towards me from out of nowhere.

"Lily, it's all wrong, honey!" She shoves a clipboard in my hand. "Fix it," she says, stepping over the handyman, and walks past me towards the desk at the back of the room.

I look down at the clipboard. There's a list a million miles long of things to do and undo. I sigh. It's going to be a long night.

I turn towards the back of the room, careful not to trip over the vacuum cleaner, and call after Camilla.

"Where is he?" I say, throwing the clipboard on the desk.

Camilla doesn't turn around. The caterer asks me if I know where a second power point is in the front room. I frown, say no, and push past her towards Camilla.

"Where is he?" I say again.

Camilla doesn't turn around. "Don't tell him," she calls back over her shoulder. "He doesn't know."

"He doesn't know what?" I call back, looking around for clues as to where she may have hidden him in this great big white room.

She lets off a huge sigh.

"He doesn't know how bad it is," she whispers in my ear.

The caterer runs over to me and Camilla stops talking.

"I've found the power point, thanks!"

I try to smile.

Camilla continues. She grabs my elbow.

"Don't tell him yet. Not tonight. It will break his heart. He thinks this type of thing is normal. Jim's called it temporary blindness or something like that. Like a side effect of the surgery. We've decided to wait till after the show. I've got a girl to look after him. He's fine. Let her look after him."

She points to the storage room door on the left behind the desk.

A voice comes at me from behind. "Can we start warming up the rolls?" I turn to see a waitress at my shoulder looking straight into my eyes. I can't focus on her face. I can't concentrate. I take a minute too long to answer her. I can't think.

"Wait twenty more minutes," I tell her eventually, hoping it's a random number that will actually work out all right. She nods at me diligently and walks away.

I elbow my way to the back and open the door to the storage unit. Suddenly, it's quiet. Sunny is sitting on a wooden chair in the middle of the room with huge dark glasses and a patch covering one eye. The glasses are obviously not his. They look like Camilla's. To the right, chairs are stacked up over my head, and to the left, the caterers' supplies are lined up on trestle tables.

An enormous woman in a tight white nurse's uniform complete with a paper hat straight from a hundred years ago scowls at me from a table a few metres behind Sunny. The buttons on her blouse barely do up over her tremendous bosom. Her tree-stump legs glow irridescent white in the poorly lit room. This is what Camilla calls a *girl?* She is pouring a pink liquid from one measuring canister to another as if that's what nurses are supposed to do. I wonder if it's just for effect or if she's really going to feed it to him. Maybe she's a stripper?

"Hi," I say, to both of them. "I'm Lily, Camilla's assistant."

The nurse scowls again, looks me up and down, and then nods her head. Sunny smiles. He straightens himself up on his chair and reaches out his hand. I close the door behind me, pull up a chair next to him, and sit down.

"Hi," I say again, taking his hand.

It's still and quiet in here. I can hear Sunny breathing. He stares straight ahead at the closed storeroom door. He twitches his nose. The white hairs of his moustache and beard around his mouth sway to and fro. They are stained yellow. I smile again, knowing he can't see me. But I don't know what else to do.

By the door stands a tower of trays, each lined with pre-cut pieces of cake: chocolate fudge, butter cake, some sort of hazelnut thing. I should know what they all are; I ordered them. I reach over and grab a piece of chocolate cake and a serviette, then I place it in Sunny's warm weathered hand.

He smiles, nods, and with a shaky hand, brings it up to his lips. But it is intercepted within seconds by Nurse Ratched's chunky fingers.

"No good," she says with a heavy Russian accent. She shakes her head vigorously. "No good for diabetes." She whisks the cake away and gobbles it down in two bites.

Sunny's shoulders droop, but he doesn't complain. He doesn't appeal. He keeps staring at the door. I smile again, knowing it won't help, and squeeze his hand. He doesn't move.

On the other side of the door, we hear Camilla talking on the phone. We sit in silence and listen.

"Yes yes," she says. "I know … I mean you know, orange, well it's the new black. It's so in right now. It's so 2010. I mean you just can't go wrong with orange. Did you see the Dunstone Retrospective last week at the MOMA? … Well, so I have one word for you: orange! … Well I'm pleased to hear that. I'll be sure to let him know … Yes very talented … Yes I know, you were very lucky! … You know what they say about the early bird … Oh, of course, yes there'll be more. There's more to come, you can be sure of that! … Okay … thank you … bye. Where the hell is Lily?"

I stand up and tell Sunny I have to go. Slowly he lets go of my hand. "I'll be back," I whisper, and open the door to the light and noise and chaos that is an hour and a half before opening.

Sunny's agent, Jim, and Camilla almost run into me at the same time. They scowl at each other.

"Lily, I have to go next door to meet the Knightly brothers. You know, the *Knightly* Knightlys. We are still negotiating *Sandflies IV.*" She pulls me close and whispers. "I know they want it."

Jim nods hello to me and follows Camilla to the door.

"Don't even think about it, Jim. I'll let you know how it goes."

He stops in his tracks and rolls his eyes.

"You'd better come back smiling," he calls after her, then mutters under his breath, "*bitch.*"

I pick up the clipboard, scroll through the job list, then slump down on the stool behind the desk. Everything will be okay tonight, I tell myself. The rolls will be hot; the champagne will be cold; the lights will be working; the place will be buzzing; the crowd will be ooh-ing and ah-ing in all the right places. Tomorrow the reviews will be published in our favour, most of the paintings will be sold for good prices, and the stress of this minute will have been forgotten. Everything will be okay.

But everything won't be okay. Sunny will still be blind.

I feel a hand on my shoulder.

"It's okay, Lily," says Jim, as if he can read my thoughts. I turn to look at him next to me. I've not seen him so close up before. He has a mean nose that seems to slant to the right and one eyebrow hair that is three times longer than all the others. His freckles are so numerous they have almost merged into one giant, killer blotch. "Sunny's gonna be okay," he tells me.

I nod, blinking back the tears.

He pulls up another seat next to me.

"It was just a little bleed, you know, nothing that we didn't expect. Very common in those types, you know, with diabetes and all that. You have to understand, Lily, his diabetes hasn't always been managed so well."

I nod again. Maybe he's right.

"There's always a risk with every operation. Isn't that what they always say? He's gonna be fine. I mean, it's only really his left eye that's totally blind. The other one hasn't been touched yet. It's chockas with cataracts and clouding over fast, though … I haven't decided yet whether it's worth doing that one or not."

I think about it. It does sound like a big risk.

"What does Sunny think?" I ask him.

"Oh no need to bother the old bloke about things like that. He'll be right. I'll take care of it. He can still sort of see, you know. And you know what they say? This you won't believe. I was reading the other day on Google, you know what? You don't even see with your eyes. Betcha didn't know that one, eh? Your eyes are just passive. It's your brain that sees." He points to his head, raises his eyebrows, and nods emphatically. "Yep! You see with your brain, not your eyes. So if you go blind as an old bloke, this is what they say, then you can still sort of 'see' from memory. He'll be fine."

I can't believe what I'm hearing.

"Hey? Didn't old Monet have cataracts too? Didn't stop him from making masterpieces, eh?"

I look straight at him.

"Don't count Sunny out just yet, mate. He's got a couple more years in him, that one."

I shake my head. "Well, maybe you should just tell him what happened," I say.

"Nah," says Jim. "Wouldn't wanna upset the old bloke now, would I?"

Just then, Camilla pushes through the glass doors. She is clearly triumphant. She strides toward us through the chaos like nothing can touch her.

"I got the blind price," she whispers, her head nestled between Jim's and mine. But before she can run off, Jim grabs her arm and pulls her back.

"What the fuck are you doing?" he says.

"Don't *what the fuck are you doing* me," she says, shaking herself free. "Just say *thank you, Camilla,* and get your grubby little hands off me."

"We agreed we wouldn't tell anyone," Jim says.

"Remember what James McMahon paid for *Croc Dreaming IV?* Well, just add a zero – you arsehole. No one else will find out. Don't worry. Just say *thank you* and get the hell out of my way."

Jims mouth falls open and he sits back down on the stool. Camilla stands in front us and steps slightly to the left. She looks straight past us into the mirror and adjusts her dress. She pouts, smiles, then turns on her heels and links arms with the PR girl a few steps away. A minute later as the publicist is talking full steam ahead, she turns to us and winks. Jim scowls.

I pick up the clipboard and start to lose myself in the to-do list.

***

The room has already started to fill up. The who's who and the who'd love to be who of the gallery world is here. Only five kilometres away, it's a completely different world to the Oktogon of Double Bay. Women wear chunky beads and heavy coloured-stone jewellery rather than strings of pearls and diamond rings. Eyeglasses are cat-like, with thick, colourful plastic rims instead of the brown, semi-tinted shades of the café people. Women laugh loudly and wear flat shoes. Men's shirts are tucked out, their hair messy, the stubble long. I call these people *The Accessories.* They are never crucial to the business side of things, but their involvement can make or break an opening night. The arty-farty set add much-needed colour and gossip to the evening. But the Important People, the buyers, they don't stay for very long. They come, look, either buy or not, and then leave. It's not that the arty-farty party champagne sippers aren't actually interested in the art. They are up with the lingo. They tilt their head in all the right places. They admire the talent and they know what's good. But they can't even afford a miserly print. The Important People are moneyed-up. They get there early, slink past the crowd careful not to touch anyone, never take a drink, and smile and nod to everyone. But they only ever talk to Camilla. They wear ironed shirts and pointy heels. That's how you know the Important People.

But the Most Important People are not even here. They are usually given a secret, private preview by Camilla a few days before the event. On opening night, the place is absolutely spotless, but for these special previews, the messier the gallery is, the better. Canvases are taken down (if they are already up) and the more expensive ones are covered by a sheet and placed momentarily in the back room. The effort is worth it. The earlier they think they're getting their sneak peek, the more of a bargain they think they're getting, and the more they spend. They earn the right by spending big, and it always looks very impressive when there are little red dots garnishing the walls on opening night. It makes the leftover paintings all the more enticing for the merely Important People.

Things are under control. The pile of price lists has been refilled, and the drinks are going, but not too quickly. Camilla is on a high from her five-figure sale before we opened. I can breathe out for the first time in hours. And then in walk Mama and Anyu.

The volatile peace they forge for my benefit at special occasions like this one is more unnerving than the usual animosity between them. It's worse for my mother; she is allergic to Anyu's very existence. Even from the other side of the room, I can see Mama's jaw tense up, her teeth grinding, clenching, seizing. It takes all her strength and a locked jaw not to break down and tear Anyu to pieces. She's going to have a migraine tonight. Anyu fares better than her because she doesn't care to hold back. It's not her fault Mama is an *idiot*.

At least they are not yet arm in arm. That usually signals the end of civilities altogether. I've seen it a few times, Mama grabbing hold of Anyu's arm when she feels her self control eluding her. It's almost like she is hoping Anyu will hold her down.

It's time to get busy. I rush over to them, give them quick pecks on the cheek, and explain how busy I am.

"Enjoy the paintings," I tell them. "This man is a genius. He is going to be huge." That will give Mama something to concentrate on, something to brag about at work tomorrow: the "very cultural event I went to last night" spiel. I hand them both a glass of champagne and scurry away.

"Oooh how lovely, daahrlink!" I hear Anyu say as she takes a sip. Great. She'll be falling asleep in twenty minutes.

I need to check on Sunny. He must be starving by now. I need to distract Nurse Ratched. I reach the storeroom door, but it's locked. How can it be locked? I don't have a key. I look around for Camilla. She's standing in front of *Crocodile Dreaming IV* with an elderly gentleman in a cravat. Must be rich.

As I approach her, Camilla grabs my arm and pulls me in. "Oh Lily, thank God I've found you! I was just telling Mr Jamison here about Sunny's masterpiece. I do have to run, unfortunately. Lily can answer any questions you have, can't you, love?" Her eyes plead with me to stay and she turns to leave, only letting go of my arm when she is halfway across the room. I turn to Mr Jamison and smile.

"I was just telling young Camilla, dear, that there is an insurmountable distance between the viewer and the person behind the canvas, wouldn't you say? The cultural and linguistic boundaries between the two are already so vast. It's really so crucial we try to bridge that gap, eh?"

I stare at his cravat. Zsuzsi's third husband used to wear one just like it, with burgundy and paisley green designs. The milky white skin on his neck hangs loosely over the top of the silk cloth like folds of vanilla egg whites beaten until smooth and creamy. It wobbles in waves as he talks.

"The immensity of the importance of such a work is surely not to be underestimated," he continues. *Wobble wobble.* "I do so admire this attempt we are undertaking to bridge the gap."

I nod. Exactly right.

Mama and Anyu have moved slowly within earshot. I cringe even before I can hear a word. Anyu looks like she's monologuing to a middle-aged woman with bright red glasses and grey cropped hair. I nod again towards Mr Jamison and tilt my head slightly to the left to catch the end of Anyu's soliloquy.

"… you know, daahrlink, I mean she is really studying to be a *doctor* you see. This is only a part-time sort of thing you understand. I, on the other hand, wasn't allowed to study medicine you see because …"

Mama nods by her side and grabs Anyu's arm. I want to reach out to stop her ruining my reputation. I want to tackle her to the ground. Instead I nod as Mr Jamison says *bridge the gap* for the fourth time in as many minutes. *Wobble wobble.*

And then suddenly my heart skips a beat. He is here. He made it. He walks through the door and stops at the entrance, taking it all in. He looks around as if he has just landed on Mars.

"Excuse me," I say to Mr Jamison. "I won't be a moment. I have a quick message for a colleague."

I can't stop smiling as I walk toward Nixon, but I am filled with dread. This could be a disaster. In my haste this morning I forgot to remind him of the road rules: no public displays of affection, no touching the paintings, no asking questions. In fact, no talking to anyone, period. No one can know he is my boyfriend. No one can know he has never been to a gallery before. No one can know he's Hungarian. I have no time to babysit. I have no time to censor his comments. I have no time to keep him away from Mama and Anyu.

But he is here. I am happy he is here. For the first time in hours I can breathe.

"I am happy you are here," I tell him. I want to kiss him. His cheeks are flushed and his eyes bright. A friendly smile creeps onto his lips.

"Wow!" He exclaims. *Vow!* "There are lots of people here," he says.

I open my mouth to talk but he cuts me off. "I know, I know," he says. "Don't talk to anyone. What's this one?" He asks, pointing to my favourite, *Crocodile Dreaming X*. I am still amazed Camilla took my advice and had it hung right at the entrance.

"This is my favourite," I say, turning away. But he is still looking at the painting. I study his face. He is interested. This is wonderful. I grab his hand and step back from the canvas. "Come, look at the space. It's so vast. So empty. So simple. But there is something unnerving about the space. It tugs at you, somehow. Don't you think?" I turn towards him. He is still looking at the huge, orange canvas. He shakes his head.

"Maybe," he says. And then laughs. "You are more beautiful," he says. And I smile.

"Remember," I tell him. "Stay around here. And don't talk to anyone."

I go look for Anyu and Mama. They must never be allowed to get anywhere near Nixon, not even for a single second.

Lucy, my friend from the next door gallery, surprises me with a tap on the shoulder.

"This is great, Lily!" She pulls me over to the other wall. "Margot has the shits!" she says, delighted.

We laugh and I step away to keep looking for Anyu and Mama. I can't hear or see them so I'm worried. Finally I spot Anyu sitting on a chair with a piece of cake in her hand. A little part of me relaxes. But the rest is on high alert. Both Mama and Nixon are still on the loose. I need a glass of wine.

I find my mother listening in to a conversation between two gay men talking about Paris. She is hovering conspicuously like a small child. She takes small sips of wine and her eyebrows lift incredulously every few seconds as she floats around the group. They've already noticed her, I imagine, and I know it's now time for her to take Anyu home.

"Anyu's exhausted," I tell her.

She tells me to *shhh*.

Nixon catches my eye from across the room and waves. I shake my head at him. *NO!* I mouth.

"What?" says Mama.

"Nothing," I say.

Nixon starts walking towards me. He must have mistaken my message for an invitation. I panic. He is coming closer. He is smiling innocently. I don't know what to do. There are only a few metres and four middle-aged homosexuals between now and the end of my life. Mama cannot meet Nixon. I have to think.

"Oh sorry," I say, falling forward on one of the men's feet. I stumble and almost drop my glass, but it works. His wine spills on the floor and Mama races off to get me a serviette. I look around to see if anyone noticed me saying sorry before I actually fell. Nixon approaches and I send him away.

"Go away," I whisper and he does. I spend the next few minutes apologising and thanking Mama for being such a great help.

I breathe again.

I glance back to look for Nixon and almost drop my glass for real. He is talking to Camilla. I dash over there as fast as I can. He is still talking.

"*Vell*," he is saying, "you know the painting is so vast. Yet so simple. There is something unnerving …" Camilla is nodding. Her head tilts slightly to the right as she looks him up and down. She frowns a little, then turns to me and nods.

"Nice, Lily," she says. She winks at Nixon and then turns away. Nixon shrugs his shoulders at me.

"Nobody else!" I tell him.

Through the glass doors behind him, I catch a glimpse of Sunny being led to a taxi by Nurse Ratched. Jim is giving directions to the driver, smoking a cigarette.

"I'll be back in a minute," I tell Nixon and run out into the street. Suddenly it's cool and quiet and I can breathe.

"Wait," I call out towards the waiting car. Sunny stops and I reach him before he steps out onto the road. Nurse Ratched scowls at me and continues to move towards the cab.

"I've got him," I say, linking my arm through his. "You go ahead."

Her eyes narrow for a moment and then she relents. She gets into the taxi and waits.

"I just wanted to tell you how successful tonight has been," I tell him.

He smiles.

"Thank you," he says.

"I mean everyone loves your work. They are raving in there. You are going to be famous! I even heard someone talk about the next opening in Paris. Can you imagine?"

"Thank you. Thank you." He turns towards the road and takes a step.

Then suddenly he stops in his tracks, turns to me, and grabs both my arms with a terrible grip.

"I can't see," he says urgently.

"I know. I know. I'm here. I'll lead you to the cab. Don't worry, I won't let you go."

"No," he says. "You don't understand. I said I can't see."

"It's going to be okay," I say.

"Is it?"

"Sorry?" I say.

"Is it gonna be okay? Will I see again?"

He holds me tight. My arms are aching beneath his grip. The taxi beeps his horn and Sunny leans in towards me.

"Tell me, am I gonna be okay?"

I feel his breath on my cheek and his long, yellow nails digging into my skin.

Jim puts out his cigarette and steps towards us to see what the hell's taking so long. Nurse Ratched leans out of the cab with a dirty look. I look him straight in the face. It's a big, dark, crumpled face.

"Yes, Sunny," I lie. "You're going to be okay."

He lets go of me suddenly and is caught by Jim, who leads him to the back seat of the taxi. Jim closes the door, taps three times on the window, and steps away from the car. Sunny's face is turned towards the window as they drive off; I smile and I wave but I know it's no use. He can't see me. And it's just as well. It means he won't see the shame in my eyes.

***

It's only seven forty-five and I'm exhausted. These last two hours have felt like a decade. Mama and Anyu managed to get away without bumping into Nixon, and now he is sitting by himself in front of *Crocodile Dreaming VII* with a puzzled look on his face. I join him in the corner with a well-deserved piece of chocolate cake. The crowd before us starts preparing to leave, breaking into "teams" for a late dinner at the Depot, and going home to relieve babysitters. This is my favourite part of an opening: the closing. I tell Nixon why.

"This is when everyone comes together," I say. "Those ones over there, they are the artists. The one in red is a writer." I go through the ones who are left: the famous, the wannabes, the nobodies. I tell him whose name is worth remembering and whose I still don't know after months of working there. There were a good two hundred people here tonight. Some came to see; others to be seen. There were the talented, the gay crowd, the alcoholics, the politicians, the rich, the crazy, and the just plain boring. I point out the sculptors and the designers, those who paint professionally, and those who are just going through a mid-life crisis. (I leave out the group otherwise known as Lily's-one-night-stands-after-drunken-openings. He doesn't have to know everything.)

"I just don't get it", he tells me, interrupting my complex taxonomy. He shakes his head. "It's a mess," he says. "Any four-year-old could have done this with his eyes closed! I feel like I'm in kindergarten class."

I smile.

"Your stuff is better than this, Lily. It's your paintings that should be on the walls in here."

I kiss him.

Peasant.

Chapter Thirteen

It's been almost two months since the opening. Nixon wakes me with a kiss. He is warm and fragrant: sweet coffee with a hint of aftershave. He sits on the edge of my bed with neatly combed wet hair and shiny eyes.

"It's time to get up, sleepy one," he says.

I smile.

"Good morning, sleepy vun," I tease. I place my arms around his neck and pull him gently towards me. I'm not quite ready to get up yet.

He resists and shuffles his body backwards until he is almost at the foot of the bed. His leg, resting on the floor, starts to shake up and down. He runs his fingers through his hair. He is so cute when he is nervous.

"Oh Nixon," I moan, "Come on! How about five more minutes of cuddles?"

"No time for five more minutes," he tells me earnestly. "Time to get up." He stands up suddenly and starts scurrying about the apartment in a random pattern of to-ing and fro-ing that makes me dizzy. "It's late," he says. "Eva *néni* is waiting."

I sit up suddenly. "Oh shit!" I say. "You're right. We have a lesson today." Eva started scheduling our Hungarian lessons on Nixon's days off – Thursdays and Fridays only. I don't mind so much. It gets him out of the café when I am trying to learn irregular verb conjugations by heart, but the downside is that it gives me less time with Nixon. I guess Eva thought of that, too. Eva thinks of everything.

I consider getting out of bed, but the effort seems too great. I bury myself in my doona and curl up in a ball. It's warm and safe in here. Only the muted gurgle of the coffee percolator reminds me of the cruel world beyond the covers. "Maybe I'll cancel today," I say, mainly to myself, the words muffled deep from within my insulated goose-down cocoon.

Fading footsteps and then nothing. A long minute of nothing. I smile to myself. Is it possible I've won? I want to relax, but instead I strain to hear signs of life. Dare I lift this little corner of the doona, even if only for a second?

A toilet flushes and then more footsteps and a voice.

"No cancelling today," comes the reply from the outside world.

The blanket is thrown off me and I am handed a warm mug of coffee. "Today you have a lesson and I have a plan for you. Plan for you and me." Nixon dashes here and there gathering my clothes, tossing them at me one by one: pink undies, skinny jeans, a black singlet top, a leopard-print scarf. I try to catch them without spilling my coffee.

"Slow down!" I say. "I'm getting up." I sit up and wriggle my clothes on one by one without actually putting my feet on the ground. I'm still not ready to get out of bed. Nixon stands over me like a guard.

"Listen to my plan," he says with excitement. "You have lesson now with Eva *néni* and then you and me have special lunch."

I raise my eyebrows. *Special lunch!* What is that supposed to mean? I've not yet seen Nixon so forceful and decisive. It feels like it's been an age of just lazing around the apartment in a bubble of lethargy and vacillation. Two months of going to work and coming straight home to loaf about in bed until the next "have to" pulls one of us out into the world. Two months of devising creative excuses why *I know it's been a long time but I just can't make it* to every single arrangement that doesn't involve Nixon and bed. Two months of blissful quiet since the stress of Sunny's opening night at the gallery which gave me enough excitement for the rest of the year.

"Okay okay," I tell him, slipping on my boots and tying back my hair. "I'm going." I still haven't moved my backside off the bed. "I'm listening to your plan. But let's make a deal: how about just one more cuddle?"

I think I'm reasonably convincing, but suddenly he's shaking out the doona in order to make the bed and elbowing me onto my feet.

"No more cuddles," he tells me, "just listening to my plan."

***

The Hungarian lesson went a little over time, but I'm not worried. I'll only end up being twenty minutes late. Nixon will probably be late himself. My lateness is exceptional; his is pathological.

We are to meet at the Watson's Bay Beer Gardens at the beach for what Nixon explained would be a super special lunch. A lunch, as he put it, that I wouldn't want to miss. So I follow his instructions to a tee. I drive straight to Watson's Bay, get a nice, quiet table by the boardwalk, and order us drinks. Champagne, he told me, order champagne.

It's unusually warm for this time of year and the terrace is buzzing with the thrill of an unanticipated Indian summer afternoon. Women peel off jumpers and jackets. Toddlers in nappies chase seagulls between plastic tables and business men in suits sweat through jugs of beer and plates of hot chips with vinegar. On the boardwalk, lunchtime joggers weave elegantly through prams and wheelchairs, negotiating potholes and discarded plastic drink bottles, while elderly men colonise weathered benches that face toward the scrawny beach a few metres away and beyond, toward the run-down wharf that's been promised a revamp ever since I was a kid. A ferryboat arrives at the pier and a patchwork of dark suits and colourful windcheaters moves towards the bus stop with a curious singularity and behind them, the shimmering city skyline rises majestically above a tired, grey sea.

I don't wait for Nixon. The champagne will go warm. I pour two glasses and take slow sips from both to make it appear fair. A middle-aged woman two tables away looks at me kindly and smiles understandingly to no one from behind her novel. I ignore her and take two more sips.

As I slowly polish off three quarters of the bottle, I imagine detailed stories about the people at the other tables. The middle-aged Czech couple on the other side of the terrace – academics in nuclear physics or microbiology or something like that, on a day off from their annual conference in an exotic location. They're having problems with their teenage son who's recently gotten himself into trouble with drugs, but they're on holidays now, and look at that, the view is magnificent and the prawns are so fresh! There's the WASP mother–daughter combination in the corner politely sipping their third glass of Chardonnay between thin-lipped fake smiles. The daughter has her iPad out, finalising arrangements, I imagine, for her engagement party at home. There are the petit fours to order, the young girls to help with the dishes (Filipino or not?) and (what do you think?) maybe a violinist? There's the mothers' group right in the middle blocking access to and from the bar with seven space-buggy prams in an assortment of nauseating pastel colours that probably have more features than my car. But they have every right, no? They're mums, after all. Today they're good-naturedly competing about the number of daily washing loads until a blonde one, who is by now almost standing, announces a weekend of stomach flu. The group almost bursts into simultaneous applause, except for the quiet, skinny one next to her who ever so discreetly inches her chair away and showers her baby with antibacterial hand wash. And then it suddenly dawns on me: Nixon's not coming.

So I jump in the car to go straight home. I'm offended and I'm drunk. I should never have gone to the bloody Hungarian lesson. I should never have listened to his super special plan. I should never have gotten out of bed.

The drive home is a blur. I grip the steering wheel tightly with two hands as familiar streets and intersections whiz past the windscreen like in a video game. I don't know how I get back to North Bondi in one piece, but my focus sharpens instantly as I turn the corner onto Blair Street. I'm still a little way off, but I can see them both very clearly; there is no mistaking what I see. I decide not to go any closer. I pull over behind an SUV half a block away from my apartment building and catch my breath.

They are standing on my front steps, *our* front steps, the security door propped open by Nixon's foot. She takes his hand. He looks right, then left, and takes a step back, shaking his head. She turns away and starts walking across the street. Nixon takes out a cigarette, lights it, and starts to wave. He must be saying something because she stops bang in the middle of the road, turns her head, and laughs. He is still waving as she gets in her car and drives away.

I didn't see her face front on, but I know it is her. I saw her in that very dress at the gallery only last week! She told me all about her shopping adventure, how the designer was actually in the shop when she had tried it on. She said to me, "Lily, what do you think? It cost me two months' rent," and I said, "You know me, Camilla. Orange is not my thing." *Double-crossing bitch!* I should have told her what I really thought.

Camilla is long gone and Nixon is still standing on the step in the same spot. His hand has stopped waving now but it holds its position at shoulder height for an uncomfortably long time. He looks to the floor, smiles, punches the air with a joyous sense of victory, turns back towards my building, *our* building, and reaches into his pocket for his mobile phone. He dials.

I don't answer. I'm not crazy. Suddenly the contents of three quarters of a bottle of champagne starts bubbling inside of me and I want to be sick. I open the car door and lean over the edge, but nothing comes out. The phone is still ringing and Nixon disappears inside.

Without thinking, I start to drive. Just drive, Lily, drive. I cross Mitchell Street and head out on automatic pilot towards the alley behind Anyu's apartment block. Second right, first left, second left again. There it is. I park the car, reach for my bag, move to open the door, and then, without warning, in a most spectacular fashion, I collapse on the steering wheel in a pool of tears. I cry and cry, and then I cry some more.

When I eventually stop, I do feel a little better. I consider going upstairs, but then I catch myself just in time. Is this really what I need right now? Am I crazy? Or just plain stupid? Am I really going to go upstairs now and cry on Anyu's shoulder about the Hungarian peasant from Eva's bistro who – yes, a Hungarian Hungarian – no, not Jewish – yes, from the Oktogon – no, just a waiter – yes, *that* Eva – no, I'm not kidding – yes, who cheated me, deceived me, humiliated me – and no, I'm really not an idiot. I am not in the mood for explanations. I'm not ready for *I-told-you-so*'s and *how-on-earth-could-you-*

be-so-stupid's. I don't need Anyu's wisdom, nor another Monologue. I don't need a sermon or a roasting or an endless bout of Twenty Questions. I need another drink. That's what I need. My phone rings again. I fumble to turn it off, turn on the engine, wipe away my tears, and then flounder through an awkward ten-point turn in the excruciatingly narrow back street behind Anyu's apartment, and head straight to the pub.

The Golden Sheaf is only fifty metres from the Oktogon, but it may as well be a world away. Another Double Bay institution, it feels more like the backdrop to an American television series about law school students on spring break than a place of Old World soirees and rendez-vous. It's a world of arrogant, good-looking, drunken "nice" boys in pink business shirts who watch rugby union, play poker, snort cocaine only on weekends, fuck their private school friends' mothers, and settle down with a pretty girl in pearls with a big trust fund and a father who'll look after him at the office. It smells like money, but it's not the Double Bay of heavy accents and heroic stories of making it from nothing; it's thirty years younger and exclusively Australian-made. It's fun and rowdy and almost tolerably obnoxious because this world looks beautiful, sounds smart, feels important and always, and I mean always, includes sex.

I guess that's why I'm here now. I sit at the bar and order a tequila shot. And then another. It can't be too early, can it? I lean over the stool next to me to get a glimpse out of the window. It's just starting to get dark. Good. Another shot please. I look around. I don't know anyone. I need someone with me. I turn on my phone, ignore the seven missed calls from Nixon, and start dialling Sam's number. But I don't press send. What I need now you can't get from your gay best friend. I scan the room again. How is it possible that the bar is filled with losers? I sigh. I guess that's me included.

A guy I know from high school is playing pokies in the corner of the players' lounge. It's dark and noisy and I consider going up to him, but it's too much effort. I couldn't bear the whole *how-I-left-medical-school-for-a-job-as-a-gallery-assistant-where-my-boss-fucked-my-Hungarian-non-Jewish-boyfriend-today* saga. And besides, I don't think I'd be able to walk straight anyway.

I shake my head. How could Nixon do this to me? And with Camilla of all people? My boyfriend with my boss? In my own apartment? How stupid could I be? *Meet me at Watson's Bay,* he told me. *I may be a little late, but order champagne anyway and just wait. Just wait.* Always a safe bet to leave Lily alone with a bottle of alcohol if you need to buy time. I wonder if he ever intended to meet me there at all. Did he plan to come after his date, but just got carried away? Did he forget the time? Did he think I'd wait there all day? Did he think I'd forget about it? Did he think it would be okay?

It isn't okay. And neither am I. One more shot please, bartender.

Out of the corner of my eye, I notice a middle-aged man sipping scotch at the end of the bar. He is not bad looking, for an *old guy*, that is. He's got to be close to forty. What's it called again? The distinguished look. Like Richard Gere. All right, not exactly like Richard Gere, but he's old. It can't be all that different to a twenty-five-year old, can it? Or do pubic hairs go grey, too?

A hand taps me on the shoulder and startles me from my profound inner dialogue.

"What are you doing here, Lily?"

I turn around. The bar swims around my head and when I finally manage to turn my eyes towards the voice, I notice there are two, or is it three, young men taking a seat next to me.

"Jeremy!" I say to all of them. "Hi." I smile as sweetly as I know how, but really, all I want to do is throw up. "I haven't seen you in ages."

"Are you okay?" he asks.

I nod. "You'll do," I think, or do I say it aloud? I don't know anymore.

Jeremy smiles. "What are you drinking?"

I point to the empty shot glasses on the bar. Luckily there are more than one because my hand wavers all over the place like a tired metronome.

"Another round please, bartender," Jeremy calls. I smile and put my hand on his shoulder. It's more to steady me than anything else.

"I thought you had a new boyfriend," he says.

"Me too," I say, clinking glasses. "Me too."

***

Before I know it, it's already too late. My jeans are around my ankles and my stomach is scraping the stone wall across the street from the pub. Bang bang bang. I wish that I could say that I feel numb, but it's not true. Bang bang. Come on! Don't stop, Jeremy. *More. More.* What do you think of this super special plan, Nixon? Hey? What do you think of this? Bang bang bang. Do you think it's special? Bang. No more time for cuddles? Bang. Tell Camilla I'll be late for work tomorrow, will you? Bang. Don't stop. Harder. Harder! Come on! Tell Camilla I'm not coming. Bang bang bang. Don't stop. Oh no, I'm coming. I'm coming.

I manage to get my pants on all right and then gracelessly throw up all over the ivy on the wall of the antique store. I laugh. The world has finally stopped spinning. I move to the other side of Jeremy and we share a cigarette in comfortable silence while I mull over the situation in my head. Fucking Jeremy! This is all his fault. Taking advantage of me when I can hardly even stand up. Surely I shouldn't blame myself. Ha! I'm not the one who did anything wrong! I blame Nixon: if only he hadn't deceived me so violently. And then there's Camilla (my boss! my mentor!) for going behind my back. I blame Eva for introducing me to Nixon. I blame Sam for not protecting me from Eva. I blame Anyu just for good measure. Surely somehow this could all be her fault. Surely she has some part in this crazy world of secrets and lies. I want to blame someone, because somehow I am scared that this means *The End.*

But if I really think about it, it's probably none of their faults. Out of the corner of my eye I catch a glimpse of someone new to blame. The truth is that if I had just managed to block out all that happened today, then everything would have had a chance to go back to some kind of "normal". If only it wasn't for Peter *bácsi* the chef who, on a random cigarette break from the heat of the kitchen, sees Lily daahrlink fucking a complete stranger against the stone wall of the carpark right in the middle of Double Bay.

Chapter Fourteen

I can't go home. Absolutely not. It's Nixon's home too. And Jeremy's place is out of the question. I was done with him before he could even do his fly up. Everyone else I can think of will probably still be awake, so *she* really is my only choice this early in the evening. She'll already be in bed and I can slip in quietly without her noticing. It will give me time to recover and sober up, time to think, time to sleep, time to forget. By the time Anyu realises I am there, it will already be a brand new day.

I've spent many a desperate night in Anyu's cosy apartment. The last couple of times I slept on the couch. It's a little short and limp. My feet hang off the end and the middle cushions have lost most of their original bounce, but it's not quite as uncomfortable as it sounds. The upholstered covers are worn just to the brink of perfection, smooth as silk, that magic point that only cotton knows just before it falls apart. They've been at that stage as long as I can remember. There's always a knitted quilt draped over the armchair for a blanket. I'm not so certain of the last time it saw the inside of a washing machine, but in the state I'm usually in when I sneak into the apartment, anything will do.

When I was a young girl, I'd crawl into Anyu's bed and sleep with her through the night. She had an elaborate bedtime routine that I loved to watch. First she'd brush her hair and fasten it all back with a silk scarf. Then there was the face wash, the eye cream, the lip balm and the moisturiser. She then took two long, red capsules and a small white pill with a quick swig of whisky (she didn't think I saw her) followed by a toilet stop. On the way to bed, she'd check that the gas was turned off on the stove, and then halfway back to the bedroom, she'd turn around and go back to the kitchen to be absolutely certain. The same procedure every time and she never even made me brush my teeth! What a treat! If I wasn't too tired, I'd change the pillow-slip on my side of the bed so as to avoid being smothered by last night's cold cream, and then I'd sink like a baby into the soft, powdery sheets as the familiar smell of hairspray and musk lulled me to sleep.

Anyu's apartment was a great place for a kid. We'd play cards till way past my bedtime and eat potato chips for dessert. I'd listen to her monologues over and over like old records and try on all her jewellery. *Tell me the one about the crazy next-door neighbour, pleeeaaase! One more time!* There were the occasional evenings during the week when Mama had to work late or, even more seldom, when she went out on dates, and when I was really young, when Papa was still alive, Anyu's place was where I was sent when he wasn't feeling well, when he was too sick to have a nosy, tiresome little girl running around the house making too much noise, asking too many questions.

I park the car and collect my things: my purse, my cigarettes, my jacket, and the hairbrush and can of deodorant I leave in the glove box for emergencies just like this one. I stuff everything into my handbag, and get out of the car, even remembering to take off the parking ticket from under my windshield wiper. That's all I need at the end of a day like today. My head is pounding. I can hardly stand straight. I guess I must be slowly sobering up, stuck in that headachy halfway house at which one either has to go straight to sleep or else have another drink. My shoes are killing me. I plod up the stairs and with my last surge of energy, ready to collapse, I finally put my key in the door. And that's when it hits me like a freight train: rummy night.

Three pairs of raised, tattooed eyebrows (and one pair of huge sunglasses) greet me from the table. Zsuzsi cries "*Jaj*", Punci drops her cigarette on the green felt cover, and Dotsi jumps up and scampers off down the hallway to the toilet. Her bowels are never good with surprises and sudden noises. Anyu's face is a mixture of delight and irritation and then quickly turns towards the hole Punci's cigarette is creating, eating away at the felt cover in neat, concentric circles. Zsuzsi panics first, upending her soda water on the table cloth, successfully drowning the fire and the entire pack of cards. "Imbecile!" she cries. "Are you trying to kill us all? It's only Lily for God's sake!"

How could I have been so stupid? Thursday night has been rummy night, only for the last fifteen years!

If I hadn't been so preoccupied with my own misery, I would have already smelled their overpowering presence from the stairwell and been able to escape the circus just in time. But here I am standing in the middle of the room and there's no turning back. I wilt melodramatically on the couch, the entire contents of my bag toppling like an avalanche onto the floor. Anyu races to my side.

"Lily, daahrlink, are you … what's this?" She picks up the yellow envelope from beside my feet. "*Vot?* Another parking fine? Are you mad? How much this time?"

I grab the fine from her hands and stuff it in my pocket. "Doesn't matter, *now*." Those miserable eighty-seven dollars I wasted parking illegally at the pub are the last thing on my mind. "I'm exhausted," I say. "Can I sleep here, Anyu? Do you mind?"

"Well, of course not, daahrlink, well, you know …" She stops and looks me up and down. "Lily, are you okay?"

"Let me guess," chirps Zsuzsi triumphantly from across the room. "Boy trouble!"

They all look over in anticipation. I cradle my head in my hands and feel my pulse drum against my eyelids. I'm sure they can hear the thump thump thump of my temples.

"I knew it! I told you, didn't I? Lily, it's boy trouble isn't it?" How is it Zsuzsi can be so proud of herself at a time like this? I desperately want to lie, but I don't have the strength for another story.

"They are all the same, daahrlink. Don't worry about it. Men are pigs, right, Agi? Pigs!"

"Who's a pig?" Dotsi is back from the bathroom.

"Never mind, Dotsi. Lily's upset," says Punci.

"Lily's not a pig. How could you say that?"

"Men, Dotsi, men are pigs, not Lily." Zsuzsi is always the first to get exasperated with Dotsi's ditziness. "Well, daahrlink, I told you to call that Bloomberg boy. Didn't I tell her, Dotsi?" She turns to Anyu and continues. "An accountant, mind you."

I manage a half-hearted mumble from behind my hands. "Don't worry, you wouldn't understand." But I have already anticipated the response. Between them, there had been six husbands and God knows how many more affairs and disappointments and vindications. This isn't the first time Anyu has been called upon to nurse a broken heart. I have heard it all before. How things were different in those days, in the good old days; *love* was different then. *Love* meant something else then. People spoke of loyalty and family and "doing the right thing". People spoke of appropriateness and success, propriety and convenience, suitability and opportunity. Oh sure, there was romance, but *love*? They didn't have time for love. They called it love: that warm, flirty look from across the busy marketplace, the letter lined with poetry sent to the front, the prenuptial nooky at the water's edge. They called love a pretty bouquet of flowers every day for a month, a playful midnight dance in the summer rain, a tearful set of promises as the train pulled out of the station. I know what it was like in the old days: people met, got married, and then fell in love. Sometimes even with each other.

"You know what your problem is, Lily. *Vell?* You want to know?"

Here it comes. Monologue Number 63.

"Let me guess." I mouth out the response. "It's not just me ... it's my entire generation."

"It's not just you ... it's your entire generation!"

"Poor Lily, oh daahrlink." Dotsi comes over to the couch and holds my hand. She is a bit flaky, a bit goofy, but she does mean well. She always takes my side, so to speak, when the ranting starts. She doesn't always stay there, mind you, but that's another story.

"Your generation is so spoilt. I can't believe how fussy you people are," Anyu continues.

"Fussy? What's wrong with an accountant?" Zsuzsi has to put in her two cents' worth. "He already has his own apartment. In Rose Bay, mind you."

"Oh pleeaase! How boring."

"You see what I mean? Fussy. This one's too fat. That one's too skinny ..."

"Boring? What do you mean, boring? In our day, we didn't have time to be bored!"

"If only we had the luxury of being so choosy!" It's Punci's turn to join in the fun.

"In our day, we did the right thing!"

"In our day, we did as we were told!"

In our day ... in our day ... I can't stand it anymore. "In your day ... you know what, in your day you were all miserable!"

"And you're so happy?" Anyu holds her hands up to the sky. She looks over at the others. "*Na!* So tell me!"

The three of them nod to themselves and each other.

"We did what we thought was right, that's what we did!" exclaims Zsuzsi. Anyu, Zsuzsi and Punci are now gallivanting around the room like Shakespearean actors on a stage, hands flying all over the place, heads flinging noses upwards to the sky. The drama is too much.

"You people treat men like a cheap pair of shoes. You try them on, and when they're out of fashion, you just throw them away. Plomp!" And with a quick flick of her hand, Anyu performs her favourite line. Her eyes say serious, but her dimples give her away. I can see the pleasure welling up in the corners of her mouth. Here come the puns. Oh, she is so very pleased with this one. "I know, I know, let me guess: you get sick of them. What do you call it? You are *over* him? Well, let me tell you something, young lady. May I suggest to you that *you* are over it, my dear, over the hill! That's all you are over."

Punci nods to Zsuzsi. It seems as though they have all heard this one before. The one about how at twenty-two I am over the hill. The one about my people's puerility. The one about my generation's lack of staying power.

In their world, things may have been old and imperfect, but they were built to last. Relationships, culture, philosophy, art: everything was meant to endure and, like this monologue, to be endured. She loves to rant about *what the world has come to ...*, that infuriating built-in style obsolescence that renders everything in my generation expendable, disposable. Friendships, studies, men, everything. Even the old Sydney she so hated was never built to last: the school I went to is now being sold off the plan as townhouses. The playground I used to roam about in is the car park for a shopping mall. The hospital I was born in is a cinema complex and the hall I had ballet lessons in burnt down from an electrical fault. Cheap and nasty! No respect! Even Budapest, after two world wars and a revolution, even dirty old Budapest had enough decency to remain the same. Where's the stamina in the world today? Nothing lasts five minutes in this bloody world.

Punci and Zsuzsi mumble along, butting in emphatically every few minutes with a word or two for emphasis.

"Cheap!"

"Nasty!"

"No guts!"

"No heart!"

And a final, triumphant, "What's the world coming to!" from an over-excited Zsuzsi.

Meanwhile, I mouth the words to the second verse along with Anyu.

"She doesn't know how lucky she is! *Jaj!* If only you knew, daahrlink. What I would have given to have been allowed to study medicine ... like my father. Two years and you've had enough. Is that it? Simple as that! Enough?" She turns to me with her hands on her hips. "Enough! I'll tell you all about *enough*. There weren't *enough* places for Jews! You get given a place on a silver platter and then you give it up. Just like you give up everything and everyone!"

Dotsi kisses my hand in sympathy, but the other two just stand there nodding. *That's right! Give it all up.*

"I don't think he's a pig, daahrlink," Dotsi says, out of the blue. Her kind, innocent, pale eyes stare straight into mine. She is just being sympathetic, but we all know the truth: she is only having a little trouble following.

"Shhh, Dotsi, come on. You're just making things worse," says Punci, leading her back to the rummy table.

Meanwhile, nothing can stop Anyu. "In my day, we knew when we were onto a good thing and we held on like super glue! None of this mucking around, I tell you. When we found a decent boy, we bloody married him! That was that!"

"What's all this mucking around for?" I mimic, predicting the next line.

"*Vell*, what's all this mucking around for?" Anyu says.

I'm just sick of the same words again and again. I'm getting a real feel for the meaning of the word endurance. The emptiness of her sermon is making me crazy. This one-size-fits-all monologue isn't going to work this time. This isn't about *me*. This time it's not my fault. This is about Nixon! I found a decent guy. I wasn't ready to give him up. I didn't do anything wrong! (At least, I wasn't the first one.) I wasn't the one who was making secret rendezvous behind my partner's back. I wasn't the one who was making arrangements and then not turning up. I wasn't the problem here. This time was different. I was ready for the long haul. I was happy!

"What's to decide? What's to think about? I don't understand you people. What's the bloody problem here?"

I take a deep breath. "I tell you what the problem is, Anyu. The problem is that you don't listen." I pause slightly for effect. And to think. Urgently think. I have never said anything like this to her before.

I don't know exactly where I'm going with this, but I have her attention now.

"Come on," I say. "I've heard this all a million times. I'm just sad, Anyu, just plain sad. I'm in love and it's probably all over. Can't I be sad for a change? I've had a rough day and, quite frankly, I'm exhausted."

"What could you possibly have to be so exhausted about?" she says.

I guess that wasn't going to do it.

But this certainly is. Dotsi and her big mouth.

"Well, I think he looks like a lovely boy. Good-looking."

"It's okay, Dotsi, my dear, don't worry …" Punci starts comforting her at the table. Anyu looks at me, about to begin again, but I don't acknowledge her. I just nod towards Dotsi.

"I know," I say, mainly to myself. "He is lovely."

"Who's lovely?" Zsuzsi asks Anyu with a sense of urgency. "What's-his-name, the accountant?"

Anyu shrugs her shoulders. For once she's stumped.

"The boy," says Dotsi, squirming to free herself from Punci's clutches. "The young boy from the Oktogon. Isn't that who you're all talking about? Lily? Someone? The young Hungarian fellow, what's his name? Reagan?"

Silence. A long, uncomfortable silence until confusion sets in. They are all so used to summarily dismissing Dotsi's blubbering and muttering that they almost don't process her comment. But there is something unnerving about her words that makes them disconcerted, unable to simply cast off her claim as the usual rambling. I don't know whether it was mention of the Oktogon or the *young Hungarian fellow* that did it, or maybe it was the strange sounding name. Or alternatively, and more likely, it could have been the fact that I ever so gracelessly crumpled to a heap on the floor.

Then everyone goes crazy. I can see it in their faces. How can Lily possibly know someone from the Oktogon? And what the hell is she doing on the floor? How can Lily love a Hungarian fellow? And is it possible that Dotsi is the only one of them who knows what the hell is going on? Anyu starts looking from face to face searching for clues, trying to understand. I can almost hear the wheels turning in her head: and what does Eva have to do with all this, anyway? What does Eva have to do with Lily? Can someone please tell me what the hell is going on?

And then I start to cry. Before I have to explain, before I have to answer any questions, before I have to give the whole thing away.

I cry with all my heart. I cry for everything that I can manage to muster up. I cry for all the boys I tried to love and all of those I left. I cry for leaving university so early and I cry for ever having started it in the first place. I cry for the career I'll probably never have, the illness I'll never make sense of, the father I'll never know. I cry for loving Nixon so easily and losing him just the same. I cry for trusting a complete stranger like Camilla, and then deceiving my very own grandmother. I cry until I can't cry anymore.

And then I'm finished. I pick myself up from the floor. I know that it's time. I'm ready.

I tell her everything. I tell her about Eva and the Hungarian lessons. I tell her about Peter and Nixon. I tell her about Camilla and the lunch. I'm not so happy about confession time in front of the Three Stooges, but I have no choice. They would probably hear all about it sooner or later anyway, and I'd rather they hear the original version straight from the horse's mouth instead of who knows what type of revisionist story from Mrs Goldberg at the Double Bay Bridge Club. And I guess that little Dotsi already knew! How about that!

To my surprise, Anyu sits patiently and quietly through the entire story. It's a good one, I think, one of betrayal, disloyalty, and forbidden love. I think it is exciting, nail-biting stuff, an edge-of-your-seat type drama, but she hardly even blinks an eyelid. She hardly even moves. And even now that I have finished, she just sits. She stares in my general direction with those sleepy, glassy eyes of hers. Just sits and stares.

Finally she stirs. I don't know whether to be afraid or relieved. She walks slowly towards the table, takes out a cigarette from her silver case, and then casually reaches across for the lighter. Every movement is painfully executed, deliberate, and excruciating.

"Your generation ..." she says. It's the third attempt and still the lighter won't work. She puts the cigarette down on the table to fiddle with the lighter mechanism, and when she picks it back up, it is soggy from the soda water. But she doesn't seem fazed. Ever so casually, she reaches across to her handbag. I can't take it. Neither can Zsuzsi, who, probably out of impatience rather than kindness, gives Anyu her own half-smoked cigarette to share. Anyu takes a long drag and then slowly exhales. "... your generation has no idea."

I can't believe it. Another monologue. After everything, this is what she is giving me?

"You wouldn't understand, Lily. You think you know everything, don't you? Well, maybe it's not you, maybe it's your entire generation. In my day ..."

Another one-size-fits-all sermon. This is too much. I can handle anything else, anything at all: condemnation, reprehension, exclusion, even damnation. I just need something, either a hug or a curse or a smack in the face. I need her to be *awfully mad.* Anything but this – empty, repetitive words. This isn't a conversation; this is a performance. This isn't a fight. This is noise, another hollow exchange. It's like I am looking at one of those Roy Lichtenstein prints, the ones with a comic book type text bubble, a jumble of cynical and sarcastic comments devoid of any real emotion, any profound meaning, anything at all.

"Well for your information," I tell her, "for your information, Eva told me ..."

"Eva? Eva? Come on, Lily, you don't know anything about Eva."

"I know she talks to me! I know she tells me things! I know more than you can even imagine! I know real stories!"

"Stories? You want to know stories? I'll tell you stories about Eva, daahrlink, don't you worry about that. I'll tell you stories that will knock your bloody socks off!"

There's a sudden bout of whispering and shuffling in the corner. Zsuzsi, Punci, and Dotsi start packing up their things and slowly tiptoeing towards the door. I've never heard them so quiet before. Nor have I ever imagined them running from a scene. I walk over to the table, pour two glasses of soda water, our traditional *Hungarian Champagne,* and watch Anyu follow them in silence through the lounge room and then close the door behind them.

I wait.

Anyu goes over to the table and starts cleaning up the mess.

"Tell me," I whisper. "Tell me about Eva."

"You see there are so many things you couldn't understand, Lily. Well, how could you, daahrlink? Things were so different then. *Jaj!* It was such a lovely time, you know. Such fun! We were a sensation! We were the most elegant place in Sydney, Lily, can you imagine that? The most popular bistro in town. Every Friday and Saturday night we were booked out, not a spare table in sight. They came from everywhere. Women in fur coats and long dresses, men … imagine, men really knew how to dress in those days. There were none of these thongs and dirty t-shirts in my time, I tell you. People used to look in the window just to see what they were wearing in the Oktogon. We were a sensation!

"Bert Newton, you know Bert Newton? Well, he had a permanent table in the corner. Can you believe it? And I served them all, I did, Gough Whitlam and Joan Sutherland and Dawn Fraser. They all knew my name, you know, they said *Agi darling, you can arrange something nice for us, can't you? A nice one by the window tonight. Be a doll, would you? Agi darling*, they called me. *A doll.* Imagine. And then I'd run around like mad trying to fit them in because I understood. The Oktogon was the place to be. I'd run around making sure the food was hot and the drinks were cold. I'd be in the kitchen and on the phone and at the front door all at the same time. I'd clean tables and wash dishes and make coffees until my feet would bleed. *Bleed.* That's what I did, Lily. I did everything.

"But Eva, ha! Your Eva. Eva had other ideas. Other crazy ideas like how the place was hers. When Ivan died, when he died, you see, Eva went bananas. Just like that. She couldn't deal with it. She always had a problem with reality, you know. She blamed everyone she knew. You see, she remembered things so differently.

"She had all the papers and all the records, but how can that be enough? It was me who did all the work, daahrlink, it was me who ran the place."

Anyu gets up and goes to that little corner of the bookshelf where she keeps her albums. I hold my breath. Surely she can't be looking for the green one, the one with Eva torn out of every page, the one I had taken last year. But she doesn't look like a woman on a mission. I've never seen her quite like this before. She is gentle, almost listless; her passion and anger spent, giving way to a melancholy stillness that's calming even me. Her monologues are not shows: she is remembering the hard times when somehow life was better.

She starts sorting out the wet playing cards from her half-finished rummy game. "Three aces, I had, Lily. Would you believe it? Three aces and we didn't even get to finish. Just my luck! I was going to win! I would have won!" Then she pauses. "Look," she says, "look at the mess in this bloody apartment! I can't stand this place." She sits down, her hands still full of cards, and covers her eyes. "Eva, huh? You want to know about Eva?" She sighs. "Well, if you want to know the truth, Eva is the reason why this place is such a dump. Eva, my daahrlink, is the reason we are so poor."

I can't move. I don't know exactly what I was expecting, but it certainly isn't this.

"The Oktogon," she continues. "You say you fell in love in the Oktogon. Well, the Oktogon used to belong to me." She emphasises the *me* with a pounding of her chest from a tight, strong fist. "Me."

I am listening.

"I was the one who used to sit all day in that little office and make plans. I was the one who rang the cash register and paid the bills. I was the one who cleaned the fridge when everyone went home and sat up at night worrying about the menu. Me, Lily, it was me.

"Who do you think decided every day what Peter would cook for the specials? Who do you think made sure he didn't drink away half the profits and steal the rest? Who do you think used to charm the famous clients when they waltzed in demanding the best table on the terrace without a booking? I tell you who. I tell you who did all the work." She pounds her chest with her fist to the beat of her accent, the thump thump thump on the first syllable of every word. "Me."

"Eva, well, you want to know about Eva. Eva was always there, of course. She came and went as she pleased. She was my partner, my teammate, my friend. Some friend! But she didn't have a clue. I tell you! Lily, the Oktogon was my creation."

She suddenly gets up and moves her chair next to mine.

"You don't remember this, daahrlink, but we had a nice big house, you know, with a view of the water and a swimming pool. Imagine. And your father, well, he wasn't so sick yet and your mother had such dreams. She went back to school, you know, and was working so hard. You were so very little, Lily, such a gorgeous little thing. And so funny! Always the clown. She loved you very much, you know that, you were Eva's favourite. She'd tell you jokes and then you'd rehearse them together. She liked to shock, she did.

"*My Lily*, she used to say. *Tell me a funny joke, my Lily.* But even that didn't stop her. She turned into a monster. Just like that. Ivan was dead and there was no one left to remember the truth. Her word against mine. Always her word against mine. It sounds like it's still her word against mine.

"That's how it happened. So your father, what a good boy, your father thought he could fix it all. But bless his little soul, he didn't know what he was doing. He had a heart as big as a lion's, you know. You would have been very proud of him, a real softie, but Lily he was in no condition to fight. Not for me, not for the Oktogon, not even for you. Lily, he was already fighting for his life.

"And then the bloody lawyers started to send their bills. They just kept coming and coming. There were barristers and solicitors and this expense and that cost. *Shysters*, every last bloody one of them, thousands of dollars for photocopying and pencil sharpening and none of them could help us. I kept telling them, *one more month*. I tell you Lily, one more month and we could have won! But so many bills.

"First your Mama had to quit school and she got a job at some office. That's why she's so angry at you for quitting too. That's why she's so angry with me. Well, someone had to pay for it all, no? Then it was the car and then the house. It just never stopped. And your father was so sick by that time. It was too much for him, daahrlink. All of it. The court dates and the lies and the doctors' appointments. He wanted to handle it all by himself, a sweeter man you'll never find, Lily. But he was hopeless with money. What can I tell you? And there was so much fighting. Fighting Eva, then fighting your mother, then fighting his illness. Lily, he just couldn't fight anymore.

"We didn't realise how sick he was. He didn't want us to know. That's what he was like, your Papa, such an angel."

Suddenly she finds what she was looking for on the shelf. She pulls out a picture of Papa, one I have never seen before. She points to his eyes.

"Look at this, Lily. Look at him." His face is so pale, almost grey. He is thin and gaunt and fragile, his eyes empty of life. "He just couldn't fight anymore, Lily, no more."

I know those eyes, those lost, hurt eyes. I see them every day when I look in the mirror. I, too, am sick of fighting, fighting Anyu, fighting men, fighting myself.

Anyu sits back down at the rummy table. "Three aces," she says. "I would have won."

I look over at Anyu. It's just the two of us again, disappointed, irritated, exhausted, but somehow not alone.

I kiss her on the cheek and feel her softness fall into me.

"I'm sorry, Anyu," I say. "I'm so sorry."

"I know," she whispers. "Oh, Lily daahrlink, I know."

Chapter Fifteen

I don't know what I'm doing here. It's the morning after and I have driven straight to the Oktogon. At the door I think about it. It's not too late. I can easily just turn back and disappear into my old life. But something compels me to walk straight in and sit myself down in my regular booth like I've done a hundred times before. Like I did yesterday. It's my seat, after all. The vantage point. The very heart of the machine, from which all the café's comings and goings can be observed, discussed, appraised, judged. So I sit down and just wait.

Peace. A few moments of peace before life will force me to choose between character-defining strength or a forced attempt at indifference. I look around. Everything looks the same as it did yesterday. The same row of cakes hovering in the display cabinet, the same smell of cleanser seeping from the kitchen door, the same crunch of grinding beans coming from the coffee machine. Could everything Anyu told me last night be true? Is this *her* cabinet, *her* kitchen, *her* coffee machine? How could this place that I have grown to love be the seat of a battle so bitter that it could tear apart a friendship that spanned war and revolution and emigration? How could this pleasant, but largely insignificant, little European café in the heart of Double Bay be the very reason I grew up in a small apartment without air-conditioning, the reason my grandmother lost everything, the reason my mother had to leave school, and the reason my father couldn't fight anymore? Could this be the same place I found an unlikely friend in an elderly Hungarian woman who was my family's nemesis, the same place I found the courage to ask questions, the same place I fell in love?

"What are you doing here, Lily? Don't tell me … you've forgotten!"

I look around. I hear the click click of heels. I smell the waft of perfume, but I didn't see her coming. A black coffee lands on the table in front of me and then suddenly there's Eva, arms folded across her chest, seated on the bench opposite me. It is almost like magic.

"It's Friday," she says after a few long seconds. "You know you won't find him here on a Friday. So why don't you just drink your coffee and go home?"

I look her straight in the eyes. I scan her face for clues. It's definitely the same Eva *néni*: the same grey, pallid eyes lined Cleopatra-style with a thick black bar, the same wry lips that quiver ever so slightly when she thinks, the same laugh lines around her eyes that stay even now when she's completely serious. What does Eva *néni* know? What does she know about how the past twenty-four hours have turned my life upside down?

Or is it the right way up?

I don't know what to do. So I pick up the cup, take a sip of coffee, and tell her straight up.

"Give me a Hungarian lesson, Eva *néni*."

That is what I am doing here, isn't it?

She laughs.

Not a happy laugh. Nor her usual sarcastic snigger. It's a bitter gesture, hostile and disrespectful. But I am relieved. It's what I need to hear this morning.

So it's true. This woman is a monster. Maybe she's right about one thing: maybe I should just go home. How could I have been so disloyal to Anyu? How could I have been so stupid? There I was dismissing her petulance as part of the eccentricities of an old, lonely woman. How could I have been so generous? I should just leave. No. I should just ask. I should fight.

Instead I take another long sip of coffee.

Eva waits, and then gets up.

"Go home, Lily," she says, walking away. "I don't think I have anything to teach you today. We are both of us tired." She walks slowly towards the kitchen door. "I have to work," she says.

I put down my coffee.

"I'm not tired," I call after her. "And I'm not going anywhere. Anyway," I say, "you don't own this place. You can't tell me when to leave. It belongs to my Anyu."

Eva turns to me and laughs that awful laugh again. She laughs so hard it turns into a guttural, uncontrollable coughing fit.

I wait until she regains her composure.

"Isn't that true, Eva *néni*?" I say.

"Isn't what true? What?" She walks over to the coffee machine and I stand up to follow her. She starts rearranging the milk jugs. She grabs a sponge and wipes down the spout. "Isn't what true, Lily?"

"I know everything," I say, this time in Hungarian.

"Everything, huh?" She answers, in English. She runs her sponge over the coffee bean grinder. She smiles to herself. "Oh don't worry, my dear, I also knew everything at your age."

"Anyu told me," I say. "She told me about everything, so there's no need to pretend anymore."

Eva casually takes the sponge to the sink and washes it clean. She squeezes it tight, then washes it again.

"Everything?" she says, still at the sink with her back to me. "Which everything did she tell you, daahrlink, the everything about me or the everything about her?"

"I know it all, Eva *néni:* the lawyers, the court case, the fighting until they couldn't fight anymore. So let's not bullshit around, here. I just came for my Hungarian lesson in my grandmother's café, that's all, so give me a Hungarian lesson please."

Eva suddenly stops and puts down the sponge. She looks straight at me. "Well, my dear, it sounds to me like you've already had enough lessons for this week, doesn't it? And I can see you've been such a good student, haven't you? She obviously taught you all about men and how to screw them real good and proper. Now you've been such a good girl, daahrlink, you've learned it all by heart, so go back to Agi and tell her what a good girl you've been."

"What are you talking about?"

"Who's pretending now, Lily? Listen my dear, you're not the only one who knows everything."

I can't believe it. She can't be talking about last night, can she? Not yet, anyway. Then I remember Peter *bácsi.*

"That's none of your business," I tell her.

"Really?" she says. She puts her hands on her hips.

I stop for a moment. Is it any of her business or not? I don't want it to be, but I just have to know.

"And Nixon?" I ask.

I feel sick.

"Nixon, *na!* Nixon knows everything too, daahrlink. What did you think would happen?" She shakes her head. "I knew it from the very beginning. You are just like she is. You just can't keep your legs closed." She sounds like my mother. "You just can't stop screwing."

This is so unfair. I feel like crying. This is not about me.

"Talk about screwing," I say. "Have you asked Nixon who he screwed lately? Have you forgotten how it was you who screwed up my life?" I'm angry now. I'm not ready for this. I didn't come here for this. I came to talk to her about the Oktogon. Eva is the monster. Nixon is the monster. This is not about me.

Eva turns and walks into the kitchen. I follow her through the swinging doors.

"What?" she says, over her shoulder. *Vot?*

"Tell me what he said," I say, following her.

"I thought it was none of my business," she sniggers. I hear a latch switch and turn to see Peter *bácsi* leave through the back door. Eva leans against the counter top and sighs. "He said what I thought he'd say. He said, 'Eva *néni*, you were right'."

"What did you tell him? What did he say? Eva *néni*, tell me!"

"He said, 'Eva you were right. You can't trust her.' So you don't have to worry about Nixon anymore, Lily."

I take a breath. "Right about what?"

"Right about how you people just can't keep your legs closed. You, Agi, you're both the same. I told him, I did, I told him from the very beginning, but he didn't want to believe me."

"This has nothing to do with Anyu. She's suffered enough. She lost everything – her café, her money, her house, her son!"

"And what about *her* friend?"

"What about her friend? The friend who fought her till she had nothing left? The friend who stole everything that meant anything to her? Is that the friend you mean?"

Eva coughs and looks to the floor. She clasps her hands together and squeezes until her knuckles are white. She coughs again before taking a deep breath.

And then she tells me.

"What about the friend who stole my husband from me, huh? What about that friend?"

Wait. Stop. I try to think. What's going on? What is she talking about?

"What are you talking about?" I say.

"I thought she told you everything, Lily."

And then it suddenly clicks. Ivan. Of course, *Ivan the Terrible. Everything happened when Ivan died. Eva couldn't deal with it. Eva blamed everyone. Eva went crazy.* This wasn't about me. It wasn't about Nixon. It wasn't about the Oktogon.

"Ivan and Anyu?" I whisper.

"Ah, the genius!" she quips, both arms in the air. "Of course Ivan and Anyu," she says. She smiles and turns to lean on the kitchen bench with both hands. I move to stand by her side. I can see she really is tired. Too tired to fight anymore. She shakes her head. "Ivan and Agi for forty years, Lily, for forty bloody years. So don't talk to me about stealing things. Nothing was ever enough for that woman, nothing. She had everything she wanted, but it wasn't enough because she had to have what I had too. She had to have my friends, my café, my husband. Everything." *Everysink.*

My head starts swimming. I'm not prepared for this.

"You think this is all fun, don't you, my dear?" She turns her head towards me. "Playing grown-up games, fucking this one and then fucking that one, discovering this secret and then discovering that one. Are you really sure you want to know the truth?"

Of course that's what I want. That's what I have wanted all along. The truth! So I could stop making things up and stop being called an idiot. There are some things I might never be ready for, but I need it nonetheless.

Eva continues, "You know what the truth is: I tell you the truth. It's my fault. I fell in love with you the day you asked me to teach you Hungarian. You said 'Teach me Hungarian, Eva' and I thought I'd laugh my head off. You were always so funny. You are still that funny, naughty little girl. You had come back to me. You had left her, Lily, and you had come back to me. Silly me. But did I really think it would be so easy to be friends? You and me? Ha! You know, daahrlink, I told Nixon that you were probably like Agi and I'm not proud of that. I probably shouldn't have opened my big mouth, but deep down I was secretly hoping to be wrong."

Wait! I can't think. Nixon knew about Anyu and Ivan? Nixon knew about all of this before me? How could she have done this to me? Wait a minute!

But she isn't waiting.

"But it's not about goodies and baddies anymore, daahrlink. That's only in the movies. We're watching real life, now, you know."

Wait. Stop.

But she's not waiting. She's not stopping. "I'm sorry about many things. Sorry about things I did and things I said. I'm no saint, I know that. I have a big mouth and I say what I think. But there's one thing I'll never be sorry about: I'll never be sorry about fighting back, fighting for my Oktogon. Until last year it was the only thing I had left, until last year, Lily. Until last year when you came back into my life. I nearly lost the Oktogon once! I lost my husband and I lost my friend. And I'll be damned if now I'll lose you too."

Half an hour ago, Eva told me to go home. Maybe I should have listened. And now she won't stop. She can't stop. My head doesn't stop, either. The questions keep growing and multiplying, overtaking my brain. Or are they answers? It's all too much.

Anyu stole away Eva's husband; Eva stole away Anyu's café; and then Papa couldn't fight anymore. Eva told Nixon I would sleep around. Then she told him I did. My questions are being answered, but things aren't making any sense. I can't see out from this monstrous web. I went behind Anyu's back seeking answers; Anyu went behind Eva's back seeking love; Eva went behind my back seeking confirmation; Nixon went behind my back seeking the inevitable; I went behind Nixon's back seeking revenge; Anyu went behind Eva's back seeking to keep her share; and Eva went behind Anyu's back seeking to take it all back again. I just can't keep things from spiralling out of control. Is it all true? And if it is, is this what I really wanted to know?

Eva keeps talking and talking but it has all become just words, isolated, meaningless words: *told, me, fight, him, daahrlink, right, and, then, know, truth, feel, but, dear, see, girl* ... hollow, absurd, silly little sounds that my brain can't put back together into any sort of lucid or significant pattern. *Time, so, many, love, little, lie, she, gone, find, say, don't* ... and I can't. I can't listen to them anymore.

***

It's not so much what Nixon took from the apartment that makes me fall to pieces when I get home from the Oktogon; it's what he left behind. Gone are his shirts hanging in my cupboard, his toothbrush from the bathroom cup, his violin and his pillow. Even his packet of muesli and special lactose-free milk are cleaned out. I wander around the room, desperately checking drawers and shelves and window sills for remnants of yesterday's world. It is only when I collapse in a heap on my unmade bed that I come across a pair of navy blue satin boxer shorts tangled up in the doona cover. And that's when I decidedly and categorically break down.

I try to think. I start to panic. When had he come home? What time? Where was I then? Was it last night when I was with Anyu or this morning with Eva at the café? I feel sick. Did he come ready to move out or was he planning to talk about things? Surely he must have thought I would be there or at least come home and catch him in the act. Did he wait a while before packing things away or did he arrive all ready to go with boxes and cases and bags? Did he pack slowly, carefully, lingering over every coat hanger and pair of socks? Was it a deliberate, drawn-out muster hoping I'd catch him mid-suitcase, hoping I'd stop him in his tracks, hoping I'd block the doorway and beg him to stay? Could I have stopped him? Would I have tried? Was *she* with him? Where did he go? Where is he now? Do I even care?

I clutch onto his shorts and hold them tight. I cry. I lie down and try to sleep. I sit up and try to think. I throw his shorts across the room. I stand up to make coffee and then pour it straight down the sink. I hide under the covers. I cry again. I crawl to the bottom of the bed, rummage on the floor until I find his shorts and take them back to bed with me. Their edges are fraying and they smell mildly of mildew. I clutch them tight.

I light myself a cigarette and look around the apartment. Is this how Eva felt when she found out about Anyu and Ivan? Even with Nixon's stuff out of here, our relationship is unresolved. The more answers I was given, the more questions were spawned. Did he fight Eva when she told him I would betray him? Did he whisper our sweet Hungarian nothings to Camilla? Did he think he could get away with it? Did he leave my unfinished portrait of him here on purpose to haunt me? Did he ever love me?

His unfinished eyes stare at me from the easel in the corner near the window: sketchy and half-done; vague, almost random strokes and lines barely even visible from where I lie. Yet another incomplete canvas to add to my already overflowing pile of unfinished tales. The stories of my life. The story of my life. Pieces held loosely in place by other randomly gathered pieces. These are the pieces of my life: medical studies half-completed, a job completely unsatisfying, a career unfulfilled, an illness unexplained. Boys that come and go, a pair of disjointed women I am forced to call family, a crazy friend. There are other pieces too: a murmur overheard from behind closed doors in a strange language, a torn-up photo album, a chance slip of the tongue, a sharp retort, a rumour. There are fantasies and Hungarian lessons, fears and secrets and regrets, an eternity of indecision punctuated by spontaneous moments of passion, half-asked questions, and half-finished answers. It is a life, quite literally, "under construction". It's me, a girl always stuck at the same stage: the preliminary sketch. Am I doomed to float around in a comfortable non-descript no-man's land? But then no-man's land is a place I am used to: with boys, with Anyu, with Eva, with my career, with my illness. I let myself be miserable for years in a world of studying which was alien to me, in a life lived for others, so they could complete their dreams, so they could live them through me. The place in medical school taken unjustly from Anyu just because she was a Jew, a satisfying career my mother gave up to pay for Anyu's legal bills. And when I finally took that giant step out of denial and into truth, their disappointment and shame outshone my courage. I didn't step; I stumbled. And now I've fallen.

After three years of sketching and painting, I sit today crying in a room full of half-finished canvases. I spend all my time with Camilla, a miserable double-crossing boss who treats me like a doormat and then fucks my boyfriend. She doesn't even know I paint. There's Sam, whose craziness just drives me crazy, and Georgie, the handsome father-figure who can't even look me in the eye because he knows what I know and doesn't have the heart to say it. *One more test, Lily. Nothing is confirmed. Let's just have one more test.* It takes a drama of crisis magnitude for a real conversation with my grandmother and I can't keep a boy interested in me long enough to finish his portrait. I have swayed like a pendulum from denial to bravado, but the swinging has broken my back. Lying on my bed, exhausted and alone, I feel the swinging stop.

It's time.

I get up out of bed and I make my way to the easel by the window. I unfasten Nixon's portrait from the shelf and slide in a brand new canvas. Then I carefully manoeuver the contraption from beside my bedroom window around the foot of my bed, and towards the bathroom door. The mast gets caught in the doorway and I wrangle it to and fro until I am standing both in front of the mirror and my new clean slate. I look at myself; I smile to myself. And then I start to paint.

I paint and I paint. For the first time I let myself paint what I see, not what I feel, not what I want to feel, not what I want others to feel, not what I want others to think I am feeling. I paint me. Lily. Me.

I don't stop. I can't stop.

And when I finally do, I see Lily. Not the Lily of fantasy. Not the Lily of dreams or dramas. Not the happy Lily, the hurting Lily, the sick Lily, the hoping Lily. Just Lily. Just me.

I look again in the mirror and I want to laugh and cry at the same time. I am covered in paint from head to toe: green streaks in my hair, violet earlobes, orange toes. My arms are lined with blotches of colour, a smear of red on my forehead, blue on my neck. I am filthy. I am hungry. I am exhausted, but when I look at the finished canvas, I am happy.

I peel away my clothes and crawl through the H-frame of the easel to the shower. I let the hot water run over my face and wash away the stains. It burns and soothes. Suddenly I know what I have to do. I have to finish it. I realise how sick and tired I am of my half-baked world, a world in which questions are left not only unanswered, but unasked. A world in which I don't have the strength, the courage, or the discipline to follow a track all the way to its end.

I dry myself off and look again at the self-portrait. It is the eyes that confirm it for me. My eyes, Papa's eyes. I have been avoiding it for months, maybe even years. I have always known it lies inside of me. I can feel it in the middle of those sleepless nights when only painkillers and sleeping tablets make it go away. I can feel it every time I think of my father. I fight it, not like one would normally fight an illness, with tests and hope and trust. I fight it with the only thing I am good at: denial. I spent years hanging out in Georgie's office content with scheduling another test, arranging another appointment, waiting until the next time. But now I have to know. I don't want to end up like Papa who couldn't fight anymore. I want to know. I want to live.

Chapter Sixteen

It's beautiful blue skies and I'm hoping this means a quiet morning at the surgery, an unanticipated lull in the cold and flu season, a time to enjoy a weekend outdoors instead of the inside of a waiting room. Georgie doesn't take appointments on Saturday mornings. It's first come, first served until lunchtime. I'm hoping the wait is not too long. I'm ready to hear it all. I'm ready for the truth.

I push past the glass doors and my heart jumps. The waiting room is almost empty. There's only one patient, a middle-aged man in tracksuit pants playing on his iPhone. I take a deep breath.

It's almost over, I tell myself.

The receptionist is standing behind the front desk dancing from foot to foot and rapidly turning the pages of a magazine. It takes a minute for her to notice me in front of the counter. She snaps shut the magazine and smiles at me.

"Lily!" she says. "I'm sorry I didn't see you there. You okay?" She sits down on her stool, swivels madly from side to side, and then suddenly stands up. "You want to see George?"

"Thanks, Mary," I say.

"You okay? You look pale." She looks at me and squints, then tilts her head upwards to get a better look through her reading glasses.

"I'm fine," I say. I try to smile.

She tries to smile back. Her gaze lingers a little longer than necessary. She shakes her head and turns to the filing cabinet behind her.

"How's mum?" she asks half-heartedly. "Oh! I almost forgot!" She spins back around and waves her hands about in front of her. "I was meant to call you last week, but it completely slipped my mind! You left this here last week, your new script and some samples – the Valium. George wanted me to call you to pick them up. Good that you came in today!" She scratches her head and then fumbles through a pile of papers and pill packets on a tray on her desk. "Fekete, Lily ... Fekete, Lily ..." she mumbles. "Wait a sec. Here we are. Got it." She hands me the plastic tube, sits back down, stands straight back up, and scratches her head. She turns back to the filing cabinet and searches for my file. "Fekete L ... Fekete L ... ummm, Fekete J ... Fekete V ... wait

wait, here it is! George is just in with a patient at the moment, but he won't be too long. There's only one before you." Then, leaning forward, she looks left, looks right, and whispers, "I can put you next if you like." She glances over at the other patient. He doesn't look up.

"Thanks," I say, trying to mean it.

She takes my file and puts it on top of the man's file next to her on the counter.

She looks at me for a moment, then nods to herself. "Okay," she says. She smooths down her skirt and skips around the desk to my side. "Lily, listen, you don't mind, do you? I'll only be a minute. It's not too busy. You see Kathy called in sick and I've just got to go … you know, at my age it can be … urgent. Can you just stay here at the counter for a minute while I go to the loo? I won't be a minute. Do you mind keeping an eye on things for a sec?" She's holding both my hands by the end of the speech.

"Not at all," I say. "Go, I'll be fine."

She glances down at her watch, smiles at me with a tilted head of understanding, and then dances off through the glass doors. I pick up the samples and the prescription and place my bag next to my file on the counter top. More sleeping pills! How much longer will I need these, I wonder. I put them away in my bag and glance down at the file.

Fekete, L. That's me. An ordinary, run-of-the-mill beige cardboard manila folder holding the story of Fekete, L.

I will never fully understand the workings of fate, the whys and wherefores of that great machine that keeps the world turning even as we sleep, the accidents and adventures and coincidences and events that happen to us and because of us, changing us into who we are. I could spend years analysing and evaluating the actions that brought me to this moment in my life. There are the purposeful ones, like asking Eva to teach me Hungarian or jumping a Hungarian waiter as he finished up work. There are the accidental ones, like being caught red-handed by Peter *bácsi* the chef or having Mary the receptionist need to go to the bathroom at just that very moment. Call it courage, weakness, fate; I'll never fully understand exactly what makes me open up my file as I wait for the doctor on this beautiful Saturday morning.

I finger the edges of the cardboard for a brief moment, and then casually open the top.

Fekete, L.

I quickly leaf through the file, pages and pages of print-outs and hand-written notes, pathology reports, referral letters, copies of scans. I'll never have time for any of this! I glance back at the glass doors for a glimpse of

Mary coming back from the bathroom. I look at the man on his phone. He hasn't stirred. I turn back to the file. I flip to the first page, held loosely at the top by rusted paper clips, and glance at the hand-written notes.

And that's when I see it.

I read it and reread it and reread it again.

It must be a mistake! I don't understand. Even with my better than average knowledge of medical terminology, I am completely confused.

Then I feel sick.

I look to the door; Mary is nowhere to be seen. I look to Georgie's door; there's not a sound. I check: the world is still turning. But all of a sudden it seems to be going backwards. I reread the last two entries again. How can this be? My head is swimming. I feel dizzy.

> *3/5/88 Rx Nembutal -25, 500 mg oral.*
> *5/5/88 Coroner finding – suicide by overdose*

Again.

> *5/5/88 Coroner finding – suicide by overdose*

I check the cover.

> *Fekete, L.*

How could this be? I turn to another page, this time a typed letter to Dr Horvath.

> RE: Fekete, Lesley. b 6/7/43

I feel sick. I look up. Suddenly Mary is walking through the glass doors. Everything feels in slow motion. Papa! *Fekete, Lesley, born 6/7/43.* I can't see straight. The room is no longer in focus. The blurred body of Mary comes towards the counter. She is smiling, talking. What is she saying? It's just a dull, muffled, droning murmur. She is drowned out by those handwritten words swimming around in my head. *Coroner, Suicide, Nembutal, Overdose, Fekete, Lesley, Suicide, Papa.*

I have to move. I have to run. I have to scream. I have to go. There are so many reasons for me to be here, so many questions I have to ask, so many other things I have to know. But right now, I just have to go. I slam closed the file and bolt past Mary. The world is dimming, fading. I am confused. I feel crazy. The shapes and colours and sounds of the street melt into one long, dizzying swirl. *Suicide. Nembutal.* I don't know how I make it home. *Coroner. Suicide.* I try to think, to reason, to understand. I can't. I need to sleep. I try to think again. I try to say the words but I can't. I can't talk. I have to sleep. My head is on fire; it won't stop. I have to stop.

I don't know how many of them I take – is it five or six in the sample pack that Georgie left for me? One pill? Two pills? More? I just need to sleep. I just need to stop thinking and come back afresh. I need to stop thinking now. I need a break. I need blackness. I need to stop. I need to sleep.

And then, finally, peace.

***

I awake slowly to the rhythmic, high-pitched beeping of the machine by my bed and the familiar brew of perfume and stale cigarette smoke. I open my eyes. It smells like home but everything around me is a pale, nauseating shade of beige; the walls, the curtains, the bedside table, the plastic chair by my feet. All around me a watery, pallid, lifeless shade of beige. The television on the wall in front of me is on, muted, blurred; I squint to make out the scene – a police car, blaring lights, a freeway, a black man in a suit – I close my eyes again. Peace.

When I open my eyes again, the beeping has stopped. A fat Chinese woman with a funny white hat fiddles with my elbow.

"I just take blood pressure, no hurting, no worry. Okay?"

I nod. And close my eyes. I feel the gradual tightening of the band around my arm and then the final squeeze. I hold my breath. Release. Where am I? I try to sit up. My head is so heavy and my legs! I can hardly move my legs. It's as if someone weighed them down with warm sandbags.

"Good. No move, okay? Sleep good. Sleep now."

I relax back into the starched pillows and hear the plastic sheets rustle and crackle beneath me. I close my eyes again. *Sleep good. Sleep now.*

It's an intense half-whispering in Hungarian that accosts me when I eventually come to sometime later; two voices, strained, slightly guttural, almost frenzied, talking at the same time. The blurred outlines of Mama and Anyu hunching over a gaggle of plastic shopping bags. I am not used to seeing them in the same room together. I try to sit up. When they see me struggle to my elbows, they simultaneously look up, stop talking, drop what they're doing, and rush to my side. Then the squabbling resumes. I manage a smile. It's timed to perfection, their little choreographed manoeuvre. *The Desperado Ballet*, I think, as they each take hold of one of my hands.

"Lily, *my* Lily! You're all right!" they cry, at exactly the same time. Then look at each other, annoyed. "Oh thank God, thank God, oh thank you, God …" continues Anyu, looking up at the beige, cardboard ceiling. "Thank God, everything's okay."

"It's going to be all right, Lily. Oh you scared us so much, my darling. Are you okay?" Mama smiles and touches my forehead.

"Where am I?"

"You're at St Vincent's, darling. Are you feeling okay?"

"I'm tired. I have a headache. My legs are so heavy."

"Oh thank God!" cries Anyu. "Her legs are heavy! Did you hear that, Judy? Her legs are heavy!"

"How ... ? Why ... ? Mama, what happened?" I don't know what to ask first.

"We don't know what happened, Lily darling. We don't know anything. Only that you're okay now. You're going to be okay. It was a nice young Hungarian boy who called us, Lily, from the hospital. He brought you here this afternoon. He found you at home. Oh Lily, I'm so glad you're all right." Mama squeezes my hand.

I suddenly perk up. "Nixon?"

"Lovely boy."

"Lovely boy, huh?" grumbles Anyu. "Some boy! Look at her ... she's lying half dead in a hospital bed and you say lovely boy! *Jaj!*"

"Anyu, please, I already asked you. Now's not the time."

"The time? Now is the only time. She finds herself a peasant Hungarian boy who works for the monster herself and ends up in hospital! Ha! Some lovely boy!"

Mama throws Anyu a look.

I try to sit up. I let go of their hands and start to run my fingers through my hair. "Nixon? Here?"

"Darling, he brought you here. He found you." Mama's voice is clear, but a little shaky. I feel a calm wash over me. *He found me.* "He stayed until they knew you were okay. Lily, it's okay. He didn't want to be here when you woke up."

I fall back down again, deflated. I try to swallow. My throat is on fire. I close my eyes. *He didn't want to be here when I woke up. He found me.*

At last, a bit of quiet.

But only for the briefest of moments. The squabbling starts up again almost immediately, hoarse, venomous whispers backwards and forwards over my head, mumblings and vicious little sputterings. I just want to rest. I just need a break. But the buzz won't stop. I try to swallow. I try to lift my head, but someone must have come while I was asleep and injected lead into my veins. I can't move. I keep my eyes closed. Maybe it will all just go away if I keep my eyes closed.

There's peace and then a knock at the door. More mutterings. Hungarian mutterings. Backwards and forwards, getting louder and louder. Three voices all at once. I can make out a few words Eva taught me. *Shhh let her sleep. She's slept enough. Enough sleeping. She needs to rest. Something something downstairs. Sleep. Not long. Something something dying. Sleeping. Something sick. Let her sleep. Maybe tonight. Tomorrow …* There's a man's voice, a strong voice, a sure, clear, bold voice of reason somewhere in the mix, getting louder, getting bolder. *It's not your fault*, I hear. *Nem a te hibád.* It's not your fault.

I'm exhausted. I just need to rest. But the noise won't stop.

"Stop!" I cry, suddenly, and with all the energy I can muster, the words somehow coming to me in Hungarian. "Stop all the words. All this Hungarian is making me sick!"

I open my eyes. Mama, Anyu and Georgie are standing over my feet. All three of them suddenly stop their whispering mid-sentence and look at me. Then Mama gets that look and turns to Anyu.

"Don't look at me, daahrlink. It wasn't me. It was *her*. I told you."

Mama sits down on the plastic chair by the window, exhausted, deflated, finished. She stares out the window.

"Tell her, Georgie, please," Mama says. "Tell her what you told me."

"Lily, sweetheart, everything's going to be okay."

Anyu nods reassuringly, but she has tears in her eyes.

"Stop telling me everything's okay. Nothing's okay, nothing. I'm sick. Look at me. Tell me the truth. Mama? Anyu? Someone? Tell me what's going on. I can't stand it anymore. I can't stand all the whispers and all the Hungarian and all the secrets. Tell me what's wrong with me! I can handle it. I can handle more than you can imagine. I need to know. I need to know the *truth!* That's why I was coming to see you today, Georgie. The truth!"

"The young fellow found you at home. He got scared. That's all. He found the packet, the empty packet on the floor by the bed and he got scared. He called an ambulance. They took you into Emergency and most of it is out. But not all of it. That's why you still feel like this. I'm sorry. But now it's all over."

His voice is clear and loud, but I have trouble following. I can discern words, but the general sense of what he is saying is blurred. All I hear is *The End. Not all of it is out. That's why you feel like this. I'm sorry. It's all over.*

"It's all over?" I repeat. I can't believe it. What does he mean? What's not all out? What's going on? I swallow hard. I look around. And then I go for it. The question I should have had the guts to ask years ago.

"How long have I got?"

Silence.

"Georgie? Please ..."

"I don't know, Lily. We don't know." He looks at Mama. "A day, two days, maybe tomorrow. Everything will be over tomorrow." He goes over and stands next to Mama. He put his hand on her shoulder. I can't look at them.

I close my eyes. So that's that. Tomorrow. Everything will be over tomorrow. It's just a silly little word, but it means so much. I suddenly know why they haven't told me sooner.

"So that's it, then? Today or tomorrow?" I am calm. I am much calmer than I thought I'd be. Slightly removed, remote, dispassionate. Even stoic. Whenever I'd imagined this conversation previously, in those darker moments, it had been completely different. In my thoughts, this final, defining moment was always fraught with panic and fear. I envisaged violent, angry outbursts, followed by inconsolable depression and despair. Or the classic denial everyone talks about. I certainly didn't picture *this*: this emptiness, this nothingness. An eerie sort of peace. I know. I finally know. Tomorrow, everything will be over. I'm not afraid, I'm not worried. I'm not upset. I finally know.

"Is there anything we can get you, Lily, you know, until then? Anything you need to make things more comfortable?" He can't look at me. None of them can look at me.

I look over at Mama. Finally she comes over to the bedside and squeezes my hand. She smiles. But still she can't look at me. I can tell she is trying to keep a brave face. Anyu is pacing up and down at the foot of the bed, her eyes fixed on the floor, red, swollen, moist. I am floating, hovering just above the bed, it is as if I have already left my body. I can see everything, just like on TV. I can see the actors pacing up and down, surrounding the central character in the middle. I see my body, pale, gaunt, wax-like, almost completely swallowed up by the starched hospital-grade shroud. I am watching it all from a faraway place, slightly muted, slightly blurred. For a moment, it is already over.

Until Anyu suddenly starts up the conversation again, this time in Hungarian. She turns to Georgie, and even in my highly surreal state of being, I strain to make out a few words here and there. *Arrangements, ask her, don't ask her, organise, arrangements, Rabbi, phone calls, Rabbi? No Rabbi. Too expensive.*

"Please, I understand everything. I know you don't want to hear it, Anyu, but Eva, she taught me everything. She told me everything. I want to be involved. I want to be a part of it. You don't have to protect me, Anyu. I can handle it. I'm okay."

Mama answers for Anyu. "Lily, you don't have to worry about anything, darling, just let us handle the arrangements. We still have time. Nothing's happened, yet. How do you feel, darling? Are you okay? Do you need anything?"

"I want to be involved. I need to be involved. I'm fine. I've known it for a while now. It's taken me a while to accept it, to admit it, to believe it, but I'm ready. Please." My body feels numb, there is no more pain, no more fear, no more strain.

But I still have questions.

It's now or never.

"I need answers, Mama. Before I go, I need to know. About everything. About Eva. About my illness. About Papa. Tell me about Papa."

"Oh my God, now's not the time, Lily."

"Now's never the time, Mama. It's not fair. I have to know what happened." I take a deep breath. "I have to know before I die."

Georgie laughs. "I guess she gets it from you, Agi, all this melodrama." Even Mama manages a smile.

"Gets what? What do I get? I never get anything. That's why I'm here. Tell me. Georgie. Tell me. What's Nembutal?"

"Nembutal?" Mama suddenly has a panicked look in her eyes. "Where did you get Nembutal, Lily?"

I look at Georgie. "Tell me."

But Mama pushes past him to my bedside. "Lily, look at me, darling. Is that what you took?" She shakes my shoulders. "Tell me. Where did you get it?" Then she turns straight to Georgie. "Is that what you gave her? Georgie, what the hell is going on?"

Georgie shakes his head. He smiles at her. "Relax, Judy, there's no Nembutal. Lily, what are you talking about? Judy, listen, that stuff's illegal now. I'd never do anything like that. Come on!"

"What's Nembutal? Why won't anyone answer me!" This is why I never asked questions.

"Nembutal's a drug, Lily, a very dangerous, potent drug. A barbiturate, a sleeping pill. Tell me, where did you get Nembutal?"

"Is that what I need? Will it make it easier?"

"What are you talking about?"

"Dying. Will it make it easier?"

Georgie looks puzzled. Mama looks horrified. Anyu just looks awfully mad.

"Lily, you're a little light-headed from the sleeping pills." Georgie's voice is the voice of reason. "No one said anything about dying. You're going to be fine. You'll have a good rest here overnight and then maybe tomorrow you'll go home. Tomorrow it'll be all over."

Tomorrow. Tomorrow it'll be all over. Going home?

"What about my illness? My disease? The family disease? Like Papa?"

"I don't know what you're talking about, Lily. What family disease? Your father was sick, that's true, but it's nothing to do with you. Your father was sick and he chose to end it all, his choice, his decision. It wasn't about you."

I stop for a minute.

Then another minute.

"So I don't have Papa's disease? I'm not sick? I'm not dying? There's no lupus?" For a minute I don't know whether to be relieved or irritated. I don't know what to think. For as long as I can remember, this has been my life. The fear of death has accompanied me everywhere, like a friend, like the skeleton atop Frida Kahlo's four-poster bed. Death and Lily, together, always.

Georgie rubs his forehead. "What a mess. Oh Lily, I've spent years telling you you're okay. You've never believed me, have you?" He turns to my grandmother, who just shrugs, and then to Mama. He is looking for an answer.

Mama speaks first. "We never told her, Georgie. We just said he was sick. That's all. Just sick."

Georgie shakes his head.

"They never tell me anything, Georgie, nothing! I thought you were just the same."

"There was never anything to tell, Lily! There was nothing wrong with you! Every test confirmed it, but it was never enough. I should have known why. I should have understood. You don't have your father's disease. Your mum's right, he was sick. Very sick. But it's nothing to do with you."

"They never tell me anything! I even had to go to Eva to learn Hungarian. To Eva! Imagine! Out of all people ..."

"And look where you end up!" shouts Anyu, piping up all of a sudden. "One thing I've always told you, Lily. One thing I've always said: that woman is a monster! She's a maniac. My baby died because of her and now look what's happened ... I'm visiting my only grandchild in hospital after she plays with the devil. *Jaj!* What's the world coming to!" Then she pauses. "At least there is some justice left. She doesn't have long to go herself."

"What are you talking about?" I feel like I can hardly keep up.

"She's dying! That's what I'm talking about. Dying." And with the final syllable she collapses on the armchair in a heap. Her voice breaks. "She's bloody dying."

I look around. Mama nods gently from the corner. Georgie explains. "Eva's downstairs, Lily. I thought you knew this. I thought you understood. I thought that's what you were talking about. She's very sick."

"What do you mean? What's going on? She can't be sick. I'm the one who's sick! She's fine. I saw her just the other day. What are you all talking about?" I don't understand a word.

"That's what we were discussing here before you woke up. Lily, I thought you said you understood Hungarian. Eva's been sick for a long time now. She's in the advanced stage. It looks like the end."

I squint up at him. I feel the wheels turn. The last half hour suddenly makes sense. The mumbling and whispering in Hungarian. The arrangements, the Rabbi, the *maybe tomorrow*. It is Eva downstairs in the hospital. It is almost over. For Eva. *For Eva*. I can't believe it. Eva is sick. Eva is dying. They were talking about her.

I know I'm meant to be relieved, but my heart is sinking. I need a moment for everything to register. I'm okay. I'll be leaving the hospital tomorrow, but Eva, she'll be leaving us forever. All this time it was her that was sick. All this time she sat and gave me Hungarian lessons. All this time she told me stories and translated poems. All this time she was dying and she knew it.

I try to get up, but my head is too heavy. Instead, I reach over to Anyu and hold her hand.

"She wasn't always a monster, Anyu. Surely not. She was your best friend! What happened between you? Tell me. Tell me about Eva. Tell me about Ivan."

Georgie runs his fingers through his hair and fakes a cough. "I'll be downstairs in 301 if you need me," he announces and flees before the carnage begins.

We watch him walk out into the hall and then she starts.

She starts with a big sigh.

"We did everything together, we did. It was the three of us. Always the three of us." *Sree of us,* she says. "We used to laugh at each other. We used to scream at each other. We were family. We were in love. From the very beginning we were in love."

"All of you?"

"Not all of us! Me and Ivan, you idiot! From the very beginning."

"So why did he marry Eva? Why did you marry Grandpa? Why?"

"Oh Lily, but I've tried to explain it to you. It's not as simple as that. That's just in the movies, daahrlink. You fall in love and you get married. It never happens like that in real life. Marriage is about family, about respect, about the past, about the future. Marriage isn't about love."

I can see that this isn't another monologue. This is for real. This is my Anyu.

"What about Eva?" I ask. "Was she jealous?"

"Jealous schmelous. Don't be ridiculous. Eva had other problems. And other lovers. Let's not forget, people! Eva knew from the beginning. She was there, for God's sake. She wasn't stupid. She wasn't born yesterday, understand?"

I did understand: Eva didn't know about the affair until Ivan died.

Eva went bananas when Ivan died.

"Don't kid yourself, Lily. Eva was always crazy."

My mother joins in. "Eva went crazy when Ivan left the Oktogon to Anyu. That's when it all started. That's when it all ended, too."

Ivan the Terrible.

"In his will?"

"In his will," Anyu answers. "He left the Oktogon to me."

I shake my head in disbelief. I understand. "No wonder Eva was angry," I say. "She lost her husband, her livelihood, her best friend, and all at the same time."

"She was more than angry, Lily. Angry I can understand. But the woman went mad! Stark raving mad! I explained to her at the time that nothing had to change, that we would still work there the two of us, together, like always. Things could have stayed exactly like they were before … you know, before he died. Eva and Agi running the bistro. Booked out Friday and Saturday nights. Regular table for Bert Newton in the corner. The two of us, together. But her words were strong, Lily. I'll never forget those words: *Nothing will ever be the same again.* I offered her a job. I offered her money. I could have offered her the world! I told her, we can keep this quiet. Things don't have to change, but she went awfully mad. She simply went awfully mad."

"So what happened? Did she ask for it back?"

"*Jaj!* If only she would have asked! Who knows what I would have done if only she would have asked, from one woman to another, from one friend to another, from one human to another."

Mama rolls her eyes. "*Who knows vot vood have happened?*" she mimics.

Anyu ignores her. "You want to know what she did? I tell you what she did – she went straight to her bloody lawyers!"

"She contested the will? She could do that?"

"Daahrlink, with the right shysters on your side, enough money to burn, and a screw loose in your head, daahrlink, you can do anything in this country."

"But it was his last will and testament! His dying wishes! It's what he must have wanted! He loved you!"

"Oh Lily daahrlink, you are so funny! But that's not how it works in the real world. In the real world, you see, in the real world, he was dead. There's nothing he could have done about it."

"So Eva won in the end. Is that it?"

"Well, you know, she was his wife. His next of kin. She had all the papers. She had all the money. I had nothing. I had my word. It was her word against mine."

I turn to Mama. I can see she's had enough. I smile at her.

"So there you have it, Lily," Mama says. "Feel better? Huh? The story that broke your father's heart. The story that broke your father's bank. The story you've been dying to hear. Three years in court with a crazy old bitch who couldn't hear the truth, tens of thousands of dollars for fat, rich lawyers getting fatter and richer in six-minute increments. A sick husband getting weaker and sadder until he literally couldn't take it anymore. My world turned upside down. For what? For what?" She is screaming now. She turns to Anyu with her arms in the air. "Tell me, Anyu, for an aging bistro with rats in the kitchen and a chef who can't keep his fingers out of the till for a single day? I don't think so ... For what? For a decadent and deceitful affair with your best friend's husband you dare to call love? I don't think so ... I tell you what it was for — secrets and lies. More secrets and more lies. And all this fighting to hide more of it. Tell her, Anyu. Tell her the truth! Now that we're laying it all out on the table, let's let it all out! This isn't about love! This isn't about friendship! Ivan didn't upset the status quo for a fuck with his wife's best friend. Tell her, Anyu, tell her why he left it to you."

But I already understood.

"He left it for him, for his son," I answer, mainly to myself. "Ivan the Terrible, my grandfather."

I lie back down in bed and smile to myself. It is so obvious. *Ivan the Terrible.* My grandfather. It makes perfect sense. Except ...

"Wait a minute!" I say. "That would have been enough, no? Legally, that's all you would have needed? Ivan's next of kin? Papa?"

Anyu shrugs her shoulders. "Maybe," she says.

"Maybe? Maybe?" screams Mama. "Who do you think you're kidding now? She says maybe!"

"What about DNA testing? Surely that would have proved it ..."

"DNA, SHME-N-A, come on, Lily! We're talking about twenty years ago, not last night's *Law and Order* on TV. You see, Lily," Mama continues, "it may well have worked. If only she had told the truth."

"Papa didn't know?"

"You don't understand," Anyu says. "That was then. Things were different then. Things …"

"Not much!" I say. "On the contrary, it seems nothing at all has changed. You still don't tell us the truth! You too, Mama, you never told me the truth."

"You don't know what you're talking about, Lily," Anyu says. "So get off your high horse. You were too young. You're still too young. You wouldn't understand. I couldn't tell your Papa."

"Try me, Anyu. Just try me. Tell me."

"Tell her, Anyu. Tell her what you could never tell me, what I was too young to hear, what I would never have understood."

Anyu gets up and reaches into her bag for a cigarette.

"We're in a bloody hospital, Anyu, for God's sake!"

Anyu sighs. "It was never his fault, you know." She puts the cigarette away, albeit with a hearty, flagrant reluctance. "He was a sweet boy, you know. But a little … how shall I put it? Unstable."

"Unstable!"

"Well, you know, what do you do, daahrlink, when your little boy can't stop crying? What do you do when there's nothing you can say to make him happy? It wasn't all the time, you know. There were happy times. There were smiles and jokes and weeks at a time of laughter. Tell her, Judy, you know. But there were also times when it was too much. Things were just plain too much. Getting out of bed was just too much." She pauses to look at my mother. "But things were a bit better when we arrived here, Judy, you have to believe me. I thought he was better. But I was scared. I was scared he wouldn't be able to handle things. I was scared for him. I was scared for you. I was scared for me. What could I do? I thought I was doing the right thing. I was trying to protect him."

"Huh!" sneers Mama.

"And I was trying to protect you too, Judy!"

"Huh!"

"You've never understood me."

"How could I? I was only a girl myself. I was so young, so naïve, so terrified. I didn't know what I was getting myself into. But you! You were an adult. I tell you what you could have done: you could have warned me. You could have told me what to expect. You could have helped me find him some help. We could have found him answers. We could have managed it. If only I would have known. If only you would have told me the truth. It's always better to simply tell the truth. Telling Les who his real father was, telling me that he was mentally unstable, telling yourself that he needed help."

"What about telling me what happened to Papa?" I say. "What *really* happened to Papa. How do you call it? The truth?"

"That's different, Lily. That has nothing to do with what we're talking about here."

"What? Family secrets? Isn't that what you're talking about. Or is it family lies? Which part of it is different, Mama?

"You wouldn't understand!"

"Just like you wouldn't when you were my age."

"Listen, Lily, you were a little girl. You were only a baby, darling. You didn't want to hear that your daddy ended it all. You wanted to hear that he loved you. You wanted to hear that he was very, very sick. You wanted to hear that he was a good person but he just couldn't fight anymore. So that's what we told you, Lily, what you would have wanted to hear. None of it is lying, darling, it's all true. He did love you, that's not why he did it. And his illness had nothing to do with his beautiful, little girl. He tried to hang in there but it was too much. Like Anyu said: everything was always too much for Les. There's nothing you could have done about it. Not then, not now. Nothing I ever said or didn't say would have changed the situation or how it ended. That's the difference, you see, there's nothing you could have done. I never wanted to lie to you. I never wanted to hurt you. On the contrary, darling, I wanted to protect you!"

That line! I have heard that line one too many times!

I didn't need protection.

Mama, like Anyu, thought she was doing the right thing. But what I needed was the truth because the absence of it only made a hole that grew to be so big that I needed to fill it with something, *anything*, that would make me feel whole again. I didn't know the answers, and so I just made them up. I just imagined them. I didn't need protection from the truth. I needed protection from me.

Imagine! That word I heard over and over throughout my childhood, the word that Eva taught me in our very first Hungarian lesson. I imagined answers to all the questions I wasn't even sure how to ask. And the less I knew, the more I made up: Papa's illness, the one that killed him, the one that I had inherited, the one they didn't tell me about because they knew I would suffer the same fate. I've lived my life waiting for that fate to come. And it almost happened just like that.

Almost.

But then Nixon found me.

I close my eyes and smile to myself. He found me.

Then the door swings open suddenly and there's Sam, breathless and dishevelled, standing in the middle of my room. He gasps and then, panting, puts his hand to his chest. He looks to Mama and Anyu. They smile at him kindly and nod.

But Sam doesn't smile back. He turns to look at me and then falls to his knees at my bedside. He takes my hand and starts to shake his head.

"Lily, oh Lily, no! No, no, not you, Lily!" He takes a deep breath. "You are the nice one. You are the smart one. Not you, Lily! You are the loved one."

I lift my hand to wipe away a lonely tear from his cheek.

"I know, Sam," I smile, "I know. Who would have imagined?" I tell him. "Who would have imagined that after all this time it was me that was the crazy one?"

He buries his head in the blanket by my chest and his entire body heaves and shakes as he laughs and cries at the same time.

***

The following afternoon, Anyu picks me up from the hospital. My blood pressure is normal enough that I can walk to the bathroom and back without getting dizzy, and I have kept all my breakfast and all my lunch down for three whole hours. My bags are packed, the pathology results have been checked and rechecked, all the paperwork signed and stamped. I am ready to leave.

Almost.

"There's one more thing," I tell Anyu. "One more thing I have to do before I leave. Come," I beckon, "I want to show you something."

There are mumblings and grumblings and then a reluctant consent. She waddles with me across the hallway to the lift, down to the third floor where we eventually stop outside room 301.

Suddenly the penny drops.

"Don't be an idiot, Lily," she whispers, looking around. "I can't go in there!"

"Yes, you can, Anyu. You can. You should. You must."

She sighs.

"And do what, young lady? What do I do? What do I say? What do I say to the person I hate who's ruined my life? What do I say to the person I loved and whose life I ruined? You think you know everything now, Lily, but there are still things you can't possibly understand. Some things are better left unsaid." With a flick of her wrist, she pushes past me towards the nurses' station and the lifts. "You're out of your bloody mind ..." I hear her mumble through gritted teeth.

I turn to chase after her.

"No, Anyu. You're wrong! Things are never better left unsaid." I think of all the things that were never said to me, all the things I should have said myself. "Trust me, Anyu," I say. "Just this once, trust me."

She stops for a moment and then turns towards me, almost too quickly for one who was ready to escape down the hall only a few seconds earlier. "But what do I say? Where do I start?" Is she talking to me, or to herself? She grabs my hand. She has a genuinely terrified look in her eyes. "Help me, Lily. Tell me what to say."

We stare at each other for a brief moment and then it suddenly occurs to me.

"I've got an idea," I tell her, and whisper in her ear.

She doesn't say a word. I see a tear in her eye, and with a bittersweet smile and a trembling hand, she pushes past me and opens the door to Eva's hospital room. As I walk away, I can just make out the first few words.

"Well, tell me daahrlink, what did the penis say to the arsehole?"

Chapter Seventeen

It's another two weeks before we receive the news about Eva. I'd like to say that she hung on to dear life with that sheer strength, determination, and hope that is required to fight off the wrath of cancer, but it didn't happen like that at all. After a little over a year of refusing treatment for her relatively early stage lung cancer, she quietly, and without too much of a fuss, jumped out the hospital window one evening while she still had the strength to stand upright.

I visited her often during that fortnight, bringing her coffees and magazines and drawings. Sometimes we'd translate together a classic Hungarian poem from her school days. Other times we'd simply play cards without saying a single word. At first I was tongue-tied and awkward visiting a friend with one foot in the grave. I tried to muster up as much empathy as I could. After all, it wasn't that long ago that I, too, was dying. I kept telling myself that I knew what she was going through, that I knew what it was like, but the truth is a little more pathetic than that. I had been living a fantasy. When it suited me, I would wallow in self-indulgent pity, a state comforting only to those who really feel safe. Telling myself I was dying made me feel more alive than ever; it made me feel scared and excited and wild. It simply made me feel.

***

It is indeed a Gloomy Sunday the day of Eva's funeral. Anyu and I drive in silence to the cemetery in her beat-up Datsun. I'd like to tell the story of how two former best friends rekindled their relationship on the eve of a tragedy so that neither would be left with any regrets or guilt, but that would probably be an exaggeration. I actually don't know how much forgiving and forgetting went on between Anyu and Eva in that hospital room the two weeks before she died, but I don't think that matters anymore.

Waiting for the rain to subside, Anyu and I sit in the parked car outside the Jewish section watching the mourners scuttle past. I am pleased to see such a strong turnout on such a miserable afternoon. They too must have loved Eva.

"*Jaj!*" Anyu says. "See over there? That woman in the navy jacket? Look how ridiculous her hair is!"

I smile and take her hand. "I see her," I say.

"Well, I tell you now, I'm not getting out. I can't possibly see her now," Anyu continues. "I would never give her the satisfaction! She's the one! The shyster! Eva's lawyer after Ivan died. McMillions we called her! *Jaj!* It was her idea to sue for the Oktogon. It was her idea to contest the will. It was all her! A witch!" She says *vitch!*

"And over there, the one in green," she doesn't even take a breath. "Now tell me, daahrlink, who wears green to a funeral?" I look for the green one. I see Peter *bácsi* in the front row. I want to run to him. Instead I light a cigarette. I look for Nixon again. I can't see him. Then I see the green one. "That's Lesley's best friend," Anyu says. "Imagine! Your Papa's friend at Eva's funeral! It's probably because Les once owed him money. Oh well. And the man with the hat in the back row? Zsuzsi's third husband! *Jaj!*"

She continues like this for most of the service, including through the eulogy and most of the prayers. We never get out of the car! I don't stop looking for Nixon. He is not here. But I'm strangely happy to be here, to be here with Anyu. I love hearing her stories, stories of deceit and dishonesty, of greed and cheating, of lovers and liars and bigots and bullies. For a change they are just that, *stories,* not monologues, those monologues which for years had me mouthing along to the words, the tired old sentences and clichés. She is suddenly talking, freely and openly, completely unselfconsciously. She rants and swears and even litters her sentences with Hungarian expressions she knows she no longer has to stop to explain. There are anecdotes from the Oktogon, rumours and pieces of gossip from her youth in Hungary, all funny, embarrassing, nasty, moving. She is honouring Eva's memory in the only way she knows how: bitching. Over half the funeral-goers had in some way injured or offended her to such an extent that seeing them face-to-face today is out of the question. She is not getting out of the car. So we are back at a funeral, the two of us, less than six months later. Three plots away I see Frankie's grave, the Bastard with the Tiny Shlong. I smile. I knew we would be back again soon; I just wasn't so sure it would be together.

On the way home in the car, Anyu cries.

Back at her flat, I finally find the courage to give her the present I have been working on for the last two weeks.

"It's okay," I tell her. "Take it."

But I, too, am holding back tears as Anyu leafs through the tattered green album. It wasn't easy to match up all the Evas to all the Anyus after so many years of separation. I used stray strands of hair and matching shirt collars for clues, bits of background wallpaper, the shapes of the clouds in the sky overhead. Sure, I had reunited them, Eva and Anyu together again, finally and forever, but it was more than that. I was on my way to piecing together the puzzle that would be my story, too. As I sorted through all the various fragments and clues, as I fitted them all together in my head, I thought of Nixon: another half-eaten story book with caterpillar-like holes littering the pages, a tale only half-told. What was the real story of his meeting with Camilla at our apartment? Did Eva really scare him into believing I would hurt him? Did he really know about me and my meaningless affair? How did he find me and take me to hospital? And what was he doing back in the apartment anyway?

I guess I know the answer: the truth can never be imagined. It must be discovered. And though it is often difficult to take, it'll sure sit better than any invented fantasy.

And as for Eva, I will miss her terribly. I don't know if I will ever understand her or the decisions that she made, but I do know that the language she taught me gave me the words I needed to start asking the right questions and then to understand the answers. There will still be questions (I'm counting on it), some of which may one day be answered. But whatever did or didn't happen between us, whatever was taught and whatever was learnt, whatever was given and whatever was taken, and whatever was left to remember or to imagine, I know one thing: it is okay to ask.

***

I stay with Anyu the whole night and most of today. When I get home, I collapse on my bed, too exhausted to feel anymore. I grab my mobile phone and check my messages.

You have two new messages.

Beep.

Received: Monday. 2:31 pm. Lily, honey, it's me. Camilla. So I'm back from New York! What a trip! I arrived late last night so there has not been much time to sort out the bits and pieces for your opening. Honey, the men will be there at your place early tomorrow around seven-ish to pick up the collection. I'm sure your boyfriend told you all about the plans! Have I told you how wonderful your stuff is? I still can't believe after all this time you kept this hidden from me – me of all people! Anyway, I've lost Nixon's number so I thought I'd call you. The opening will be a stunner! I'm so very proud of you! So, yeah, just call me, honey, so much to do!

Beep.

Received: Monday. 4:13 pm. Hello, this is a message for Lily Fekete. My name is Susan McMillan from Carmichael and McMillan in Double Bay. 9328 5723. I represent Eva Freedman and her estate. You probably already know you've been named as Mrs Freedman's main beneficiary and executor. I need to talk to you about some details concerning the signing over of the title for one Oktogon Café. Please call me back at your early convenience.

Imagine.

Acknowledgements

There are some people without whom this book would never have been, and to them I'd like to say thank you.

Firstly to my wonderful husband, Alon Novy, for making me feel like the luckiest person in the world. Without your love and support and encouragement and advice and patience and faith, I would never have found the courage or strength to even get started. Thank you for sitting through countless re-readings of the same paragraph for hours on end, for telling me to keep going, for believing I could do it, and for sometimes telling me what I didn't want to hear. You are the smartest, most loving, most thoughtful, most insightful person I know and I love you so much.

To my parents, Shula and Peter Endrey-Walder, for always showering me with unlimited love and support for whatever I choose to do and whenever I change my mind. Mummy, thank you for always being there for me; and Daddy, for your literary advice and help with the Hungarian. Thank you both for the way you have been so excited for me. I love you.

Thank you to my brother, Ronny Endrey-Walder, for his technical support and for always being able to see the funny side of things. To my aunties Gigi Silberstein, Nina Sekel and Linda Kopcho, for their stories about my grandmother (except the secret ones, of course) and to Gigi, for her help with Hungarian spelling. To my aunty Cathy Shadd Rosenfeld, who spent countless days and weeks diligently line editing all my drafts and for helping me see the forest in spite of all the trees. To my in-laws Eva and Daniel Novy for their encouragement and for all the help with the kids, and to Eva for those wonderful family stories.

Thank you to Naomi Gould whose thoughtful advice from the very beginning has been invaluable, and Kimmy Haimovic who helped me, especially with the first draft. Thank you to Beattie Pearlman for her editing, to Georgia Levy for her legal advice, to Jodie Lowe Ariel for 'getting it', to Jhanna Culver for being my tireless cheer squad, to Severine Farkas-Milon for that day in the cafe at Les Halles, to Michele Sweeney for her moral support, and to Micki Persky for her honesty.

A special thank you to Robert Treborlang, for teaching me Hungarian. Robi, this book is for you.

Finally a big thank you to my editor Linda Nix from Lacuna Publishing who believed in me right away and has given me a wonderful opportunity and experience.

Eva Novy,
August 2014

About the Author

Eva Novy is a writer with an insatiable curiosity about everything in general and about secrets in particular. Any secret will do – the unexplained absence at a family party, the whisper behind closed doors, the couple at the next table just out of earshot. She sees secrets everywhere, both real and imaginary, and that's what she loves to write about.

Before the writing, there were other affairs: Eva studied mathematics (her first love), French (the fling), linguistics (more of an estranged ex) and education (a good mate). She spent many happy years teaching maths at high school and linguistics at university. She has lived and studied in Australia, France and the USA but her heart will always belong to Paris.

Eva lives in Sydney with her husband and their two beautiful, spirited boys. *Darling, impossible!* is her first novel.

www.ingramcontent.com/pod-product-compliance
Lightning Source LLC
Chambersburg PA
CBHW030332020726
47493CB00004B/1244